# BOULDER POINT

# BOULDER POINT

## A Merrill Connor Mystery – Book 2

by Deborah Madar

NFB
Buffalo, New York

**PRAISE for Deborah Madar's CONVERGENCE (2014, NFB Publishing)**

"With taut prose and vivid detail, Madar creates both the internal and external world of three very different characters – a recently divorced, passive college professor; her troubled and troubling student; and her long-forgotten college boyfriend, now a married glazier haunted by his stint in Vietnam."

"This is a gripping tale, perfect in its pacing, authentic in its detail, and haunting in its perception."

"You will never forget Charlotte, Leigh Ann, and Phil! Author Deborah Madar seamlessly transports us, the readers, to small town America and throws us in the midst of these people, their complex lives and their issues."

"Madar writes beautifully, with conviction and compassion. This is a rare novel that I'll read again more slowly the second time around to savor the writing now that I know the story arc. Well done!"

"Convergence is a compelling read on two levels. On its surface it is an extremely well-written psychological thriller encompassing the lives and actions of its three main characters. On a deeper level it broaches the existential question of authentic versus inauthentic living, of the consequences of the choices one makes either consciously or by default. On both levels Deborah Madar hits the mark."

"What a great read! Deborah Madar's plot and character development are masterful. Convergence is a psychological thriller you will be thinking about long after you turn the last page. I can't wait for her next book."

**PRAISE for Deborah Madar's DARK RIDDLE (2020, NFB Publishing)**

"This book by Deborah Madar is a gentle nudge or maybe it is a sharp poke....a wake up call about the forces in our society that affect not only our young people, but our school communities, our towns and cities, and our families. It is beyond thought-provoking."

"I haven't cried in a couple of years. This book brought me to tears. It was emotionally draining. It also made me think."

"An engaging, cleverly designed plotline that addresses the haunting questions around inexplicable violence by young people. While exploring possible reasons, it does not fall into the trap of giving pat answers or pretending to know the unknowable. The characters are well developed and believable."

"Sooo good. Madar manages to weave family dynamics, school and community politics, tragedy and mystery into such a believable, readable and relevant tale for our times…It's been awhile since I "couldn't stop reading" - yet the further I went with Dark Riddle, the more I had to know now."

"Every page made me want to get to the next. I couldn't put it down. Madar did not disappoint. Can't wait for her next novel!"

**PRAISE for Deborah Madar's A DEEPER DIVE (Book 1 in the Merrill Connor Mystery series, 2023, NFB Publishing)**

In A DEEPER DIVE, author Deb Madar's new entry into the world of female detectives, is a deftly written page-turner with a compelling protagonist, delightfully sketched environs, and a pitch-perfect narrative arc. One can easily imagine Emma Thompson doing a star turn in the movie version of this compact mystery! "

"A thriller that kept me on the edge of my seat and on the verge of tears throughout this gripping mystery."

"I loved, loved, loved this book! This unputdownable novel has it all – the twisty, heart-pounding plot of a thriller plus the beautiful writing, memorable characters and heart of the most satisfying literature. Can't wait for Merrill's next adventure."

"This would be a stunning choice for a ladies' book club. So many life situations and relationships to discuss. I care about each of the characters and I'm so glad that this is just the first of the series."

"I can't wait for the next novel in the series! Merrill Connor is intriguing!"

"Not only is this an incredibly intriguing mystery, but I love how Merrill's process of healing and growth is woven into the narrative. "

"I'm excited to see where this series is headed!"

"One of the many things I loved about this novel was that Deborah Madar pursues answers to questions far more subtle and far-reaching than the usual who-dun-its."

"Good news for fans of A Deeper Dive and Madar's earlier books, Convergence and Dark Riddle. Merrill Connor will continue her popular podcast. There are more missing person cases to be solved."

"This page turner kept me guessing from beginning to end and I couldn't be happier that this was only the first in Merrill's mystery series! Loved, loved loved this book!"

"Not only are we treated to a compelling mystery but we also are witness to wonderful friendships between "mature" women."

"This is a page turner full of fascinating characters. You'll want to turn off your phone, turn off the TV and hang out the "do not disturb" sign."

"A strong, female-empowered mystery."

"Merrill's courage to reinvent herself and pursue a new passion in the latter half of her life is endearing, and it makes her a compelling protagonist for a prospective series. Her ability to engage and empathize with witnesses not only makes her a good detective, but also brings some heart to the story. A thoughtful, suspenseful whodunit with a dash of mysticism."

"Throw in Deborah's understanding of families and knowledge of music and literature; evoke a medium for a curious twist; and you have a whodunit worth your time. Deborah always gives her characters personalities and this reader hopes she'll do an even "deeper dive" into the people in Merrill's new world in her next case. Bravo."

ISBN: 978-1-953610-68-3

    Fiction > Mystery & Detective > Women Sleuths
    Fiction> Thriller
    Fiction> Crime> Suspense
    Fiction> Crime>Murder Mystery
    Fiction> Thriller
    Female Author

Cover design by Jesse Stratton

NFB Publishing
119 Dorchester Road
Buffalo, New York 14213
For more information visit Nfbpublishing.com

This book is dedicated to the helpers and the healers.

"The place of true healing is a fierce place. It's a giant place. It's a place of monstrous beauty and endless dark and glimmering light. And you have to work really, really, really hard to get there, but you can do it."

- Cheryl Strayed

CHAPTER ONE

---

# THE TABLE

JENNA BERLIN HAD a wicked hangover. Not since the morning after she had downed three shots of cheap tequila on her final night of classes at college had she felt this horrible. And that was decades ago.

Yesterday, the news that the Supreme Court might interfere in the healthcare of American women had "leaked" to the news media, and Jenna and her friends had met for their customary Thursday gathering at Larry's. The three hour discussion was hotter than the chicken wings, and this morning she was suffering the consequences of her actions. Apparently she was too old to mix outrage with vodka. As she drove toward Boulder Point, she knew that she would likely pay the price all day. In spite of the pounding headache and intermittent waves of nausea, she resolved that she would carry on with her day as planned.

Pulling onto the short beach access road, Jenna parked the Jeep along the sandy shoulder across from the empty parking lot. She had come to regard this spot on Lake Erie's shore as her own, in spite of the fact that it was a public beach. The large shale and sandstone rocks discouraged the casual beach walker, and the massive ones, situated several yards offshore, kept most swimmers further east at the other municipal beach. On occasion, Jenna would run into an intrepid photographer who had set up his tripod to capture the sun rising behind the lighthouse, or a random Airbnb tourist who had not been warned of the beach's rocky composition by his host. Today, just as she had hoped, it looked as though she had Boulder Point to herself.

A muted throbbing plagued Jenna's temples, but she forced herself to climb out of the Jeep Wrangler. "I deserve this," she said aloud as she opened the tailgate. Thankfully, she had packed her gear yesterday afternoon and hadn't had to think about it this morning. Fortunately, her shoulder bag was lightweight, as were its contents. Most important was the waterproof pouch that contained her phone. An empty tennis ball can and a couple of Ziploc bags to keep any glass treasures she found, a protein bar, and a bottle of water were all that she needed as she walked the beach.

Jenna climbed over the rocky barricade and onto the sand. Stepping over soaked chunks of driftwood, she said a silent prayer of gratitude. Lake Erie's currents could rival that of the ocean, and last night's wild nor'easter had stirred up an immense amount of tree detritus. After a sudden wave of nausea passed, Jenna tried to smile. It wasn't exactly a perfect day for lake glass gathering, but beachcombing had always been therapeutic for her. Looking up and down the shoreline, it seemed that she was, indeed, the lone hunter this morning.

A flock of shrieking seagulls began taunting her from above. Their screams increased the pain around her eyes and wiped the forced smile from her face. She pulled the tennis ball can from her bag and dropped the sack onto the sand. Jenna began her slow walk into the lake. On most days when she wasn't bogged down with a crushing headache, she would throw her canoe on top of the Jeep so that she could paddle into a hidden cove to hunt for glass. Those particular treasures especially were beyond the scope of amateur gatherers. But today was not one of those days.

Jenna's hope was that the immensity of last night's storm might have carried all manner of glass onto the beach, most of it the legacy of nineteenth and twentieth century factories that had once lined the lake's coastline. Buffalo was a major industrial center in those days, and most of the waste from the plants was disposed of in this Great Lake. People also threw their garbage into the lake back then. Broken tableware, cracked Mason jars, and other household trash ended up in the water. Careless or unfortunate boaters also donated to the bounty of sea glass, contributing the most desirable red pieces that had once been hull or tail lights.

Jenna put her hand on her forehead to shade her eyes as she looked down into the water. She avoided wearing sunglasses when she could; she found they lessened her ability to spot any glass treasures on the sand or in the water. Lake Erie was warmer than usual for early June, and she felt her breathing slowing down as she walked unhurriedly, staying parallel to the shoreline. Soft green, white, and pale blue glass were in abundance today, and although they were fairly common colors compared to the more desirable cobalt and citron green, Jenna put dozens of the shards into her tennis can. In spite of the fact that they were not rare in color, she knew they all had the potential to make beautiful jewelry.

An hour later, her headache was gone and she waded back onto the sand. Between the restorative lake breeze and the success she had had gathering glass from the lake, she felt almost normal. Sitting atop a fallen tree that had weathered to resemble a marble sculpture, she took a deep breath, and her gratitude for this morning and this particular moment washed over her. Minutes into her meditation, her growling stomach reminded her of the sandwich she had packed, and Jenna stood and stretched.

Walking back along the beach to retrieve her lunch, she looked out at the small waves that lapped gently against the three familiar offshore rocks. The second part of her gathering strategy would involve walking and then swimming out to the boulders, the ones that kept most beachgoers away from this place. On a calmer day a few years back when she had transformed from hobbyist to renowned lake glass jeweler, she had actually named the boulders. Not simply their sizes and shapes, but their personalities, as Jenna thought of them, entered into this naming process.

Jenna stopped to watch an osprey in flight. Pulling her phone out of its pouch, she managed to capture the fluid movement of the water bird against the cloudless blue sky. These moments at Boulder Point were magical for Jenna. She gazed at the image she had captured of the bird in flight. The photo was good enough to frame, and she would hang it in her shop. With renewed strength, she began walking, quickening her stride as she headed back to the parking lot to retrieve her sandwich from the Jeep. Anxious to resume collecting, she ate it as she walked back to the beach.

When she returned to the shoreline, the intrusive screams of the gulls sitting on "The Table," the largest rock that lay a dozen or so yards from the shoreline, caught her attention and she stopped to see what might be agitating the screeching birds. Last week she had spotted an oversized, possibly pregnant muskrat swimming around the huge rock. Jenna figured that the creature had most likely been carried from Canadaway Creek into the lake, given the blustery nights that had hit the area lately. Was that what was alarming the birds? She had left her binoculars in the car. She would have to walk into the lake and then swim the rest of the way to the boulder to determine what was out there.

Jenna picked up her bag and grabbed a Ziploc bag and her phone pouch and zipped each of them into a pocket of her waterproof shorts, just in case she found some glass or wanted to take another photo. Setting her bag down again, she sprinted to the edge of the water. The wind speed and the waves were picking up a bit and she felt a wave of nausea sweep over her again. She took a deep breath and fought the sensation, wading in until the water level was deep enough for her to swim. The birds took to flight when Jenna was several yards away from the rock, shrieking their disdain for the approaching human.

As she reached the edge of the boulder, there was no sign of the muskrat, but Jenna could see a patch of neon green and muddy colored algae moving against the huge rock with the action of the waves. In her years of beachcombing experience, she had found Milfoil, this omnipresent weed, was on occasion the perfect trap for sea glass – she had discovered three pieces of rare red glass earlier this summer caught in this "net" of the lake.

She wasn't crazy about the idea of swimming as the wave action grew rougher, but her excitement about possibly finding another uncommon piece of glass motivated her to stroke harder. The Table had a flat surface, the perfect place for Jenna to sit and observe. She could rest her feet on the rock's ledge that served as a natural "staircase" out of and into the water.

When she reached the boulder, she silently blessed her Pilates instructor as she pulled herself up and onto The Table. Rising to her feet, she began walking the circumference of the massive rock. On a clear day like today, Jenna knew you could see all the way to Canada from this vantage point, and sure enough, as she looked to the north, there was the Ontario land mass.

Okay, she needed to concentrate, she told herself. It was time to make a plan for gathering any glass the seaweed held before she jumped back into the water to hunt for it. All three of the boulders at the Point had sharp outcroppings that could badly cut a swimmer, so she wanted to look closely before she leaped.

Jenna got down on her knees and then lay on her stomach to get a closer look at the thatch of weed and the potential treasure it held. "Oh, my God!" she screamed. Caught on the shale shelf of the boulder was not seaweed, but brown fur. The unfortunate muskrat must have met her fate, and her body had washed up here to The Table, its final resting place. "That's what the birds were screaming about," Jenna said aloud. She combat crawled on her elbows a couple of feet to the very edge of the boulder for a closer look at the unlucky creature.

In the next moment it was Jenna's scream that filled the shoreline. What she was looking at was not brown fur.

It was hair. Human hair.

CHAPTER TWO

---

# WE'RE HERE

THE WOMAN LAY face down in the water. The life vest she wore kept her lifeless body buoyant. Jenna grabbed the vest belt and held on tight, fighting the burgeoning waves that were trying to take the body. Frantic, and still on her knees, Jenna twisted from her waist and looked up and down the beach. She could see no one. Her phone was in her pocket, but she didn't dare let go of the woman to reach for it. A wave of nausea swept over Jenna as she realized what she had to do next.

Crouching and still clutching the life vest belt, she stepped down onto the rock's ledge and prayed for strength. A moment later, the surge of adrenaline she had begged for flooded her body. At the same time, Jenna felt the vomit rising in her throat as she grabbed the dead woman under her arms and lifted her onto the ledge of the Table. Taking a deep breath, she dragged the corpse, still in the face-down position, onto the flat surface of the boulder. The effort caused Jenna to fall backwards.

Breathless and flat on her back, she unzipped the pocket of her shorts and pulled out her phone. Jenna's second call was to Deputy Sheriff Johnny Lovallo. Her first was to Merrill Connor.

"Hey, what's up?" Merrill asked, pressing the lock button on her key fob. She was late and in a hurry. She began to speed walk toward a building on the campus of Jamestown Community College.

"Merrill!!" Jenna shrieked, "Come to the beach! Now!!"

"What's wrong?" Merrill asked, trying to sound calm, even though she felt a forewarning burn in the pit of her stomach. A fleeting thought occurred to her. The class she had enrolled in, "Expanding Your Own Psychic Powers," might not be necessary. Ever since a medium had delivered a message from a dead woman who said that Merrill had innate talent in this area, she had been trying to listen to her gut more and more. As a retired librarian, a podcaster, and a rookie criminologist, she was by nature analytic and logical. But Victoria Erikson, the medium at Lily Dale, had been instrumental in helping her to crack a twenty-year-old cold case last year, and Merrill decided that she needed to be more open-minded about this ESP thing, so she had signed up for the class.

"I found a woman, a woman's body!" Jenna stammered, her usual composure obliterated by sudden sobs. "I thought it was a creature..."

Merrill turned around at the entrance of the Arts and Humanities building and began to run back toward the parking lot. "Which beach?" she asked Jenna.

"Boulder Point. My gathering beach," she gasped. Jenna had confided in Merrill, and only Merrill, that this was the spot where she found the most beautiful and rare of the Mermaids' Tears, the mythical term collectors used for sea glass. "When you see pieces in the water or lying on the sand with the sunlight making them glisten and sparkle, you understand where the term comes from," she had explained to her friend.

"Have you called Johnny?" Merrill asked, breathless, as she slid behind the wheel of her Nissan.

"Not yet. I will as soon as I hang up." Jenna struggled to take in a much needed breath. "Merrill. I'm sitting on top of the rock where I found her." She began to sob again. "The big rock, where glass can get trapped in the weeds. She's wearing a life vest. It must have caught on the outcroppings. I dragged her out so the waves wouldn't take her." The effort to speak was Herculean and Jenna suddenly felt like she might pass out.

Merrill heard the wind shrieking through Jenna's phone. "Good thinking!" she said, making every effort to sound calm. "Call Johnny. I'll be right there."

Jenna bypassed 911 and quick-dialed Johnny Lovallo's cell. "Hi, Jenna," he yelled. In the background she heard a cacophony of barking dogs that caused the somewhat deaf sheriff to shout even louder than usual.

"Can you get to the eastern beach, Boulder Point, right now?" Jenna felt the nausea rise again as she looked down at the woman's arms and legs sprawled out on the boulder. She watched horrified and fascinated, as a trickle of blood flowed into a narrow crack in the rock.

"Now? I just got to the dog park with Frank on our way to work," he yelled into the phone.

"Johnny!!" she screamed. "I need you *now*! I pulled a dead woman out of the water! The wave action is intense … I didn't want her to be carried out …"

Lovallo interrupted her. "On my way. Come on, Frank," were his last words before the click.

Jenna felt too shaky to stand. She closed her eyes and willed herself to be anywhere else except this beach, her favorite place, where now she had discovered a body. Forcing her eyes open again, she stared at the long hair that had first alerted her to The Table this morning. A wild thought came to her and her trembling became even more violent. Did she know this woman, had she known her? Should she turn her over and find out?

Jenna turned her head and vomited into the water. Closing her eyes again, she tried to focus on the fact that her friends would be here soon. She knew that Merrill would be calm and collected, comforting in her unique way. Johnny and Frank, well, that would be a different story.

Jenna had "met" Johnny Lovallo for the first time as she and her friends, Kate and Sherry had listened to Merrill's interview with him on her podcast, *A Deeper Dive*. In his official role then as the lead investigator for the Sheriff's department in the case of a missing Amish teen, he had sounded somber and serious as he answered Merrill's questions. But when he hired Merrill as a research assistant, the women came to know Johnny as a totally different character. Extremely anxious most of the time and constantly in motion, Johnny had eventually become a friend, foibles and all.

And Frank. Frank was a treasure. The four friends were gathered at their Thursday night high top table at Larry's one night last fall, when in walked Johnny, holding a black-and-tan dachshund puppy in his arms. "Who is *this*?" Kate yelled, jumping off her chair to get to him.

"Meet Frank," Johnny beamed, rotating around the table so everyone got a chance to pet the little guy.

"Frank?" Merrill asked. "What kind of name is that for a dog, Johnny?" she asked, petting the puppy's head.

"What better name for a wiener dog than Frank?" Johnny asked, getting the laugh from the women that he had hoped for.

"Where did you get him? And, more importantly, *why* did you get him?" Sherry asked, leaning back in her chair to avoid touching the little dog. "I never saw you as an animal lover, Johnny." The women knew that Sherry was not a pet owner and never would be. Too many of her Airbnb properties, she claimed, had been ruined by clients who vacationed with their animals. "I have a hard enough time with humans," she had told them.

"A couple of weeks ago," Johnny said, "I was at the office late. When I went out to my car, there was a crate on the front seat. Frank was in it."

"Imagine that. A cop who doesn't lock his car," Merrill said, never missing an opportunity to lavish some of her signature sarcasm on her boss.

Lovallo ignored her. "I called the Humane Society and took Frank to a vet to check for a chip. There was none. I posted an ad on line, and put up posters in the diner and the post office, too. No takers. So it was a *fait accompli*. Frank is mine."

"But you work all day and most of the night, sometimes," Kate said, taking Frank from his owner and holding him close to her. "What's Frank supposed to do while you solve Westfield's crimes?"

"Well, if you must know, Frank is presently enrolled in a service animal training program. While he's in the class, I can take him to the office with me. I'll be able to take him on calls, too, once he gets his certificate. And believe me, he's a fast learner," Johnny said with a parent's pride in his voice.

"So you admit it then, you *are* a bit nervous and jerky. You think that Frank can help you with that?" Merrill asked.

Jenna's thoughts regarding that night last fall were interrupted by approaching sirens. Testing her wobbly legs, she stood for the first time and turned toward the shoreline. Two Deputy Sheriff's cars were pulling onto the sand. A water rescue vehicle roared in behind them. And Johnny's old Bronco passed all of them until it reached the water's edge. Merrill appeared out of nowhere, running toward the lake as Johnny and Frank emerged from the car. Frank's little legs were faster than all of the humans, and he stood, never a fan of water, on the shore, barking his alarmed bark at Jenna.

Her heart swelled at the sight of her two friends wading into the lake with their arms outstretched. She turned and looked down once more at the dead woman. Jenna knew that in the past hour her life had changed forever.

"We're here, Jenna! We're here!" Merrill called.

## CHAPTER THREE

# MERMAIDS' TEARS

Merrill turned off the radio. It was rare that she drove without Christina Stone, her favorite XM Sirius celebrity, guiding her through decades of music, but this morning she needed to stay focused on the matter at hand. It had been three days since the woman's body had been recovered from the water at Boulder Point, and Jenna was due at Johnny Lovallo's office by 10 o'clock to give a formal statement. Her friend had accepted Merrill's offer to drive her, and more importantly, to accompany her when she recounted the details of her discovery of a body. Since that day at the lake, Jenna had not answered Merrill's many calls. She had merely responded "*Yes*" to her text asking, "*Shall I pick you up at 9:30 tomorrow?*"

Merrill pulled into the Berlins' driveway and drove behind the house to Jenna's workshop. Two months after the couple had sold their restaurant, Steve Berlin himself had supervised the conversion of the old barn into his wife's work space in the back and retail shop in the front. Merrill loved the sign Jenna had designed that hung over the door. *Mermaids' Tears* was spelled out in large chunks of multi-colored glass objects she had found in the lake, including broken blue Mason jars, amber beer and green wine bottles, and cobalt blue pieces from Vicks and Noxzema jars.

Merrill opened the door to the shop, the display cases in the front immediately drawing her to them, as they always did. Against the wall on her left was the oak case she had helped Jenna pick up from the Amish furniture maker several years ago. A framed sign done in her friend's elaborate calligraphy hung above the case. *"Been to the beach lately?"* it asked. The four shelves showcased some of the more unique items that Jenna had found during her years of hunting for beach glass. A small sign with the date and the location of its discovery stood in front of each object.

The first shelf contained a collection of broken portions of beer and ale bottles from the turn of the century. Merrill especially loved the azure blue Wise beer bottle with the raised label that read *"This bottle belongs to the wise."* There were pale green and blue pieces that came from nineteenth-century Mason and Ball jars, a few with their zinc screw-tops intact, lining the second shelf. A dozen antique milk bottles stood on the third shelf. Merrill's personal favorite was the one that still had its label which read *"Chautauqua Dairy"* in red letters. On the fourth shelf stood several amber apothecary bottles, some intact, some with chips and cracks on their surfaces. The star of the show was a medicine bottle whose raised letters spelled *"LECANTER'S MAGIC CHICKEN CHOLERA CURE."* The first time Merrill saw the container, she was compelled to do some research. Fowl cholera, she learned, is a contagious bacterial disease in birds. Farmers in those days must have been happy to have Lecanter's in their medicinal arsenal. The bottom shelf of the cabinet was labeled *"Miscellaneous Beach Finds."* Among Merrill's favorites was a beautiful blue insulator, a pocket watch, a nineteenth century Spanish coin. At the very end of the display shelf sat the piece de resistance - a set of dentures that Jenna had found washed up on the shore at Point Gratiot. That must have been a very unhappy day at the beach for the original owner, Merrill thought each time she saw it.

The beautiful mahogany display case that Jenna had bought from a Buffalo jeweler who was going out of business was on the opposite wall. Merrill's eyes took in the stunning assortment of necklaces and earrings, bracelets, and rings her friend had crafted from the lake's bounty. The variety of colors and designs always astonished her. Jenna never changed the size, shape, or texture of her finds, either. Her perfectly matched pairs of earrings were the result of her collaboration with Mother Nature. Jenna had the ability to see the possibility of a perfect match when she found them lying in the sand or water, and she never cut or ground the pieces. Over the years Jenna had become a skilled silversmith too, and wherever a metal surface provided her the space, she etched a tiny *MT* onto the piece. Serious collectors were familiar with her trademark, and that line of her jewelry was most sought after for its meticulous artistry and stunning design. It was no wonder glass and jewelry lovers from all over the country made their way to Westfield and *Mermaids' Tears.*

"Good morning," Merrill called out as her eyes took in the beauty on display. There was no response. "Jenna, I'm here," she called a little louder. When she got no response, she opened the door to the workshop, fully expecting that the noise from Jenna's equipment or possibly from her radio that was always on had drowned out Merrill's voice. But the cavernous room was unusually quiet and dark. "Jenna?" she called again into the space. She walked slowly to the back of the gigantic room where her friend sat at her desk in the far corner, staring at her laptop screen. "Hello?" Merrill called again, and watched as Jenna startled and nearly fell out of her chair.

"Oh, Merrill, I'm sorry. Have you been here long?" she asked.

Merrill looked over Jenna's shoulder and saw what had taken all of her attention. *Sheriff's Department to Identify Woman Found at Boulder Point* the headline read. Jenna turned toward Merrill. "I feel like I'm in the middle of a nightmare," she said.

"Well, you have been," Merrill said, "but you'll feel better when you can give all the details of that day to the police. You'll be able to begin to put it behind you then." The light from the computer screen shown on Jenna's face, and as Merrill stared at her friend's uncharacteristically wrinkled brow and swollen eyes, she wondered if she was right.

"Have you had breakfast? We could stop at Jack's for a bite..."

"I haven't been able to eat much since..." she looked at her watch. "No, let's not stop. If I'm late, it will make Johnny nervous."

"Hmm," Merrill said, "nothing new about that. Frank really has his work cut out for him until this is case is solved."

Two hours later after their meeting with Johnny, the women stood in the midst of the small crowd of mostly journalists who had gathered on the sidewalk in front of the Sheriff's Department. On the dais stood the Westfield Police captain, the county coroner, the Chautauqua County Sheriff and his deputy, Johnny Lovallo, who stepped up to the podium after his boss announced that he and his team would be leading the investigation. Frank followed him and sat dutifully by his owner's feet as he spoke to the group.

"Last Friday morning," Johnny began, "our department was notified by a citizen at Boulder Point beach that she had discovered a body in the water several yards offshore. The Sheriff's office, Water Rescue Team, and the county coroner arrived at the scene at 9:45 a.m., and a woman's body was recovered. As of this morning, we have not been able to identify her."

"Huh," Merrill whispered to Jenna, "fine reporting job once again by the *Westfield Journal*. The article said she *would be* identified."

"The woman appeared to be in her 40's or 50's, with long brown hair and brown eyes," Johnny continued. "She had no distinguishing features such as birthmarks, tattoos, or piercings. The coroner's findings did not indicate that she had been in the water more than forty-eight hours. There was no vehicle found near the Point, and up to this time, we've not had a missing person report that matches the victim's appearance."

A journalist from the *Dunkirk Express* called out, "Did you say *victim*, Sheriff? Is this a murder investigation?"

Johnny seemed to ignore the question. "If anyone has any further information regarding this matter, please contact our office." Although most of the people gathered in front of Johnny Lovallo could not see it, Merrill had noticed a slight flinch when the reporter had asked him about the cause of death.

"So Sheriff, please clarify. Was this a drowning or not?" the reporter from the *Express* asked.

Merrill sensed that everyone in front of the podium had stopped breathing until Johnny finally answered. "The coroner has found no forensic evidence that this is the case," he said. "As of this morning, the department has launched a homicide investigation in the matter of the death of this Jane Doe."

A collective gasp came from the crowd. This was Westfield, New York! A quiet, safe small-town harbor from the metro areas of the state and the rest of the world, for that matter. People died of natural causes here, with few exceptions. Merrill and Jenna were especially stunned. In their thirty-minute meeting with Johnny, he had not revealed the stranger's cause of death. They had assumed that she had drowned.

"So what *was* the cause of death, Sheriff?" Maria Kranz, a reporter from WKBW in Buffalo asked.

"This is an ongoing investigation," Johnny said. Merrill knew this was police-speak for 'none of your damn business.' "Once we identify the victim, we'll be on the path to discovering the perpetrator. Thanks for your attention, ladies and gentlemen." He switched off the microphone, but his, "Let's go, Frank" could be heard by everyone there.

"Come on, Jenna. We need to catch him before he takes off!" Merrill urged her friend, who stood motionless in front of the podium. She was staring straight ahead. "Jenna, are you okay?"

"You go, Merrill," Jenna said, still staring at the vacated podium. She held her right palm out and said, "Give me your keys. Have Johnny drop you off at my place, okay?"

Merrill reached in her pocket for the keys and stepped in front of her friend. Jenna looked like she could easily burst into tears, and she did not want to provoke her. Merrill had seen enough symptoms of trauma, both in her time as a college librarian and now as a research criminologist, to recognize that her friend was struggling with the aftermath of having discovered a dead woman. Worse yet, she had just heard Johnny's pronouncement from the podium that it was not a drowning. When the time was right, Merrill thought, she would call in the troops. She knew that Kate and Sherry were eager to support Jenna and to help her get past this. Through the various crises that life had thrown their way, Jenna had been there for each of them. It was her turn now.

## CHAPTER FOUR

---

# WHAT A DIFFERENCE A YEAR MAKES

"Okay, Jenna, I'll see you at your place," Merrill called over her shoulder as she began briskly walking toward the Sheriff 's department. She broke into a run when she saw Johnny take a sharp left into the parking lot. He was making a beeline for his Bronco.

"Johnny, wait up!" she yelled to his retreating back. He was obviously ignoring her. "Hey, Frank, come here, boy," she called, and being the good boy that he was, he turned and ran to his friend Merrill.

"I wish you wouldn't use my dog to get your way, Mrs. Connor," Johnny said as the press conference attendees, mainly journalists and media crews from the county and beyond, meandered around them. A few of them boldly drew nearer to the deputy sheriff and his criminologist, obviously wanting a scoop regarding the Jane Doe investigation.

"I need a ride to Jenna's," Merrill told her boss.

"Sheriff," shouted a news reporter from Channel 2, "when will you be releasing more details regarding the cause of death?"

Ignoring him, Johnny opened the car door and called to his dog, who was busy licking Merrill's knees. "Okay, you too, Merrill," he acquiesced. "Get in."

"Thanks," she answered and climbed into the passenger seat. Frank didn't have to be invited. He jumped into her lap, and she pulled the door closed. "What was that press conference about, Johnny?" she asked, as he backed the Bronco out of his parking space. "Why didn't you tell Jenna that this was a murder investigation when she was completing her witness statement? More to the point, why didn't you tell *me*, your ace researcher and criminologist, that the Jane Doe was a homicide victim?"

"Look, Merrill, we need to keep the details to ourselves as long as we can if we hope to catch the killer. The final report from the coroner came in minutes before the two of you arrived. I read it as soon as you and Jenna left my office. There was no time to fill you in before I had to address the media."

"Well, here I am. Fill me in, please," Merrill said.

Johnny pulled out of the parking lot before he answered her. "This is for your ears only, for now anyway," he began. "There was no water or foam in the victim's lungs, which excludes drowning as the cause of death. However, there were multiple, severe cranial fractures. Apparently, the woman was violently beaten to death with a blunt object and more than likely dumped at the eastern shore of the lake, possibly around Wright Beach in Dunkirk." Johnny's voice as he told her these details grew louder, a sign that his anxiety was on the rise. "Given that pattern of northeastern winds that the storm whipped up that night, she ended up at Boulder Point. If her life vest hadn't hung up on that rock, Jenna probably wouldn't have found her. More than likely her body would have ended up somewhere in Pennsylvania or Ohio." Johnny reached over and petted Frank's head and immediately the tension in his voice lessened. "So, Merrill, I can't tell you anymore, because I don't know anymore."

"What can *I* do?" she asked.

"Well, for starters, you can find out who Jane Doe is," he said. "That's essential, obviously."

"Shall I get the Divers involved?" she asked. The Divers were a core group of listeners of Merrill's podcast, *A Deeper Dive*. They were not simply fans. Last year they had been instrumental in helping her solve the twenty-year-old cold case of Grace Phillips, who had disappeared from the local mall.

"You'll have to be discreet. Say nothing about the cause of death at this point, but I think getting your listeners involved is a very good idea," Johnny said.

What a difference a year made, Merrill thought. The Sheriff trusted and even valued her research techniques now, and the Divers were a crucial component in that first case. Of course, he wasn't aware of *all* of the tactics she had employed in solving the Grace Phillips mystery. He wasn't aware, for instance, of her psychic source in Lily Dale, and she hadn't felt the need to tell him. What Johnny didn't know couldn't hurt him, his assistant believed.

No, she had not been forthcoming about Victoria Erikson, the Spiritualist who helped her solve that cold case. She wouldn't admit to Johnny that during her first reading with Victoria, a woman from the afterlife had come through and told Merrill that she had the "gift." She had discounted it then as medium mumbo jumbo, but at this point in her life, Merrill had every intention to be in touch with her extra-sensory perception. That's why she had enrolled in "Expanding Your Own Psychic Powers," a six-week seminar at the community college.

It was Merrill's nature to be analytic and logical in her approach to life, and she was still a skeptic about psychic phenomenon. But learning something new – she was always up for that, and she would see what she could garner from the class. So far, the three mediums who were teaching it had emphasized the importance of meditation in developing a heightened sense of intuition.

She had every intention of practicing this form of introspection, but she was just too busy, too involved and focused on her podcast and police work. Maybe she would have to consult a professional in the case of a murdered Jane Doe. She had a strong feeling that Lily Dale and Victoria Erikson were in her future.

## Chapter Five

# IRISH GOODBYE

Even in mid-June, Merrill's podcast space in the Prenderson Library basement was freezing. Most of the time she conducted and recorded *A Deeper Dive* interviews on Zoom, but Haley Marks had reached out to Merrill and requested that she be invited to be on a live episode of the podcast, and she made it clear in that first email that she *really* wanted to meet the host in person. As the theme music played, Merrill silently handed one of the sweaters she kept on hand to the woman sitting across from her.

The tiny storage space in the basement of the library had been converted into Merrill's workplace and the table that held all of her equipment took up 90% of the room. The janitors could barely manage to push a broom in there and they were glad to have Merrill do the little tidying up that had to be done. What a different venue from the cavernous space of SUNY Fredonia's Reed Library where she had worked for three decades. If not for her husband Richard's passing, she would not have retired from the college library staff. But she loved what she was doing now, one of the two "part-time" jobs that necessitated constant learning and contact with interesting people, people she never would have come to know without *A Deeper Dive*. One of them sat in front of her now.

She hoped she would be able to concentrate on this guest and her story. Five days had passed since her friend Jenna had held on to the body of a murdered woman in the waters of Lake Erie, and so far no one had come forward to identify her or to claim her as their loved one. But Johnny had called Merrill a few minutes before the podcast interview was to start. "I think we might have something on our Jane Doe. When can you come in?"

"I'll be there in an hour," she told him and initiated their signature phone hang-up routine – no goodbye, just a click on the other end. Now she must clear her mind and concentrate on her guest. Ever since the Grace Phillip's case had been solved by Merrill and her listeners, she had stayed true to her pledge that the podcast would be dedicated to cold cases. This day's case had already been solved, without her help, but she knew it would be one her followers would appreciate learning about.

"Hello, everyone, and welcome to today's episode of *A Deeper Dive*," Merrill said. "You may have been following my guest's intriguing journey as reported in the local newspapers and on the television news lately. I'm thrilled to welcome her to our studio today and excited to have her deliver an exclusive update to our audience. Welcome to the podcast, Haley Marks."

"Hello, Merrill. I'm glad to be here." Merrill appreciated this guest's assertive demeanor. She looked directly into the host's eyes as she spoke. Merrill's experience with other guests along with her keen intuition led her to believe that this would be a very smooth interview. "I've been an admirer of yours since the beginning of the broadcast," Haley continued. "You've actually got quite a fan base in Central New York, you know."

Merrill felt the familiar blush of embarrassment creep up her neck to her face, but she kept going. "Thank you, Haley. Let's start by telling the audience what brings you from Syracuse to our part of the state."

"Well, I had been a social studies teacher in Baldwinsville for many years. Once I retired from teaching, I traveled a bit, took a gourmet cooking class and a watercolor class, joined two book clubs and, in general, enjoyed my free time away from the hundreds of daily decisions a teacher has to make. Eventually, I found my current passion; I became enthralled with discovering my family's genealogy."

Merrill nodded in appreciation for a "sister" who had discovered that life after fifty could be fulfilling. And she was also a searcher, like herself. Even better. "I spent a couple of years investigating my maternal side," Haley said. "I even took a trip to the Sicilian village near Palermo where my great-grandparents had been born and where they resided for years until their deaths. It's called *Montemaggiore Belsito*. I actually found some distant cousins still living there."

"That must have been wonderful," Merrill said.

"It was amazing! But after that, I still had the genealogy bug, so I decided to explore my father's family, too. Unfortunately, we had been estranged since I was a young child, and I really had no contact with his siblings either, so primary resources weren't available for my search. Then one day I was on Facebook, and a first cousin reached out to me. She had limited information, but it was enough to get me started. My great-grandfather, Paul Marks, had come from County Mayo in Ireland, she told me in our first of several phone calls. Like thousands before and after him, he was more than likely fleeing from Ireland because of The Great Famine. I was so excited to find his name on the list of immigrants who left the town of Westport in County Mayo and came over on the SS Britain in May of 1852. It was the first transatlantic steamship that left Ireland and docked in New York City three weeks later. Paul Marks was listed as a twenty-year-old laborer."

Merrill heard the excitement in this woman's voice, and as a research librarian, she understood the thrill of discovery. "What kind of work did he find in New York City?" Merrill asked.

"Well, more than likely he wasn't qualified to do much of anything, and he wasn't in the city long enough to find a job," she answered. "A week after he arrived, his name appeared on a passenger list of the New York and Erie Railroad that I discovered. The line ran from New York City to Dunkirk, New York. That town, just a few miles from your studio here in Westfield, was the end of the line. It may be interesting to your audience, given what's happening to immigrants in some states today, that New York City government officials were handing out rail tickets to immigrants who had little or no knowledge of this country. They had no money, no family or friends here. The people in charge assured these folks that they would be taken care of once they reached the end point of the journey, that they had nothing to worry about. Of course, the main objective of those officials was getting these folks out of their ever expanding, over-populated city. Sounds familiar, doesn't it?"

"Frighteningly familiar," Merrill answered. "So what became of your great-grandfather Paul Marks once he got to Dunkirk?"

"He disappeared. According to the tax rolls in Chautauqua County, that is. Until his name appeared on a land tax record in the town of Sheridan."

"Really? That surprises me, Haley," Merrill said.

"Two years after he had come to a strange land, totally impoverished, and with no connections to anyone in America, Paul Marks bought a hundred-acre farm in Sheridan, New York, for four hundred dollars!"

Merrill did not miss the tone of pride in the woman's voice. "Amazing! But where did he get the money? That would have been a fortune in those days, especially for an immigrant."

"Often times when you're doing a genealogical hunt, it becomes necessary to speculate, to fill in the blanks with an educated guess," Haley Marks said.

"I can relate to that," Merrill said.

"County Cork was an agricultural region, before the Potato Famine devastated it, that is. Chautauqua County from its early days until now was, and is, an agricultural center. More than likely, Paul Marks worked on area farms until he had the money to buy his own."

"That makes sense. So where did your research take you from there, Haley?"

"Literally, Merrill, it took me a few hundred miles from home. I made arrangements with everyone in my life I needed to, got in my car, and drove to Sheridan. To Newell Road in Sheridan, to be exact. To the site of my great-grandfather's farm. Or what had been his farm. All that's left of it is a six-acre plot with an abandoned ranch style home on it. The private airfield across the road is where Paul's fields would have been."

"So you didn't find any of the original structures?" Merrill asked.

"Only one. Although the barn had been torn down, the old milk house still stood, which fortunately held a lot of clues about my great-grandfather's life. The structure itself proved that he at one time had cows. But what I found on an inside wall of the building took my breath away. I took this picture," she said, handing Merrill her phone.

"Oh, wow! We'll post this on the website so you can all see it, but let me describe it to our listeners. It's a growth chart for three children from the years 1856 to 1862. Shawn Marks, Neil Marks, and Catherine Marks," Merrill said.

"Catherine. My grandmother," Haley added. "That chart led me to the birth records in Chautauqua County during the time period. Sure enough, I located each child on the rolls. And I found the name of the woman my great-grandfather had married. Sharon Marks. I found it again in the Chautauqua County Archives. Sharon Marks (nee Murphy), also an immigrant from County Cork, died in 1862, predeceasing her husband," she said.

Merrill admired this researcher's diligence and told her so. "Great work, Haley!"

"I was so excited to find all of these documents, to see the homestead on Newell Road, to learn the names of my great-uncles and aunts. But my excitement faded when all traces of Paul's life disappeared after Sharon's death. I couldn't find anything. The taxes on the farm went unpaid from 1865 until 1900 when it was purchased again," Haley said. "I was almost ready to pack up and head home when I thought of the local newspaper, *The Dunkirk Courier*. I knew from my research that the paper has been the main source of north county news for decades. Although I had checked out of my hotel, I headed to their office on Main Street and asked if I could look at some indexes from those years after Sharon passed. Within an hour I found this article from May of 1863. Go ahead and read it if you would, Merrill."

"*Local man loses arm in farm accident*," Merrill read aloud. "*Paul Marks of Newell Road in Sheridan hitched his two horses to his wagon this past Monday and headed out to seed some fields. A critter of some sort dashed out in front to the cart and spooked the horses, at which point they reared up and the wagon with Mr. Marks in it turned over. The man lay there for over an hour until one of his boys, walking home from the schoolhouse, found him. By the time they got him to the hospital it was too late for doctors to save his right arm, and they had to perform an amputation."* Merrill stopped reading and looked across the table at her guest. "How terrible," she said.

"Losing his arm more than likely made it impossible for him to do physical labor and he probably lost the farm after that. Although I hunted online and through other sources for months after leaving Dunkirk, that article was the last trace of any document that informed me of my great-grandfather's American life. Until a year later, when I happened to come across this article in the *Jamestown Post Journal*." Haley picked up a sheet of paper from the file folder in front of her and passed it to Merrill. "I've highlighted the most important section. Would you mind reading it, Merrill?"

"Not at all, Haley. '*Three bodies were discovered on a Dewittville farm yesterday morning on the site of what had been the location of the Chautauqua County Poor Farm. For many years during the nineteenth and early part of the twentieth century, the farm housed and employed the county's indigent population. The skeletal remains of two adults and a baby were not thought to be suspicious, since 600 marked graves were also a part of the Farm. The adult remains were of a woman and a man. The man's right arm had been amputated.*'" Merrill was silent for a moment. "Oh my word, Haley! You found your great-grandfather!" Merrill said.

"I couldn't be sure, Merrill, even at that point. I contacted the county coroner's office and they sent the remains to a forensic lab. I was thrilled when they decided there was enough DNA material to perform a test and compare it to my own. And here is the latest news that I wanted to share with your Deeper Dive audience. It was a match! I had my answer and the county could now put a name on my great-grandfather's gravestone. Here's a photo I took," she said, passing it to Merrill.

"Paul Marks, born in County Cork, November 1, 1832. Died Chautauqua County Poor Farm, 1882," Merrill continued to read the verse on the headstone. '*Death leaves a heartache no one can heal. Love leaves a memory no one can steal.'* "That seems like a perfect epitaph for your great-grandfather, Haley," she said.

Merrill's guest's eyes were shining. "It's from an Irish poem," she said. "I thought it was very fitting. I was overjoyed to have found him and to be able to share my discovery with my family and with your audience."

Merrill thanked her guest and after Haley had left the podcast studio, Merrill recorded a message for her audience that would be added to the episode. "Divers, I hope you enjoyed that segment. Haley Marks was relentless in her search for her great-grandfather, in spite of the fact that time and distance could have stopped her. Today, I'd like to invite you to help the Deputy Sheriff's office to solve the mystery of the woman whose body was found at the Boulder Point beach five days ago. All we know at this point is that she was most likely a victim of foul play. If there is anyone in your life who has been missing during that time period, please contact me or the Deputy Sheriff. I know I can count on you! Until we meet again, this is Merrill Connor signing off from *A Deeper Dive*."

As the theme music played, Merrill's phone vibrated against the oak table, and Johnny's face appeared on the screen. When she answered, he skipped the hello. "Meet me at Moose Beach. I need to show you something."

CHAPTER SIX

---

# THE ORU

MERRILL HAD RISKED a speeding ticket on her way to Moose Beach, which was several miles west of Boulder Point. The Loyal Order of the Moose had purchased the lake front acreage decades before. It was a popular picnicking and swimming spot for club members and their families throughout the years. She couldn't imagine what there was at the beach that Johnny wanted her to see.

She pulled the Nissan into the lot and parked behind Johnny's patrol car. As she stepped to the ground, the sinking sun over the water outlined the profile of man and dog. Merrill decided it would make a great photo, in spite of the fact that Johnny had told her to hurry. She pulled out her phone and snapped a few quick shots as Frank barked his greeting. As she drew closer to the water, she could see lying in front of Johnny and Frank a very large one-man kayak overturned on the sand. "What's up, Johnny?" she asked, bending down to give Frank the petting he mandated each time they met.

"Sorry to bother you right before your interview, but it was important." Johnny knew how much Merrill's work for her podcast *A Deeper Dive* meant to her. It had been invaluable to the department's twenty-year search for Grace Phillips, too, and Johnny had come to have the utmost respect for Merrill's audience, the Divers, as well. "We got a call this afternoon from a woman who had brought her little kids to play at the beach. Shortly after they got here, she spotted this kayak just off shore, so she waded in and dragged it onto the sand. Then she called us."

"The world is full of good people, you know, Johnny?" He ignored the hint of sarcasm in her voice, but Merrill kept going. "Is this unoccupied water vehicle the reason you called me away from an early night with my pj's and a glass of wine?"

"That and the fact that it has a New York State registration number," he answered.

"Huh. I didn't think water vehicles without motors had to be registered," she said.

"They don't," Johnny answered. "It's optional, but given the monetary value of this one, according to my Google research anyway, the owner must have decided that it would be a prudent thing to do. I'm guessing for insurance purposes."

"Fascinating. Again, *why* am I here?"

"I couldn't help but wonder if our Jane Doe might have been in this kayak before or after she was murdered. So I traced the registration."

Merrill felt goosebumps erupt up and down her arms. "And?" she asked.

"And. We found the owner, who is very much alive. Her name is Alexandra Sheldon. I sent a couple of guys out to her home in Dunkirk when there was no answer on the phone number the DMV had for her."

"What did she have to say about her missing kayak?" Merrill asked.

"The guys said that she seemed pretty shaken up when they explained that we had recovered it. When they asked her when the last time was that she had used it, she told them she had never even been in it. That she had given it to her ex as a gift," Johnny said.

"Her ex? Who would that be?"

"Her name is Lynn Martinelli. Dr. Lynn Martinelli."

"Is she a physician?" Merrill asked.

"Therapist," Johnny answered. Merrill noticed that the sheriff's face was turning red. It occurred to her that perhaps Johnny and Dr. Martinelli had had a professional relationship. He had been cryptically candid with Merrill about the fact that Frank was not the only source of therapy that he was receiving for his anxiety. "Ms. Sheldon told Lieutenant Farrell that she hadn't seen her girlfriend since they broke up a couple of months ago. The guys took a ride to the Shore Acres address she gave them for Dr. Martinelli."

"What did Dr. Martinelli have to say about her runaway kayak?"

"She wasn't there. After five minutes of ringing the bell and knocking, our guys walked around the house and looked in. All the lights in the place were turned on, as were the outdoor lights, even though it was 3:30 in the afternoon. The mailbox was stuffed to overflowing and there were several newspapers jammed into the *Buffalo News* box. Also, on the back door there was a sticky note, more than likely from a client. It said something to the effect of 'Hey, Dr. M. I was here for my 1 o'clock appointment. Where were you?'"

"So she saw clients in a home office," Merrill said.

"Now this is why the county pays you the big bucks, Mrs. Connor." Whenever Johnny played the sarcasm card with Merrill, he called her Mrs. Connor. Really, she thought to herself, she almost felt sorry for the guy. He was such a poor match for her much sharper wit.

She pretended to ignore the dig. "Any vehicles on the premises?"

"Yes. A new Bronco with a kayak rack on the roof," he answered.

"Bingo!" Merrill said.

"Maybe. Ms. Sheldon gave us the names and addresses of Dr. Martinelli's two children. We're in the process of contacting them to see what they know about her whereabouts. Also, I have an appointment with Alexandra Sheldon first thing in the morning at my office. I want you to be there." It wasn't a question.

"Yes sir, boss!" she answered, and knelt down to make direct eye contact with Frank.

"Please," he added.

"What time?" she asked not the man, but the man's best friend. Frank's licks to her hands and face were his answer.

"Ten," was the Deputy Sheriff's reply.

Merrill stood up and checked her calendar. "I'm having coffee with Jenna at the Diner at nine, so that should be fine," she said.

"How is Jenna doing?" Johnny asked.

"Better, I hope, but I can't be sure. She seems to be avoiding face-to-face contact." Merrill felt a small twinge of guilt. Her efforts to reach Jenna were limited to mostly unanswered calls and texts. She knew she should have shown up at her house or shop unannounced so that Jenna couldn't avoid her. But to see her confident friend broken down by this traumatic event was too much for Merrill. "I guess she needs some time to process everything," she told Johnny.

"Well, it's not every day that a person finds a body at Boulder Point," he said.

"Thank goodness," Merrill said, as she turned to go. "See you in the morning, Frank," she called, and as the last of the sunlight abandoned the beach, she treaded carefully over rocks and driftwood until she reached the parking lot.

As she drove home, she thought about Jenna. She hadn't been entirely candid with Johnny about her state of mind. She seemed so fragile. Kate and Sherry had agreed with Merrill that their friend was not herself since discovering the dead woman. They took turns trying to check in with her every day, but so far she had pretty much ignored their calls and avoided seeing any of them in person.

Jenna's dodging her friends reminded Merrill of her own self-imposed isolation following her husband Richard's death four years ago. That hard shell of grief was difficult to break through, but her three friends refused to let it stand between them and Merrill. She had re-entered the world because of their encouragement, no, because of their insistence. Jenna had certainly been traumatized that day at Boulder Point, but her friends refused to let her face this alone. They agreed that they would not permit her to retreat into herself.

Thankfully, Jenna had agreed to have coffee with Merrill the next day, and Kate and Sherry were going to meet them at the beach for some glass gathering in the afternoon. Since her discovery of Jane Doe, Jenna had not been to Boulder Point or any other beach. She admitted in a response text to Merrill that she hadn't done any jewelry work either. So the plan was that her three friends would hopefully discover some gems at the beach and commission her to make pieces for them. "Just to get her creative juices flowing again," Kate had said to Merrill and Sherry.

Merrill's thoughts turned to tomorrow's meeting with Alexandra Sheldon, the owner of the runaway kayak. As she pulled into her driveway, she decided that she would do some preliminary research on Dr. Martinelli's ex. Her pajamas and an early bedtime would have to take a back seat to some online digging. Merrill was wide-awake now, anyway.

CHAPTER SEVEN

## THE EX

IN HER PRELIMINARY search, Merrill didn't find anything of note except Alexandra Sheldon's business website. The photograph at the top of the page was of an attractive forty-something in a business suit, sitting at a huge desk. According to the site, she was a self-employed IT consultant who had established her office in Fredonia a year earlier. The several comments from customers were rave reviews regarding her technical skills and business acumen. She was a Rotarian, and until recently she had sat on several village committees, including the Chamber of Commerce. Remarkable in this day and age, she had no Facebook, Instagram, or Twitter accounts that Merrill could find.

That was enough work for today, Merrill decided, sipping the last of the cabernet from her glass. She glanced around the Shed, Richard's former studio, grateful for the sense of reassurance she always took from his art work. She picked up her laptop, and on her way out of the room, she stopped in front of the easel that held her husband's last creation. Staring at the painting, Merrill took a deep breath. The watercolor of a free diver surrounded by an infinite blue ocean never failed to move her. He had painted it in his last month on this earth when his hands were immobilized by the advanced ALS, holding the brush with his mouth. Not only had she named her podcast after the painting, but she used *A Deeper Dive* as her screen saver, on her stationery, her business cards, her website. "Good night, my love," she whispered to the empty room.

When her phone rang the next morning as she was brushing her teeth, Merrill's heart sank when she saw Jenna's face appear on her screen. Was she going to cancel their outing today? Sherry and Kate had shifted some business appointments to be able to spend the day with her at the beach. "Hello," she said, not able to hide the note of suspicion in her voice.

"Hey, good morning! No need to pick me up," Jenna said. "I'm going to ride my bike. I'll meet you at the Diner."

"What about our plans to go to the beach?" Merrill asked.

"No worries. I've ridden my bike to the Point dozens of times," Jenna answered.

Merrill tried to hide the wariness she felt about this change in the plan. Did Jenna figure that she could cut the day short if she had her bike? "Okay. Sounds good. See you soon."

Over cups of the Diner's dark roast and blueberry scones, Merrill tried to assess Jenna's mood. Her friend smiled across the table as she described the new soldering iron that she expected would be delivered later today, and Merrill was encouraged. Perhaps Jenna *was* moving beyond the trauma she had experienced that day in the water.

"My treat," Jenna said when they reached the register.

"Well, thanks," Merrill said.

"You're welcome. You've been great since...I really appreciate it, Merrill."

"I just want you to feel better," was all Merrill could think to say. "I've got an appointment with Johnny at ten," she said, "but I'll meet you ladies at the beach. I probably won't be more than an hour."

"Sounds good," Jenna said, retrieving her bike from the rack in front of the Diner. "See you then."

As Merrill walked into the building that housed both the Westfield police and the Deputy Sheriff's office across the hall from it, she was still thinking about Jenna. She needed to get her head in the game and refocus, she chided herself. When she opened the door to the Sheriff's Department, the first thing she saw was the wagging black tail sticking out from under the receptionist's desk. Linda was a favorite of Frank's, and whenever the dog tired of Johnny's company, he would snuggle up to her. "Go on in," she said to Merrill. "He's expecting you."

Fifteen minutes later, after Johnny and Merrill discussed everything they had found online about their ten o'clock interview subject, Linda led a very tall young woman dressed in a chicly tailored business suit into the office. After brief introductions, Johnny began. "So, Ms. Sheldon…"

"Call me Alex, please," the woman said. Her hazel eyes were incredible, Merrill thought, and her auburn hair, cut very short, showcased an exquisite heart-shaped face.

"All right, Alex. I want to thank you for giving us the contact information for Dr. Martinelli's children. We got in touch with the local police near their Los Angeles area residences. They broke the terrible news that their mother was missing and that she might be the victim of foul play." Alex Sheldon pulled a tissue from her jacket pocket and wiped her eyes. Johnny gave her a minute and then continued. "When our department reached out to them, they told us they hadn't seen or heard from their mother in days, although they said that they didn't find that particularly unusual. Neither of them is able to get to the area to identify the body until early next week. Based on the information they gave us, we've connected Dr. Martinelli's dentist with a forensic dentist who will take a look at the x-rays the coroner made."

Merrill was not used to Johnny's "police business" voice. It made her sit up straighter in the chair. "We're hoping that they don't match those of Dr. Martinelli and that we can eliminate her as the murder victim."

"Murder?? What do you mean, Sheriff Lovallo?" The woman was obviously shaken by this information. Merrill wondered how she had missed the news of Johnny's announcement to the press. "The woman who was found at Boulder Point drowned!"

"We haven't released all of the details to the public yet, Ms. Sheldon, but very soon we will have no choice. This person did not drown," Johnny said.

Merrill observed the woman's trembling hands as she reached for her water bottle. "Can you tell us about your relationship with Dr. Martinelli?" Merrill was careful to keep her voice low and steady. "How long have you known her?" she asked.

"We met on a dating site about a year ago," she answered. "Lynn had just come out after leaving a ten year hetero marriage. Her second. Her first husband, who died very young, was the father of her children. You should talk to the kids about Peter Martinelli, though. They spent a good portion of their breaks from college under the same roof with him. And it wasn't a happy experience."

Johnny wrote something in his notebook, the one that reminded Merrill of elementary school with its black marbleized design and wide spaces. "What else can you tell us about your relationship with Dr. Martinelli, Ms. Sheldon?" he said.

"Please. I'm Alex," she said again. "Well, we started chatting online and we hit it off immediately," she said. "She and I had so much in common. We both had a passion for the outdoors. She was a runner and so was I. We found out we were both members of a cycling club in Jamestown, although we had never met that either of us could remember."

"And the kayak," Johnny said. "What can you tell us about that?"

"Well, Lynn's love of the water was where we differed. She and the kids, while they were still at home, had a speed boat and jet skis at their Shore Acres home. They pretty much grew up on the lake. Lynn was a competitive swimmer during college. But I've been afraid of the water from the time I was a child. Lynn had been talking about wanting to kayak as part of her exercise regimen, so I thought it was the perfect gift at the time." Suddenly, the woman started to sob. "Oh, my God, please don't let it be Lynn!"

Merrill grabbed the box of tissues from the top of a file cabinet and handed it to the distraught woman. "Take your time, Alex. We understand how upsetting this must be."

"Let me get you some more water," Johnny offered, and when he opened the door, in trotted Frank. His therapist instincts had been alerted, more than likely by the sound of a crying woman. He scampered toward her, and because of Alex's height he couldn't reach her knees, so he planted a lick on the sniffling woman's shin.

"Oh, my goodness," she said, looking down as she wiped her tears away. "Who are you?" she asked the dachshund.

"Ms. Sheldon, meet Frank," Johnny said, as he came back in, carrying a bottle of water.

After the introduction, Frank settled at the feet of this human who seemed to be in need of his comforting presence. "Hello, Frank," the woman said.

Johnny continued the interview. "So what do you know about Dr. Martinell's kayaking routine?" he asked.

"I knew nothing about kayaking, but after a lot of research, I bought her the Oru for her birthday. She loved it! Most of the time she had clients until 6:00 or 7:00 p.m., and she would often take it out after that, sometimes, in my opinion, when the weather conditions weren't optimal. She could put it in from her property, although she did buy a rack for her car. I don't think she ever used it, though. She told me it was more convenient to launch it from her beach at Shore Acres," Alex said. The woman reached down and scratched Frank's ears. "Lynn and I broke up right after her birthday," she said quietly. "It was a mutual decision. She said she wasn't ready to settle down, and I knew that was true. We loved one another, but we each wanted a different lifestyle."

Merrill could see how draining these questions were for Alex, and Johnny seemed to read her mind. "Alex, we want to thank you very much for coming in this morning. Rest assured, we will do everything in our power to find Dr. Martinelli," he said.

"You should talk with Peter. Martinelli. Her ex-husband. He was suing her for an increase in his maintenance and generally making her life miserable. You should talk to him."

Johnny returned to his notebook and scrawled something in it. Then he stood. "Thank you so much for your help, Alex. We'll call you if we need anything else," he said.

The two women got to their feet and as Merrill stood next to her, she was daunted by their extreme height difference. Alex Sheldon had a good twelve inches on her and probably eight on Johnny. As the three walked out of the office followed by Frank, Alex turned to them. "Please let me know as soon as you find out anything," she said.

"We will. Let me walk you out, Alex," Merrill said, giving Johnny a nod before she led the way to the main door. She was surprised to see Jenna at the entrance, about to push the heavy door open, but she continued with her goodbyes to Alex in spite of it. "Here's my card if you need to get in touch." The woman took it and spent a few seconds reading it.

"Thank you, Merrill. It was good meeting you," she said as they shook hands.

Turning back, Merrill noticed that Jenna's bike was leaning against the building, a very flat back tire quite obvious. "Oh, oh," she said. "What happened?"

Jenna ignored the question. "Who was that?" she asked, her eyes following the woman's trek to the parking lot. When Merrill remained silent, she said, "I'm just wondering because I'm sure she's a customer of mine. She was wearing a pair of my earrings. I noticed them because of the rareness of the glass. Red is extremely rare; one in 5,000 pieces is red. It takes a whole summer, sometimes, to find red glass. And that texture, those little bumps, make it even rarer."

"What would be the original source of those pieces? A bottle, a lantern?" Merrill guessed.

"Good thinking, Merrill. You'd probably be right if the glass were smooth. Smooth red glass isn't common either, but that raised texture indicates that it probably came from a boat or ship tail light. I remember the day at Boulder Point when I found those two unusual pieces. It was like winning the lottery! They were nearly perfect matches in shape and size. So I'm certain that woman was wearing my earrings. But I didn't see the necklace that went with it. She bought the whole set the day she came to my shop. They were for a special friend, she said."

"Whoa! Slow down!" Merrill said. "Did you recognize that woman, Jenna? Are you sure she's the one who bought the red set?"

"No, not when she first came out of the building. But I certainly recognized my earrings," Jenna said. "I remember seeing her at a craft fair in Bemus Point a few weeks after she had bought them. She stopped in front of my tent when she saw my *Mermaids' Tears* banner. She went on and on about how much her friend loved the jewelry. That's why I was surprised to see her wearing the earrings." Jenna paused. "Maybe they broke up. Or maybe her partner didn't like them. For whatever reason, she must have decided to keep them for herself. I must say, she has great taste. The price I put on that set was the most I've ever charged for my creations," she said.

As Merrill helped to load Jenna's bike into the back of her Murano, her thoughts were racing. She couldn't tell her friend that the buyer of the rare red set could very likely be the ex-lover of the woman whose body Jenna had discovered at Boulder Point. In the first place, that had not been proven, and in the second place, she was afraid that information would set her friend back to square one. As she fastened her seat belt, she turned toward Jenna. "To the beach we go," she said.

## CHAPTER EIGHT

---

# NO PICNIC

THE TEN MINUTE drive to Boulder Point was unusually silent. When it was obvious that Jenna had nothing more to say about Alex Sheldon and the red glass jewelry, Merrill turned the radio up. A worrying thought occurred to her while Bonnie Raitt sang *I Can't Make You Love Me*. She prayed that the yellow police tape that had outlined a portion of the shoreline was taken down by now. She didn't want Jenna to see it.

When she pulled her car in behind Sherry's black Audi, she turned her head toward the beach and saw that the tape had been removed. Breathing a sigh of relief, she reached for her backpack on the floor of the backseat. "Let's go find some glass!" she said. Jenna remained seated and said nothing. She was staring out at the mirror-smooth water, so unusual for Lake Erie. "Looks like it's going to be a great day!" Merrill said. "I'll grab your bag, too," she added, but Jenna didn't respond. She didn't move.

Kate waved from the spot yards away that she and Sherry had claimed. Her turquoise cover-up and matching hat looked fabulous on her, although the only other beach-goers that day seemed to be a class of preschoolers with their teacher, hardly Kate's demographic when it came to potential admirers. Sherry stood next to four blue striped sand chairs that were positioned close to a huge flat piece of driftwood. An osprey flew against the background of a cloudless blue sky. At that moment, Merrill thought of Richard. He would have loved to capture this scene in a painting or photograph. She took a moment to think about how far she had come since his death. The thought of her husband capturing the day with his art brought her only happiness.

Jenna seemed to suddenly wake from her daydream, and she opened the door and climbed out of the car. You would have thought by Sherry's persistent waving that the two approaching women were long lost friends, instead of people who stayed in close touch, at the very least, on a weekly basis. As they drew closer, Merrill and Jenna watched as the always dramatic Kate pointed to the cooler at her feet and pantomimed joyously eating and drinking. "Geez," Merrill said, "I guess I should have said, 'Let's find some food instead of let's find some glass!'" Her attempt at light-hearted banter went unacknowledged by Jenna.

"Hey, you two," Sherry called out. "You're late!" She towel-dried her long brown hair as she continued. "I think Kate and I have picked up every cool piece of glass on the beach! Look at these beauties," she said as she approached Jenna, picking out three cobalt blue pieces from her small collection bag and showing them to her friend. "Do you think you could make me earrings and a bracelet with these?"

"Sure." Jenna's voice was uncharacteristically flat and barely audible. She wasn't looking at Sherry's treasures. She was staring out at the lake.

Kate stopped in the middle of setting up their picnic lunch on top of the driftwood table. "Jenna, are you okay?" she asked gently. God, Merrill thought, leave it to Kate to come right out with it.

"No. I'm sorry, girls. I'm not," Jenna answered. "Would you take me home, Merrill?"

"What?" Kate said. "No. Don't go Jenna! I thought we were spending the day together." But Jenna had already turned toward the parking lot.

"I'm sorry," Jenna repeated as she walked away from her friends.

Kate and Sherry followed them to the car in silence. Merrill could see how shocked they were at Jenna's behavior. This was the first time they had seen her since she had discovered the body at this beach.

As Merrill and Jenna buckled their seat belts, Kate yelled, "Put the window down. I want to ask you something." When Merrill complied Kate leaned in and asked, "What are you two doing Saturday night? I'm sitting in on keyboard with a group at Larry's. They're young, but I think they're really good. Can you make it?" She was staring at Jenna who was looking straight ahead.

"Sure," Merrill said. "Sounds like fun."

"What about you, Jenna?" Kate asked.

"I'll let you know, Kate," Jenna said.

Merrill backed out, and Kate and Sherry waved to their friends, one more forlorn looking than the other.

As Merrill drove she tried to respect Jenna's silence and said nothing, but her mind was racing. Jenna was so distraught, so unlike her calm Zen-like self, her usual temperament so different from those of her three frenetic friends. In this moment, she seemed to be very far away, as if she were in a trance. How could she help her friend? Merrill felt desperate for the answer. Until last week, Jenna was the most confident of the four of them. She had always known what she wanted. It killed Merrill to see her this way. She would have a talk with Jenna's husband Steve to find out what he thought about his wife's state of mind. Maybe she needed a vacation. Sherry could help with that. Maybe a girls' getaway weekend, or maybe a few therapy sessions would help her get beyond this trauma.

Her anxious thoughts were interrupted by Jenna's voice. It was barely a whisper. "Why me? Why did I have to be the one who found her?"

Merrill knew that Jenna didn't expect an answer. She understood what it was like when logic did not prevail and truth was elusive. She had discovered last year as she worked on the Grace Phillips case that not all facts were obtainable using only the power and reach of an analytic mind. That was why Merrill had enrolled in the community college course on psychic development. But so far, she had missed the last two classes because of the Jane Doe murder. Suddenly, Merrill had a vision of the white iron gates of Lily Dale.

Before she pulled out of Jenna's driveway, she quick-dialed Kate. "What do you know about Inspiration Stump?" she asked.

# CHAPTER NINE

## THE STUMP

LAST YEAR, FOR *A Deeper Dive* episode on the local area's connection to Spiritualism, Merrill had done some preliminary research on the services held in Lily Dale at The Stump. But she believed that primary resources were most times superior to a written recounting, and she just happened to have a close friend who qualified as an expert on all things Lily Dale. The evening following their failed beach outing, Merrill had called Kate and invited her for a salad and a glass of wine on her patio.

"So, what should one know before attending a Stump service?" Merrill said, while she performed the last maneuver on the corkscrew.

Kate held out her wine glass. "Well, first of all, how much do you know about the Fox sisters?" she asked.

Merrill answered as she poured. "Probably what you would call the basics. Maggie and *Kate*," she said, barely stifling a chuckle, "the Fox siblings, were instrumental in the development and popularizing of Spiritualism and its practices in Lily Dale beginning in the 19th century. They supposedly found..." Merrill saw that the word *supposedly* had raised Kate's hackles, so she corrected herself and continued. "They found that each of them had the keen ability to beckon and recognize spirits, especially those who rapped to get the attention of the living." Merrill demonstrated the technique, rapping her knuckles three times underneath the patio table. "This was the method the spirits used to reveal their presence to the sisters and their clients." At that moment, Merrill was tempted to reprise the Sugar Hill Gang classic *Rapper's Delight*, but she didn't want to offend Kate, who had a sincere reverence regarding all things mystical *and* musical. Instead, she continued her narrative about the Fox sisters. "That particular talent made the siblings, and Lily Dale, famous. Of course much later in life, because she was old and impoverished, Kate Fox began to grant interviews for money. She told several journalists that she and her sister had been fakers all along."

"That's mostly accurate, Merrill," Kate commented, a slight tone of approval in her voice. "Although the faking, as you call it, has been disputed by some other historians."

"Well, you know what Napoleon said about history, don't you?" Merrill continued.

"No," Kate said. "What did he say?"

"He said: 'History is a set of lies agreed upon.' Anyway, apparently the Fox sisters did their best "work" while their followers sat in a circle around a stump or a tree trunk deep in the woods."

"The woods are called the Forest Temple," Kate said. "People gather there to get in touch with those who reside in the Afterlife."

"I've read about that. You've actually been to the Stump, right?" Merrill asked, although her ESP assured her what the answer would be.

"Many times," Kate said. "Even though I've never had a message from Spirit at the Stump. The gathering is somber and serious. You need to understand, Merrill, this is a religious ceremony, as solemn as any other church service."

"How are the messages from the spirits delivered?" Merrill could hardly believe these words were coming out of her mouth.

"*Spirit* is the more correct term, Merrill, not spirits."

"Alright," Merrill said. "I stand corrected. *Spirit.*"

"There is a medium, usually more than one, presiding over the prayers and connecting with those in the Afterlife," Kate answered. "But not every one who attends receives a message. My first experience at Lily Dale was at the Stump. After no medium came to me that day, I made my initial appointment with Victoria."

The last time Merrill had seen Victoria Erikson was at Grace Phillip's funeral. She still had her doubts about psychics and their ability to reach those who had passed on, but she had come a long way from being a complete skeptic. She owed that to her experiences with Victoria. Although she knew that Jenna was neutral on the subject of mediums, Merrill was fairly sure that her friend wasn't in the frame of mind to have a reading any time soon.

"The weather is supposed to be beautiful for the next few days. I'm thinking of inviting Jenna for a ride around Cassadaga Lake. It's conveniently located near the Lily Dale Assembly. I'm not sure I want to tell her my main objective, though."

"Which is?" Kate asked.

"To take a walk around Lily Dale and eventually wander into the Forest Temple. Just to observe a Stump service. I'll see if that entices her to eventually make an appointment with a medium."

"You've come a long way from your Doubting Thomas days, Merrill. I'm proud of you, and it sounds like a good plan to me," Kate said, clearing the table as she spoke. "And speaking of plans, don't forget I'm playing at Larry's on Saturday with the trio of kids I told you about. They call themselves *The No Names*. They're very good, even though their sum total age is, well, almost as many years as any one of us."

"I'm looking forward to it, girl," Merrill said, opening the kitchen door to the outside for Kate. "You'll get no judgey ageism from this lady."

As soon as Kate left, Merrill took a deep breath and called Jenna. She was surprised and relieved when Jenna picked up and even more pleased when she accepted her invitation for the next day. It wouldn't be the first trip to the Spiritualist community for the two of them. Jenna had accompanied Merrill to Lily Dale last winter when she had had a reading with Victoria, just to keep her friend company. Although Merrill didn't think that Jenna was a doubter like she was, or rather, had been, she certainly wasn't a devotee of Spiritualism like their friend Kate.

The afternoon Stump service started at 1p.m., and when Jenna climbed into her car at eleven, Merrill had already decided to tell her the truth about today's venture. "I just thought we might enjoy the sunshine with a dash of Spiritualism mixed in," she said.

Jenna was silent for a few seconds. "I guess I need a distraction from what's been going on in my head these days. Steve totally agrees with that, too. But I'm not interested in making an appointment with Victoria or any other medium, Merrill," she said.

"Yep. I get it," Merrill said.

As they drove, she and Jenna talked about many things. Dina, Merrill's daughter who was pregnant with her first grandchild, Jason, Merrill's son and his new living arrangement with his partner, Craig, Jenna's plans to teach some classes on jewelry-making at her shop, the Saturday night plan to see Kate at the Larry's gig. "She just can't be stopped, our Kate," she said. Jenna agreed. Before they realized it, the sign on Route 60 pointing to the left turn to Lily Dale was in front of them.

It took them a good five minutes to pay for admission and pull through the gates. Lily Dale was a much more popular place during the summer season, Merrill realized. The last time she and Jenna had been here, the lake was frozen and a serious snow was falling. Most of the cars in the long line in front of them today had out-of-state plates from all parts of the country.

Merrill pulled into the parking lot closest to the small lake. Signs pointing to *The Trees of Lily Dale* and *Leolyn Woods* were posted just beyond where they had parked. She sat on the tailgate of the Murano and took off her shoes and put on the sneakers she always kept in the back seat. Looking down at her friend's feet, she said, "Those flats are cute, Jenna, but will they work for our walk?"

"I'll be fine, *Mom*," Jenna said, displaying the wide grin she was known for. Merrill felt relief flood over her. It was the first time in a long while that she had seen her friend smile. "Hey, the brochure says there's a shop called *The Crystal Cave*, specializing in unique glass objects. That's right up my alley."

"That sounds interesting, but let's get a walk in first, shall we?" Merrill said. "Oh, look at that sign, Jenna. It says *Fairy Trail*."

"Okay, follow that arrow," Jenna said indicating the wooden staked sign.

The two women strolled with dozens of other hikers, stopping along the way to admire the little fairies and gnomes charmingly arranged in their tiny houses or arrayed on low-hanging pine branches. Merrill heard "*oos*" and "*ahs*" as they walked, and when she looked at Jenna's face, which registered nothing but pleasure, she began to feel like she had made the right decision.

The next arrow pointed toward the Pet Cemetery of Lily Dale. As the women approached the memorial to the pets that had passed on, they saw all manner of grave markers, ranging from crude to artistic. Jenna stood in front of the sign and read aloud. "*The Lily Dale Pet Cemetery is the oldest known of its kind in the United States. In 1900, a beloved team of horses and their driver went out on the lake to cut blocks of ice. That spring there was an early thaw, and Topsy, one of the horses fell through the ice and drowned. This spot is dedicated to her spirit and the spirits of all the beloved creatures whose memories are consecrated here.*" Merrill and Jenna spent several minutes reading the many tributes to the animals that lay below.

"We should keep moving," Merrill said, looking at her Fitbit. "We don't want to miss anything."

They continued to follow the growing crowd that suddenly diverged toward the woods. A sign read *Inspiration Stump*, and Merrill crossed her fingers as she spoke to Jenna's back. "So this is supposed to be one of the highlights of the Lily Dale experience."

"I read about it in the brochure. It sounds interesting," Jenna said as they walked into the clearing. Merrill let out the breath she had been holding.

As she and Jenna entered a clearing, Merrill was surprised at the number of people who were already there. They sat in a large circle that surrounded a tree stump. Apparently, according to the Lily Dale brochure, there was no real proof that this was *the* Stump presided over by the Fox Sisters, but it was intriguing for Merrill to imagine that possibility. "Let's get a seat, Jenna. It's almost one o'clock."

As they sat among the one hundred or so people, the only sound that could be heard was birdsong. Merrill wasn't sure why she was so nervous. Was she jittery on Jenna's behalf, or because of her own apprehension upon returning to Lily Dale, the place where her dead husband had come back from the grave to speak to her? Whatever the cause of her disconcertedness, she had made up her mind before the trip that she would try hard to be receptive to any spiritual energy at this gathering. Taking several slow breaths, she began to gain a kind of serenity, which was not her usual mode.

Entering from the clearing in the opposite direction that the visitors had come from, several women and men approached the Stump. One of the women stepped up on top of it and addressed the hushed crowd. "Welcome to Inspiration Stump," she said. Merrill was somewhat surprised to see a microphone in her hand. "My name is Amanda and I am a Spiritualist and a medium here at Lily Dale." The woman went on to briefly explain that some people who practiced Spiritualism were intermediaries between the living and the dead. "These folks behind me have a variety of backgrounds. Some of them are permanent members of our Lily Dale Assembly. Some are visiting mediums."

Suddenly, from the clearing behind Amanda, another woman emerged. Her purple caftan with the belled sleeves gave the impression that she had floated through the Leolyn Woods and gracefully landed here. Merrill slid lower in her seat and stared across the way at Victoria Erikson. "And some are student mediums. Think of them as well-educated interns," Amanda said. She peered behind her and welcomed Victoria to the circle. "Now, we mediums will most likely not receive messages for everyone here today, so please prepare yourself for that possibility. Remember, you can always make an appointment for a private reading with one of our many mediums here at Lily Dale," Amanda said.

One of the students led the group in a prayer, inviting Spirit to join the assembly. After a minute or two of silence, a medium who Amanda had introduced as Carl reached out to take the microphone from her. His eyes were closed tightly for a few moments until he spoke. "A lovely lady is telling me that someone here has a secret. Spirit tells me Cher, or Sheryl, is wondering if she should share it. Does anyone here believe that description fits you?" A young woman sitting a few rows in front of Merrill and Jenna let out a gasp. "Raise your hand if you'd like me to come to you," the medium said.

As Carl approached the young woman who had raised her right hand, he asked again, "Would you be alright with receiving a message from Spirit?"

"Yes," the woman said, not sounding entirely alright.

"Cher?" he asked, placing the mic in front of her.

"I'm Cheryl," she said. Appreciative murmurs spread around the circle.

"I see the woman who is with Spirit is cooking and saying she's making your favorite meal. Pasta with her red sauce, she says. Do you know who this is, Cheryl?" he asked, handing her the microphone.

"My nana," she answered, releasing a single sob. "She died last year. We were very close."

"She's telling me that you have a secret and you're wondering if the time has come to share it." Carl paused and then pulled the mic close to his mouth. "Nana says, 'The time has come!'"

Cheryl turned to the small group of women sitting next to her. Carl handed the mic back to her. "I'm pregnant!" she said, and her family and friends, as well as the dozens of strangers at the Stump, broke into cheers.

One by one, these human dramas, large and small, conveyed to the circle of strangers by the mediums brought both laughter and tears to the people gathered at the Stump. Messages from beyond included everything from *"your little dog (deceased of course) says you need to see an ENT for that sinus issue," "your sister-in-law isn't crazy about the guy you're dating," "your husband says he misses you, too."* From the corner of her eye, Merrill could see that Jenna was totally engrossed in these unfolding scenes.

But the spell for Merrill was broken when Amanda said, "Victoria," as she handed her the microphone. Merrill felt panic rise in her chest. She had admitted to no one but herself that Victoria Erikson and her gift had gotten inside her head. It had made the analytic librarian consider puzzling questions in a different, mystical light, and this unnerved her.

As Victoria Erikson stepped over the low fence and onto the Stump she said, "Now, I can see you all." Her warm smile captured everyone's attention. She didn't close her eyes, as the others had, but instead, she looked up at the branches of the old oak that stood above her. Slowly, she began to speak in a halting manner. "I see a woman surrounded by water or... tears... no... maybe not tears. Could they be jewels? She isn't revealing to me who she wishes to speak to from the circle. She says the person will understand that the message is intended for her." The crowd reacted to this mysterious statement made by someone in the Afterlife. Heads turned to their left, to their right, and over their shoulders, accompanied by a subtle questioning murmur. Jenna stared straight ahead, but Merrill heard her breath catch. Then Victoria spoke again. "The woman surrounded by tears or jewels is speaking." The medium closed her eyes and was silent for several seconds, and then she spoke. "The woman says, 'You didn't lose me. You saved me.'"

Merrill thought that even the birds were silent in those moments following Victoria's delivery of the cryptic message. And the spell did not seem to be broken until Amanda stood in front of the assembly and led them in a final prayer at the Stump.

Jenna was silent as the two followed the crowd out of the woods and back to the parking lot. As Merrill sat on her tailgate and changed shoes, her friend finally spoke. "Victoria was talking to me, wasn't she, Merrill? 'Tears.' 'Mermaids' Tears.' 'Sea glass.' 'Jewels.' But I *did* lose that woman! I didn't save her! What did Victoria mean?" Merrill was trying to think of the best answer to give her desperate friend to assuage her rising anxiety. Before she could do or say anything, her phone vibrated in her pocket. The text from Johnny wiped every other thought from Merrill's mind.

**"Jane Doe = Dr. Lynn Martinelli. Her children are here. Get to my office, ASAP."**

## CHAPTER TEN

# CORONER'S REPORT

"JENNA, I'M SORRY, but I have to get to the Sheriff's department. We'll find some time to talk about what happened today, I promise," Merrill said. The twenty minute silent drive to Jenna's house was unsettling. "See you soon," Merrill said, as Jenna got out of the Nissan. There was no reply. As she sped off to the village center, she tried not to think about what had just transpired at the Stump.

"Sorry I'm late," she mumbled, as she opened the door to Johnny's office and sat down next to him. It was obvious that the interview with Dr. Martinelli's children had reached a crucial and emotional point and Johnny did not want to interrupt it to make introductions. Merrill observed a young blonde woman sitting across the desk from the deputy sheriff, and a man with a deep tan and handsome features sat next to her. The woman could barely be understood through her sobs.

"Who would want to hurt, to *murder* our mother?" Merrill heard the click-clack of nails on the tile as Frank left Johnny's side. He knew a human in distress when he heard one. Positioning himself at the woman's feet, he stared up at her face. Through her tears, Shannon Kramer smiled down at the little dog. She blew her nose and asked the sheriff, "Is it okay if I pick him up?"

"He would love that," Johnny said. "Let me help you." Once Frank was situated on the distressed woman's lap, Merrill watched as a kind of calmness settled over her. "This is Frank, our service dog, and this is Merrill Connor, our research assistant," he said.

What Merrill didn't know until after they'd left Johnny's office was that Tim Kramer, Shannon's older brother by seven years, had been silent during the thirty-minute ride back from the morgue, where Lynn Martinelli's children were asked to identify the corpse. Her oldest child had last spoken as he looked at the body lying on the slab. "Yes, that's our mother," he said.

The Kramers had flown in from Los Angeles the night before, just hours after Johnny's call to Tim Kramer notifying him of his mother's death and the suspicious circumstances surrounding it. Johnny told her later that he had wanted Merrill to be present at this interview so that he could bounce his impressions off of her. He wanted to compare her judgements with his own. This had become their work routine ever since Merrill had been instrumental in solving the Grace Phillip's case. It wasn't that Johnny's surly anxiety and Merrill's sometimes biting sarcasm weren't a toxic mix of personality traits from time to time. But in the long run, their work together had yielded results, ones that made the Westfield area a safer place to live.

This was only the second murder case for Merrill, and Johnny thought her inexperience might work in their favor. Her impressions would be fresher than his, and her research skills could fill in gaps in the case, should they arise. Recently, she had passed the civil service test with flying colors to qualify as a criminologist. The fact that she had hundreds of *Deeper Dive* fans who loved to be involved in solving crimes was the icing on the cake, as far as Johnny was concerned.

At the moment, both Merrill and Johnny were laser focused on Tim Kramer, who had finally broken his silence. "Look, Sheriff, our mom was a helper. She was dedicated to the service of others. This was true in her personal life with her friends, as well as in her professional role as a therapist. She was a lifeline for troubled people. She counseled couples, families, individuals who were in crisis. As a kid, because her office was in our home, it sometimes bothered me that there would be all kinds of people coming and going. As I matured, though, I came to understand what a difference she was making in the lives of those who were troubled." Tim Kramer took a deep breath and looked at his sister before continuing. "I decided it was what I wanted to do with my life, too. That's why I chose the field of psychiatry after medical school. Our mother had no enemies, Sheriff Lovallo," he added.

"Unless you count that bastard Peter Martinelli," Shannon said, as Johnny scrawled something in his notebook.

"Who is he?" Merrill asked.

"Mom's second husband. After our dad died suddenly of a brain aneurysm, I think she was terribly vulnerable for a while after his death. We were both away at school on the West Coast when she met Peter." Her bitter tone could not be missed. "And as soon as Tim and I spent time in his company, we saw what our therapist mother ironically couldn't see, or maybe didn't *want* to see. The guy is a raging narcissist, Sheriff Lovallo. Not a good match for our mom, or anyone, for that matter. And then there was his propensity to spy on her."

"How did he spy on her?" Johnny asked.

"Over Christmas break one year, he let me use his computer, since Mom had hers in her office that day. I admit I did a little spying myself. His email contact list had a sub group: it was labeled *Nut Cases*. It looked to me like he had harvested all of the contacts in our mother's address book. After they broke up, she asked him about it, and of course he acted like he didn't know what she was talking about."

"And what about the tracker you found on Mom's car?" Shannon said.

"Yeah," Tim said. "I showed it to Mom right in front of him, and he denied that he had anything to do with it. Said it was probably one of her crazy clients who had put it there. That was the last time I saw the creep. Mom dumped him soon after, thank God."

The only sound in the room after Tim Kramer had told them about these incidents was Johnny's pen scratching against paper. Merrill couldn't wait for him to finish, so she asked the question first. "Shannon, Tim, you obviously don't have any respect for the man, but do you believe that Peter Martinelli had a motive to murder your mother?" Merrill asked.

"If there was a way that he could get his hands on more of her money by killing her, then yes, he would have a motive," Shannon said. Merrill made a mental note to check the benefactors on Lynn's life insurance policies, although she doubted that an ex-husband would be named as one. "The rat was actually taking her to court again next month after he'd already been denied a raise in his maintenance payment..."

Her brother interrupted Shannon. "That's why it doesn't make a lot of sense that he would want Mom dead. The money-making machine would stop for him. But he *was* jealous of our mother to the point of obsession, so I can't rule it out. Not until there's proof that someone else did this." His concerned glance at his sister forewarned of the gravity of Tim's next question. "Sheriff Lovallo, how exactly did our mother die?"

Merrill felt hot prickles of dread rise on her scalp. The Kramers, she guessed, were close to her own children's ages, and she could imagine the horror and shock of this moment from their perspective. Johnny handed her and each of the Kramers a copy of the coroner's report. Tim looked at his sister. "You read it," she said. "Out loud, please."

Her brother scanned the single sheet that Johnny had given him. "Are you sure?" he asked his sister. He waited a few seconds after Shannon's assenting nod, and began to read. "*On the morning of June 10th, 2022, at approximately 9:30 a.m., the body of a deceased Caucasian female, later identified by forensic dental records and confirmed by family members as Lynn Martinelli, age 55, was found in the waters of Lake Erie off the Boulder Point shoreline in Westfield, New York.*" Tim Kramer stopped reading and looked up at his sister.

"Keep going," she said.

"*External Examination: Water was not found in the lungs. The victim did not drown. Rigor mortis was present and fully developed in all major muscle groups, indicating that death occurred approximately 12-18 hours prior to the discovery of the body. The cranium exhibited multiple severe lacerations and blunt force injuries. Extensive swelling and hematoma formation were observed, consistent with repeated blows to the head.*" Lynn Martinelli's son stopped and asked Johnny, "That kind of violence would only come from pure hate, wouldn't it Sheriff?"

"I would have to agree with you, Dr. Kramer. The viciousness of the attack indicates that the killer more than likely knew your mother. And the fact that she was murdered while getting ready to set off in her kayak that evening indicates that it was a planned attack and not a robbery. Our initial search of her home verified that. More than likely, the perpetrator knew her routine, and we believe the violence probably took place on the water," Johnny said. "And yes, I agree, it was a very malicious act."

Merrill was amazed at Johnny's ability to combine facts with empathy when delivering news like this. She suspected that his having to share the horrible details of their mother's death with the Kramers pushed his anxiety button, but she realized, he was like her in this way. The truth came before everything else, and so, to these grieving strangers, he showed no signs of the stress that he felt.

Shannon closed her eyes and hung her head as her brother read the report's conclusion. "*Based on the examination findings and preliminary investigation, the cause of death of Lynn Martinelli appears to be homicide. The investigation into this case is ongoing and updates will be provided as additional information becomes available.*"

There was a sense of heavy finality in the room. The only sound that could be heard was the voice of Linda on the phone at her reception desk. Frank seemed to stir on Shannon's lap in response to the somber atmosphere, and he licked the woman's arm. "Have you found Mom's cellphone?" Shannon asked. "She always took it with her when she was on the water."

"Not yet," Johnny said, "and it might not ever be found if it ended up in the lake. The only thing that we've recovered is the kayak. We have a follow-up search of your mother's home and office planned for later today, including her tablets and computers. I'm sorry you can't go into the home until the search is completed. The investigation will be complicated, legally speaking, because her treatment notes will be a part of our search..."

"How will that work, Sheriff?" Tim Kramer asked. "If Mom were alive, you'd have to petition her with a court order to release her patients' files. But since she's deceased ..."

"We'll have to petition the court and get permission from each of her clients, as well, in order to get information from those treatment notes," he said. "We'll let you know how that goes."

"I can imagine that that will be very time-consuming. It will definitely delay your work, Sheriff," Tim said.

"I'm afraid you're right. The wheels of justice…" Johnny answered.

Shannon stood and gently set Frank down on the floor. "We're done here, right, Tim?"

Her brother recognized the toll this meeting had taken on his sister and said, "Yes. Let's go back to the hotel. You need to rest."

When Johnny returned to his office after seeing Lynn Martinelli's children out, he observed that Frank had gained another comfortable seat, this time on his criminologist's lap. "You okay?" he asked Merrill.

"I'm not going to pretend that witnessing shock and raw grief like the Kramers' compares to my old days in the quiet stacks at SUNY Fredonia," she said as she petted Frank's head. "As a mother myself, that was tough."

"It's one thing you never get used to in this line of work," Johnny said, seating himself across from her. "Now that we have a positive identification and the family has been informed, we need to get the news out to the public." He looked at his watch and continued. "I'm doing a news conference in two hours. In the meantime, I'll get a court order to search Dr. Martinelli's home and electronics. I need you to do some research on the doctor, in terms of her profession."

"What do you mean?" Merrill asked.

"What kind of therapy did she practice?" Johnny said. "The answer to that question might lead us in the direction of understanding who her clientele was. I also think it would be helpful if you made an appeal for information from your Divers."

"Will do," Merrill said, setting Frank down on the floor. "What about Peter Martinelli? Shannon and Tim seem to think he could be a suspect."

"Yep. I'll have Farrell reach out to him. We may need to interview him here, depending on what the lieutenant finds."

"Okay." Merrill gathered her bag and the coroner's report. "See you, Frank," she said and headed out the door.

## Chapter Eleven

---

# UP EARLY, OUT LATE

The next morning as Merrill was drinking her first cup of coffee, her phone vibrated on the table in front of her. Johnny Lovallo's face stared up at her from the screen. "You're awake pretty early, for an old guy," she said, omitting the traditional greeting.

He was becoming an expert at ignoring her snarky remarks. "I wanted you to know that I sent Farrell to Dr. Martinelli's home at seven this morning. The locksmith the department uses met him there. Once they got in, they found that the alarm system had been disconnected…"

"Oh, oh…"

"Nothing on the main floor was disturbed, except that her desk in her office had been rifled through. Files were strewn all over the floor, but her computer was untouched."

"Weird," Merrill said.

"It didn't take long for them to discover a broken garage window, which was probably the point of entry."

"Your guys didn't see that the other day when you first sent them to the residence?" Merrill asked.

"Nope. Farrell was there that day, and he said they checked every door and window. Someone broke in after we released the news that the victim was murdered."

"I wonder what they were looking for," Merrill said.

"That's the question on my mind, too. At the press conference, I'll be announcing that Lynn Martinelli was the murder victim and I'll detail the cause of death. At this point I don't see any reason to divulge the details of the break-in," Johnny said.

"So I'll keep that fact to myself when I do the podcast," Merrill said.

"For now, yes."

"What's your initial guess? Who would want to get into her office, but leave her computer?" she asked him.

"The ex-husband? A client? A random thief?" Johnny said. "When will the next airing of *A Deeper Dive* be, by the way?"

"I'm heading to the Prenderson as soon as I finish my coffee. I have an interview I recorded earlier, but I'll add the information about Dr. Martinelli at the end of the podcast. By the time I post it, your press conference should be over."

"Let's go, Frank," Johnny said, and hung up. For at least the hundredth time, she wondered if the man had ever been taught proper phone etiquette.

As she rinsed her coffee cup, her phone vibrated again and Sherry's face appeared on the screen. "Good morning, gorgeous," Merrill said. "Where has the world's busiest travel agent landed today?" she asked.

"I'm home in Westfield, believe it or not! I had some business in Sedona, but I cut it short to be able to get to Kate's gig tonight. I'm wondering if you want to ride to Larry's together," Sherry said.

"Absolutely!" Merrill answered. "Have you called Jenna to see if she needs a ride?"

"I did. This won't surprise you, but she didn't pick up, so I texted her," Sherry answered.

Merrill felt that sinking sensation again. It registered on the scale of bad feelings somewhere between disappointment and guilt. Ever since their Lily Dale venture, she had reached out to Jenna on multiple occasions, but she had gotten no response. In her heart, she knew that Jenna was ignoring her friends' efforts to be in touch, possibly because of what happened that day at the Stump. It seemed that she didn't want to talk about that, or about anything else, for that matter. "Okay, Sherry. What time shall I be ready?" she asked.

It was a beautiful June morning, so after settling on a plan with Sherry, Merrill opted to walk to her library studio. She no longer had to lug a bag full of equipment, including a laptop. *A Deeper Dive* had increased its subscription base by a few hundred customers since last year, so her son Jason was not only her tech guy, but her sales manager too. The podcast was now sponsored by several county businesses, and she had decided she could afford to buy a second laptop to keep in the studio.

Today's episode was a recorded interview Merrill had done with two siblings from Fredonia, both in their 60's, whose father had not returned to the states from his duty in Vietnam, at least as far as the family knew. The official record from the United States Marines, however, stated that he was very much alive on the day in 1968 when he was discharged. But his wife and children had not heard from him since weeks before that date. His daughter concluded the episode with words that broke Merrill's heart. "We don't know what happened to him. Maybe he met someone over there. Maybe he's had a new family and a happy life all this time," she said. "We just want to know. That's all."

Before her sign-off, as she and Johnny had discussed, Merrill spoke to her audience about the woman found at Boulder Point. "As you may know, Divers, a woman's body was discovered at Boulder Point on Lake Erie in Westfield, New York, last week. This morning, the Sheriff's department is updating the public about her identity and the cause of death. Her name is Dr. Lynn Martinelli. She was a respected therapist who lived and practiced in Dunkirk, New York. Dr. Martinelli was murdered. According to the coroner, she was struck on the head with a blunt object and died from multiple cranial fractures. A kayak registered to a friend of hers and gifted to Martinelli washed up on the Moose Beach shoreline soon after her body was found. The doctor was known to be a frequent kayaker. Put out your feelers, Divers. If anyone has any information about Dr. Martinelli's untimely death, you can reach out to the Sheriff's department or to me at *A Deeper Dive.*"

When Sherry pulled into Merrill's driveway that evening, her first words were, "I can't believe that therapist was murdered! Poor Jenna. She texted me a few minutes ago and said she wouldn't be joining us tonight. Finding the body seems to have rocked her world. In a bad way!" She took a breath and added, "My Airbnb clients throughout the county are feeling shaky about losing renters. Murder is not good for the economy."

Merrill adored her business-minded friend, but sometimes her unintentional insensitivity rattled her. "So what do you think about Kate gigging with these kids tonight?" she asked, hoping to change the subject and the tone of the conversation.

"I think Kate will always do Kate, and that's why we love her."

Merrill was glad she had thought to reserve a high-top table near the stage, closest to the vintage Hammond B organ their friend would be playing tonight. All of the tables and the bar were full and there was an unusual buzz of excitement in the air. Larry's had not featured live music in months, and the loyal townies were joined by the many tourists who flocked to the lake during the summer. At this point, Merrill noted, Sherry's prediction about a lagging tourist economy hadn't happened yet. Her friend ordered a pitcher of Southern Tier Nu Haze and three glasses. She poured one and immediately got up and handed it to Kate, who was leading three young musicians onto the stage. As the crowd roared their welcome, Kate raised her glass to the audience.

"Hello, everyone!" the band's drummer shouted into the microphone. "We're *The No Names!*" He smiled as applause filled the room. "Tonight we have a musician who is actually an important name everywhere in the music world. Some of us were lucky enough to have her as our music teacher before she became the famous and sought-after studio musician that she is today. We're so excited to have her with us tonight! People of Larry's, please give a warm welcome to Ms. Kate Sterns!"

Kate stood and took in the standing ovation she was being given before having played a note. Merrill marveled at how comfortable her friend was being in the limelight. She would have suffered a heart attack if people had stood and clapped for her. Merrill did her best work in the basement of the library, alone with her laptop, headphones, and microphone.

"Thanks, everyone, and thanks to Derrick, *The No Names'* drummer and my former student, for inviting me to sit in tonight," Kate said. "And thanks, guys, for letting me pick the opening number. I think the audience will understand my choice."

Kate played the singular riff that opened Steely Dan's *Hey Nineteen* and the crowd in Larry's went wild. When she leaned into her mic and sang the chorus, half the room got up and danced. *"Hey, nineteen. No we can't dance together, no we can't talk at all."*

The first set was over before anyone in the crowded room was ready for it, but Kate was happy to join her two friends at their table. As Sherry poured her another beer, Merrill leaned across the table. "Kate, you sound amazing!" she said.

"Thanks! I love playing with these guys. The energy is...hey, Derrick," she called, waving the young man to their table. "Come on over and meet my friends." Kate introduced the drummer to the women, and as he shook her hand, Merrill could see a light of recognition in his eyes.

"Merrill Connor. *A Deeper Dive*, right?" he asked, as he took the stool next to her. "My mother loves you." His face flashed red with embarrassment. "I mean my mother is a listener and she turned me on to the podcast during the Grace Phillips investigation. I really enjoy your program. I'm a subscriber."

"Thanks, Derrick," she said. "And thank your mother for me too."

After their break, as the two musicians headed back to the stage, Sherry and Merrill agreed they would stay for the second set. They ended up staying for all three. By one in the morning, they had danced at least ten times and finished a pitcher of beer. When Kate joined them, she insisted that Sherry leave her car and the two ride home in her Z4. "I'll put the top down, Merrill, and you sit on Sherry's lap. It's a two minute drive to your place. I don't want Westfield's Chamber of Commerce Person of the Year to end up with a DUI. Or worse."

Five minutes later, Merrill unlocked her back door and stepped into her dark kitchen. *"Hey nineteen, that's 'Retha Franklin,"* Merrill sang. As she switched on the lights, an unexpected bolt of loss hit her. Sharing her life for so many years with Richard, a song, a scene from a movie, an evening spent with friends was bound to bring back memories of the love of her life. Tonight it had been the music. They had both loved Steely Dan and her husband had every album and later every CD. Four years ago, she would have fled from this memory and done everything in her power to take her mind off of it. Tonight, she challenged herself to keep singing. *"The Cuervo Gold, the fine Columbian, make tonight a wonderful thing."*

Merrill peacefully drifted off to sleep at 2 a.m. with the thought that yes, Richard was gone, but they had shared such a rich life, he would never be forgotten.

## Chapter Twelve

## PHONE CALLS, EMAILS, TEXTS

Merrill awoke Sunday morning feeling surprisingly rested after only five hours of sleep. Lately, she had joined her peers who belonged to the league of lousy sleepers, nodding off easily, but waking several times in the night, leaving her groggy much of the next morning. Maybe the remedy for this dysfunction was late nights of drinking and dancing, she thought, as she turned on the water in the shower.

Dressed and ready for the day, she decided that coffee was not going to be a sufficient breakfast, and as she watched and worried over the poached eggs she was attempting to perfect, her phone rang. Johnny typically texted, unless he required her immediate attention. "Yes?" she said. "I'm making eggs benedict," she lied, "so please don't lollygag."

"Lollygag! I haven't heard that term since elementary school!" It was nice to hear Merrill's nervous wreck of a boss laughing out loud.

"And yet you're lollygagging right now," she said, retrieving an egg with a slotted spoon and placing it on top of the English muffin. Thank God for speaker phones, she thought. "How did the press conference go?"

"As per usual. I told them just what I needed them to know and they tried to drag more details out of me. It was over in five minutes, so that was good. The press release went out all over the country, and Linda tells me that most of New York State dailies have run it on the front page."

"Hopefully, that will work in our favor," she said.

"Yeah. Okay, so I'm not going to keep you from your breakfast," he said.

"By the way, you don't strike me as someone who actually knows how to make hollandaise sauce," he added, not waiting for her response. "I just wanted you to know that Lynn Martinelli's children spoke with me yesterday after the private graveside ceremony they had for her. They'd like an opportunity to meet with Jenna. To thank her for, well, you know what for. Can you arrange that?"

"Let me think about it after I've finished eating. I'll let you know." Johnny gave her Tim Kramer's number, and as usual, without any fanfare he hung up.

As she ate her breakfast, Merrill thought about the failed day at the beach she and Kate and Sherry had experienced. And the Lily Dale trip to The Stump that seemed to make Jenna retreat from the circle of friends entirely. Merrill hadn't talked to her since dropping her off that day. It was telling that she hadn't shown up at Larry's last night. She went to the sink with her plate and stood staring out the window at her backyard.

She was not used to this feeling, and it made her squirm. What was it? Inadequacy, she decided. In her work life, past or present, she could usually find a solution to most problems either through investigation, persevering in the face of obstacles, digging deeper. But Jenna's state of mind since discovering Lynn Martinelli's body felt impermeable to her. Merrill inhaled deeply and resolved once again not to give up. She picked up her phone and dialed Jenna's shop number instead of her friend's cell.

"*Mermaids' Tears*. Good morning. This is Jenna. How may I help you?"

No, Merrill thought, how may I help you? "Hello, friend," she said.

"Merrill?" Jenna was obviously surprised to find her on the other end of her business line.

"Yes, it's me. Just checking in. How are you?"

"Okay, I guess. What's going on?"

"Well, we missed you last night," Merrill said. When Jenna remained silent, she decided she might as well come out with her question. Merrill was shocked at Jenna's quick acceptance when she told her Johnny's news about the Kramers' request to meet with her before they returned to California.

"I'll text you some times that will work for me," Jenna said.

"Great," Merrill answered, trying hard to mask the surprise she felt.

"And Merrill," Jenna said.

"Yes?"

"Thanks for being such a good friend."

Feeling comforted by Jenna's response, Merrill poured a second cup of coffee and began scrolling through her *Deeper Dive* emails. Her son Jason had been encouraging her to hire an assistant to help her with these and other tasks that took her away from her research. But Merrill was not convinced. Most of the messages contained words of encouragement and admiration for her podcast. Sometimes the emails were more than that, though. The last one on the list written at 6 a.m. this morning from drummerderrick caught her attention.

> *"Hello, Mrs. Connor. It was nice meeting you last night. After gigs, I usually have a hard time falling asleep, so I typically listen to a podcast or two. When I got in, I decided to listen to A Deeper Dive – your latest episode. And I think I might know something about Dr. Martinelli that could help. Here's my number. Give me a call if you're interested.*
> *Derrick"*

If the Grace Phillips murder case had taught her anything, it was never to overlook the potential of a *Diver* to be of help. Merrill set down her coffee cup and dialed. The musician answered on the first ring. She could tell he was as suspicious of an unknown number as everyone from his generation by the question mark at the end of his hello. "Hi Derrick. It's Merrill Connor."

"Oh, hi! Thanks for getting back to me so soon, Mrs. Connor."

"You can call me Merrill if you like," she said.

"Okay. Merrill. Like I said in my email, I often listen to podcasts after a gig. Your last one about the children of that Vietnam vet really got to me. But your announcement to the *Divers* about the death of Dr. Lynn Martinelli kept me up the rest of the night. I couldn't sleep until I reached out to you."

"Yes, it's very unsettling. We think of ourselves as living in a haven, a place where something as horrible as murder doesn't happen. We were fortunate to have the ID made so quickly, but that and the coroner's report is about all we have to go on at this point. Did you know the doctor, Derrick?"

"I didn't. But I have a young drum student who does, did. "

"Oh?" Merrill said.

"Yes. I have a private studio. Teaching is a way to make a steady income, as opposed to the sporadic bookings the *No Names* get," Derrick said.

"I see. What can you tell me about your student and Dr. Martinelli?" she asked.

"I've been giving him lessons for about a year, and he's always seemed pretty messed up, emotionally, I mean. Moody, even for a teenager. But in the past few months, he's been noticeably agitated most of the time. When I questioned him about what was bothering him, he told me that his parents were divorcing. He said he was vehemently opposed to the break-up. His little brother was having a hard time with it, too. He believed his mother and father could have worked it out, and he blamed their therapist for their decision to split. I mean, he's a sixteen-year-old kid, and as someone who went through my own parents' break-up when I was fourteen, I could understand his frustration, and I told him as much. From that point on, he began to share some pretty fucked–up...oh, sorry, messed-up visions he was having."

"Visions?" Merrill said.

"Yes. Violent ones. With the therapist as the victim. And to make it worse, he often created a drum track to capture how he felt. He played them for me. All kinds of Black Sabbath anger came out of that kid. He would punish the kit every Saturday."

"Do you know if your student ever met with Dr. Martinelli?"

"He did. He had several sessions with her, he told me, a few with his parents and several by himself."

"And do you know how he felt about those meetings?" Merrill asked.

"He told me he hated them and he hated the bitch, sorry, he hated Dr.

Martinelli. He said when she talked to him she tried to make his world falling apart seem like a normal thing. That really frustrated him."

Merrill had walked out to The Shed and grabbed her notebook from her desk as the musician spoke. "What's your student's name, Derrick?" she asked, putting pen to paper. She became aware of several seconds of silence.

"Dave. David Michaels. He actually has a lesson with me in a couple of hours," he said.

Merrill felt a shiver run up her spine and onto her scalp as she scrawled the name in her notebook. "How would you feel about asking him a couple of questions? Specifically, would you ask him where he was on that Thursday night before Dr. Martinelli's body washed up at Boulder Point?"

Derrick seemed to be thinking his answer over while Merrill waited. "Yeah. I could do that," he finally said.

"Great," Merrill said. "Let's talk tomorrow. What's a good time to call?"

When they hung up, Merrill made sure she had written down every pertinent detail Derrick had shared. She tapped her pen against her bottom lip as she thought about whether she should give Johnny a call. A strong intuition convinced her not to. Not yet, anyway. She did text him, though, minutes later when Jenna got back to her.

*"Tell the Kramers that they can meet with Jenna at my place tomorrow morning at 10. Feel free to join us, if you'd like."*

## Chapter Thirteen

# HEALING

"I made blueberry muffins," Jenna said, standing at the kitchen door. Merrill could see that her friend's hands trembled as she handed her the tray.

"Come in! Oh, they smell wonderful, Jenna," she said. "Coffee?"

"Yes, please."

Merrill was uncharacteristically quiet after she greeted her friend. She didn't want to scare Jenna away with speculations about how good this meeting would be for her. After all, she had shown up this morning, and that was a good sign. They each pulled out a chair and sat with their coffee cups and the platter of muffins in front of them. The distinct galloping sound of Frank's short legs negotiating the stairs to the upper deck soon broke the uncomfortable silence. The women turned to look as Johnny opened the door for the dachshund. Frank greeted each of the women with his signature knee lick.

Merrill walked to the pantry shelf where she kept the peanut butter treats she baked and kept on hand whenever she was going to see Frank. She knelt down to his level. "You are the best dog," she said, and added under her breath, "for putting up with *him*."

"Good morning," Johnny called out and headed for the coffee pot. "Jenna, I'm really glad you came. From the first time I spoke with them, the Kramers have said that they wanted to meet you."

"I'm very nervous, Johnny. I'm here out of respect for them and their..."

Frank's single bark alerted them to the Kramers who stood on the deck looking in the window at the group. Merrill hurried to the door. "Welcome," she said.

Shannon Kramer handed her a small bouquet of blue hydrangeas and an envelope. "Thanks for having us, Mrs. Connor," she said.

As the five gathered around Merrill's farmhouse table, Johnny made the introductions. After serving coffee to all, Merrill sat down across from Jenna. Her friend's tension was palpable. Tim Kramer, who seemed to be the spokesman for the two siblings, began. "Mrs. Berlin…"

"Please. I'm Jenna."

"Jenna. Shannon and I wanted to thank you for what you did that day at the beach, what you did for us and for our mother. It had to be very difficult for you." Merrill studied her friend's face as Tim Kramer went on. "We are so lucky that you were there. If Mom's body had been carried out further into the lake, it might not have ever been discovered. If she had gone missing for a longer period of time, it would have only increased our anguish." He paused for a moment, looking around the table at each of them until his gaze returned to Jenna. "Yours was an act of such kindness and bravery…" Jenna had grabbed a napkin off the table and dabbed at her eyes as he continued. "Because of you, our mother wasn't lost. In a way, she was saved."

Once again, in the short time that Merrill had known her, Victoria Erikson had been right. She locked eyes with Jenna and she could see that her friend, too, was thinking about the message she had received at The Stump. She dabbed at her tears one more time, and then sat up straighter in the chair. Merrill thought that her friend had resolved something in that moment.

"That is a beautiful necklace, Jenna," Shannon Kramer commented, and soon the brother and sister were asking about her sea glass gathering and jewelry business. The atmosphere in the room went from funereal to pleasant.

"We have to get going soon," Tim Kramer told them. "Our flight out of Buffalo leaves in three hours. Sheriff, I hope the judge rules soon on the subpoena for Mom's treatment notes."

"I hope so too," Johnny said, attempting to sound much more optimistic than he actually was.

As they stood to say their goodbyes, the brother and sister reminded the sheriff and Merrill that they would be only a phone call away if they needed anything from them. Merrill walked the Kramers out, and Johnny and Jenna, with Frank wrapped around her feet, sat at the table in silence. When Merrill returned, Jenna spoke. "Thank you, Johnny and Merrill, for arranging this meeting. I don't know if I'll ever feel the same about looking for glass at Boulder Point, but after listening to the Kramers, I feel like a weight has been lifted off my chest."

After Jenna left, Johnny stood and stared out the window at Merrill's backyard. "Your husband's sculptures, right?" he asked.

"Yes. Those pieces are my favorites of all Richard's sculptures. Come on. I'll walk you two out," she said.

At the bottom of the deck steps with Frank at his heels, Johnny headed toward the two metal sculptures that, years ago, Richard had created and installed in their yard. They were large, abstract pieces that stood several yards apart. "I can't tell if they're human or not, but I can't stop looking at them," he said.

"I know what you mean," Merrill said. "Staring at them is almost hyp-notizing, isn't it?"

Johnny didn't answer. Instead, he headed to one of the two Adirondack chairs that she and Richard had bought as newlyweds on a road trip to Ver-mont. To Merrill's surprise, he sat down and gestured for her to join him. "Is it hard to be surrounded by so much of what was a part of him, a part of your lives together, now that he's gone?" he asked as she sat down in the chair across from him.

Merrill was stunned. This was the most personal question Johnny Lovallo had ever asked her, and likewise, she had never mixed her private life with police business, especially when it came to her relationship with him. She wasn't sure what to say, but she immediately rejected her customary sarcasm. Reaching down to pet Frank, she took a deep breath and attempted to answer Johnny. "At first, it was crushing. His artwork is everywhere, inside and outside of our house, at the college, in buildings throughout the county. I spent that first year after his death squinting at his work. It hurt too much to look closely." Johnny was leaning forward, attentive to her every word. "But eventually, its presence everywhere helped me to heal."

They sat in silence for a long time. And then Johnny spoke. "Did you know that I was married once?"

The question made Merrill dizzy. For a minute she found it impossible to speak. "I didn't know that, no," she finally said.

Frank walked toward him and whined at Johnny's feet. The sheriff signaled for him to make himself at home on his lap and the good dog was happy to oblige. "Yes, I was. A long time ago. I married my college girlfriend in 1979."

Merrill was afraid to respond. She didn't want to break this spell that Johnny was casting here in her backyard, but at the same time she was rattled to her core. "Melissa," he said. When Merrill didn't say anything, he continued. "We lived in Jersey. That's where we both grew up, in a little shore town there. The house we found after we married was actually a ramshackle cottage that had been abandoned. We couldn't get a mortgage because of that, but our parents helped us out. We spent two years renovating it. I was in the Academy at the time, so Melissa was pretty much in charge of making it a home. She did a great job. That fall she got a job teaching social studies at the high school."

Her head spinning and her voice quivering, Merrill attempted to speak in a normal tone. "I remember when you were hired by the Department in the early 90's. I read about it in the newspaper. But I don't remember knowing that you had a wife. What happened to Melissa, Johnny?"

"She left me before I came to Westfield."

Merrill felt a rush of resentment toward the woman she hadn't known of until five minutes before. Johnny Lovallo was her friend. And Merrill always had her friends' backs. She was about to lambaste this Melissa she had never known, but Johnny spoke first. "After the baby died. She left. She couldn't cope. She tried for a year, but she couldn't stay with me."

"Baby?" Merrill couldn't catch her breath.

"Rose. Rosie. She was six months old."

Merrill felt the instant sting of tears. "Oh, God, Johnny. I'm so sorry."

"SIDS. Sudden Infant Death Syndrome. Back in those days, they weren't really sure what it was, or how it could be prevented." Frank was profusely licking Johnny's hands and then his face. "I'm okay, Frank," he said, and suddenly the dog was in Merrill's lap. "Yeah. So solving Dr. Martinelli's murder is especially important to me. A shrink played a huge role in my attempt to find my way again after I lost Melissa and Rose. I want to find the piece of crap who killed Lynn Martinelli." Johnny stood up and Frank jumped off Merrill's lap.

She felt the vertigo wash over her again when she tried to get to her feet. "Johnny," she said and her voice was not her own.

"I know, Merrill, I know. Cherish these sculptures and everything else Richard left you. You must feel his love for you every time you look at them." His tone changed suddenly to his boss voice. "I'll be in touch in the next couple of days about the subpoena for the doctor's records. Let's go, Frank."

It wasn't very often that Merrill's feelings overrode her thoughts, but that was what happened in her backyard that morning. She couldn't have told you how long she sat there, staring at her husband's sculptures, and thinking about the tremendous sorrow in Johnny Lovallo's heart.

When she finally had the impetus to walk up the deck stairs to her kitchen, the first thing Merrill noticed was the pretty bouquet on her counter. She chose the cobalt blue vase in the pantry and filled it with water. Still feeling like a sleepwalker, she picked up the envelope and opened the card the Kramers had left. Something fell onto the floor. Merrill bent down and picked it up. On the counter, the card lay open.

"I'm afraid I have a confession to make. Shannon wanted to take a last look around the Shore Acres property. I still had a key to the house, so we drove out there last night and spent a few minutes saying goodbye. I hope you'll understand. It was the last place we saw our mother alive. My mom had a locked compartment inside her desk. When she and Martinelli were going through their ugly divorce proceeding, she told me about the drawer and where I could find the key. When I unlocked it last night, the only thing in it was this thumb drive. Hope it's useful. TK"

## Chapter Fourteen

# INFORMANTS

Standing in the middle of her kitchen, Merrill stared at the thumb drive in her hand. What was Tim Kramer thinking? He knew as a professional himself that the confidential information in a therapist's notes, including treatment plans, could not be disclosed without a court order. She hoped she would not find personal information about the doctor's clients on this drive. Panicked, she decided she had to get ahold of Johnny and tell him. She looked around the kitchen for her phone, but she didn't see it. She turned with the intention of checking for it in her bedroom, but before she could, she heard it vibrating loudly against the granite counter.

Who with a California area code would be texting her, she wondered. It took Merrill just seconds before she knew. "*Hello, Merrill. I wanted to share this information with you exclusively at this point. I believe this was copied by my mother from texts and perhaps emails that she received, not as a therapist, but as a private person. Why she did this, I don't know. I'll leave it up to your discretion if and when you need to turn it over to Sheriff Lovallo. Thanks for having us today. T Kramer.*"

Merrill hurried to her desk in The Shed and stared, this time at the USB port on her laptop. She was a paid employee of the Sheriff's Department, an official researcher and criminologist, but Johnny was her superior. She had meant to tell him about her phone conversation with Derrick the drummer regarding Dr. Martinelli's hostile teen client, but between the emotional meeting with Jenna and the Kramers followed by Johnny's heart-wrenching story about the loss of his child and his failed marriage, the timing was not right. Shouldn't she call Johnny now and tell him what Tim Kramer had left for her? Although she had not completed the *Expanding Your Own Psychic Power* course, she felt a strong hunch that told her what she should do, or rather when she should do it. Not yet, she decided, as she inserted the thumb drive into the port.

Within seconds, two folders appeared on her screen. The label on each one backed up Tim Kramer's theory that these communications were private messages. She breathed a small sigh of relief. Perhaps what she was doing was not violating the law and Johnny's trust in her. Perhaps.

She opened the first folder titled "*PM's texts.*" There were a dozen or so files in it. As she read the first one, given Shannon Kramer's intense hostility toward her mother's ex-husband, Merrill made an educated guess regarding the identity of the author.

**PM:** *Lynn. I don't like being put in this position where I'm forced to beg and cajole, but I can hardly be expected to take this bullshit lying down, can I? I'd like to settle this without lawyers, but I'm warning you, if I have to get the best, the most cut-throat expert in spousal maintenance issues, I will.*

**PM:** *You were the bread winner in the relationship, there's no question about that. And then you broke, no, you demolished our marriage vows. You definitely owe me, Lynn.*

**PM:** *The judge in our divorce case was a personal friend of yours, of course.*

**PM:** *Why should I have to lower my principles and my standard of living because you felt the need to come out of the closet??? I will give you exactly a week to do the right thing and raise my monthly check by two thousand. I'll take cash if that is one way to get around the court order. I'm warning you, Lynn, you will pay one way or another.*

Merrill read a few more of Peter Martinelli's texts, most of them in the same accusatory vein. The final one sent shivers down her spine.

**PM:** *Listen, you bitch. Once again, you've managed to use your status and your connections to keep what is rightfully mine. I promise you this. I will ruin you! I will use every social platform, hell, I will even put an ad in the* *newspapers, I will expose you for the FRAUD that you are! If you don't pay me what I deserve, I suggest you do us both a favor and climb into that kayak of yours and drown!*

Merrill sat in front of her computer screen, stunned. Shannon Kramer had detested this guy, and based on his hateful texts to her mother, she had good reason. Had Lynn copied these and kept them in case her phone eventually went missing? As a therapist, in spite of what her daughter had thought, Dr. Martinelli must have certainly recognized the sociopathic nature of her former husband, and that final vicious text was enough for Merrill to concur.

She actually jumped up from the chair when her ring tone jolted her back to reality, although for a second, when his name came up on the screen, she couldn't remember who Derrick was. "Mrs., er, Merrill. It's Derrick. I'm sorry to bother you again, but I think this is important."

"That's okay. What's up?"

"David Michaels just left the studio. Before his lesson even started. As soon as I brought up the murder of Dr. Martinelli, the kid spilled everything," Derrick said.

"Everything? What do you mean by that, Derrick?"

"Everything.  What she told him during their three sessions together, how she wanted him to understand that her office was a safe environment. How she wanted him to be open to feeling and saying everything that was in his mind and in his heart about his parents divorcing. That change would be hard on everyone in the family, but maybe mostly for him, she said. She understood that. So David told her exactly what he thought he knew. That it was Dr. Martinelli's fault. That before his parents started seeing her, they argued a lot, but they never talked about divorce. Now, because of her, he and his little brother would have to move. Their lives would be like those of many of their friends whose parents had split, uprooted and miserable."

"Wow! He totally unloaded on her, didn't he?"

"He did. Dr. Martinelli told him that she understood how hard this was for him, but that the decision to divorce had been his parents' choice. That as a therapist, she couldn't tell them what to do." Derrick paused to take a breath.

"What was David's response to that?" Merrill asked.

"He called her a liar. And a hypocrite."

"Why would he call her a hypocrite?"

"He found out from his friend who babysits for Dr. Martinelli's neighbor that the therapist was divorced. He said he was so pissed when she told him that it was his parents' choice to stay together or split, he got up and left. But, and this scared the shit out of me, Merrill, he told me *he went back to her house that evening*! The evening she went missing!"

"Oh my God, why would he do that?" Merrill asked. "What happened when he went back? "

"I don't know. He bolted out of the studio before I could ask him. Grabbed his music off the stand and was screeching tires out of my driveway before I could stop him."

After Merrill hung up, she walked from one end of her house to the other, trying to decide what to do with these two discoveries. Peter Martinelli's menacing texts were certainly proof of his hatred for his ex-wife, but whether he had been to her Shore Acres home during that window of time when she was attacked was not known at this point. His last text gave no indication that he intended to show up at her house. Now that David Michaels had admitted to Derrick that he had actually *been* at Dr. Martinelli's house on the Thursday evening that she was likely bludgeoned to death, Merrill did what she was obligated to do.

Three hours later she was sitting in Johnny's office with Frank lying at her feet. Across from the two investigators sat Lorna and Bob Michaels and their teenaged son, David.

## CHAPTER FIFTEEN

# COGNITIVE BEHAVIORAL THERAPY

THE MICHAELS WERE an attractive middle-aged couple, both blonde and athletic looking, dressed impeccably in expensive brands of active wear. But their stiff postures and strained expressions made it evident to Merrill that the two had suffered a great deal of emotional strain and upheaval lately.

Their young son appeared to be even more distraught than his parents. "Wait!" he shouted. "Let me get this straight. Derrick told you things I told him in confidence! I trusted him! My mistake. I should have known better!" Tall and lanky, wearing jeans ripped at the knees and a Foo Fighters t-shirt, David sat on the edge of the chair and leaned across the desk staring belligerently at the two investigators. He ran his fingers through his long, dark hair over and over again throughout the interview. At one point, he drained the bottle of water Linda had brought him in three loud gulps.

In her former life, Merrill had been in the company of many a college student who suffered from depression or anxiety. Each year, the faculty and staff were required to attend workshops and in-service trainings on these mental health issues that plagued a large portion of their student body. As Johnny questioned David, she thought that the kid looked and acted as though he was in some sort of manic state.

"Calm down, son," Johnny said. "I'm sure Derrick had nothing but your well-being in mind when he spoke to us."

The kid scoffed at the thought of it. "Yeah, right," he said.

Johnny continued in spite of the glaring teenager sitting across from him. "David, you told your music teacher that you had…" At this point, Johnny looked down at his notes and read from them, "'*an intense dislike*' for Dr. Martinelli. You blamed her for your parents' impending divorce. Is that right?"

"Yes! Yes, I blamed her! Some therapist! She's the one who encouraged them to fight and argue…"

"David, that's not true. We've tried to explain this to you. Dr. Martinelli used an approach with us…"

David interrupted his mother with a shout. "Yeah, yeah, I know! CBT." For some reason, he had turned to Merrill now and spoke directly to her. "Cognitive Behavioral Therapy."

"The method teaches you to identify negative patterns of thinking and behavior …" Bob Michaels began.

"That's all my brother and I ever heard from the time they started to see her last year," he said to Merrill. "Negative behavior! Yelling, screaming, and then leaving. Sometimes for days." David turned and glared at his father.

"It was a very intense time in our home for several months, that's true," his father said. "Sometimes it was best for everyone in the family for Lorna and me to go to separate spaces." Mr. Michaels turned to his wife for her feedback, but she remained silent.

"David, you told Derrick Stevenson that you had an appointment with Dr. Martinelli at her office on Thursday afternoon, June 10th. Is that correct?" Johnny asked. The teen looked frustrated or confused, Merrill couldn't tell which emotion it was.

His mother pulled her phone from her purse and answered for her son. "Yes, I see that on my calendar. June 10th, 2 p.m." Her son said nothing.

"You also told Derrick that you went back to Dr. Martinelli's house later that same afternoon." Merrill noted the kid's sudden far-off stare and clamped lips. His body language told her that he was determined to remain silent for as long as it took to get Johnny off his back.

"David, our forensic investigation into the doctor's murder has concluded that she was killed sometime before 11 p.m. that evening. Did you see or talk to Lynn Martinelli after your appointment with her that day?" Johnny's stern voice roused Frank and he pattered over and sat at his owner's feet. The boy said nothing.

"As I explained to you and your parents, David, this interview was entirely voluntary. I appreciate you and your family coming in. However, I have every right to petition you with a subpoena and question you on the record if you don't cooperate and answer my questions." The kid remained unresponsive. "Okay, David. You're leaving me no choice." Johnny stood up and walked around the table. He leaned down until he was eye-to-eye with the kid. He raised his voice and it echoed back from the high ceiling. "As lead investigator in Dr. Martinelli's murder, I can summon you to court to answer these questions and more." Johnny was shouting now. Merrill had never seen him lose his temper in his official capacity, but she could see he was close to doing that now. "Do you understand what I'm saying, David?"

Merrill heard David's muffled "yes" and breathed a sigh of relief. She was uncomfortable in the presence of Johnny's "bad cop" persona, even though she understood why he was using this technique with the stubborn adolescent.

"Good," Johnny said, standing up and walking back to his chair. He turned to David's parents. "Is there anything else you'd like to add?" he asked the Michaels.

"David is a good, kind kid, Sheriff Lovallo. He's an honor student, a baseball player, a musician. He could never hurt someone in the manner that Dr. Martinelli was attacked," his father said, "no matter how much he disliked them."

Johnny turned to the boy. "David? Is there anything else you'd like to add?" Shoulders hunched and head down, the teen remained silent. Johnny got to his feet again and shook hands with the parents. "Expect to hear from us soon. It looks like we'll need to question David in a more formal setting," he warned them.

After the Michaels family left his office, Johnny turned to Merrill. "Well, what do you think?"

"I think the kid's father shouldn't have mentioned that David plays baseball. A bat is one way to end a therapist's interference in your family's life," Merrill said.

"Hmm. That's a horrible thought, Mrs. Connor," Johnny said.

She shrugged her shoulders and watched as the sheriff reorganized the papers in front of him. Merrill was aware that ever since Johnny had shared his personal tragedy that day in her backyard, something in their dynamic was shifting. She couldn't have explained to anyone this change in her feelings for him. When she tried to sort it out for herself, one word kept surfacing. Protective. Merrill felt protective of Johnny Lovallo.

"What's the rest of your day look like?" he asked her. One of the benefits of working for the Deputy Sheriff was that she was on an as-needed basis. Merrill had made it clear from the beginning that this condition was the only way she would accept the job.

"It depends. What do you need?"

"I'd like you to accompany Lieutenant Farrell in canvassing Lynn Martinelli's neighborhood…"

Merrill interrupted him. "To find out if any of the neighbors might have seen a tall teenager snooping around the doctor's place after office hours."

"Yes," he said.

She was picking up her bag and notebook when Linda rapped on the office window. "Sure. I'll clear my schedule for the next couple of hours," Merrill said.

"Come in, Linda," Johnny called, and Frank crossed the room to greet her.

"Alexandra Sheldon is on the phone for you, Sheriff," Linda said. "She wants to know if you have any leads yet."

"Put her through, Linda," Johnny said. He didn't return the wave Merrill gave him on her way out the door, and she smiled, feeling grateful that some things would never change.

## Chapter Sixteen

# SHORE ACRES

Sitting in the passenger seat next to Lieutenant Mike Farrell, Merrill was carrying on an internal monologue about the merit of keeping the existence of Lynn Martinelli's thumb drive to herself. After all, Tim Kramer had entrusted it to her, but now Johnny had assigned her to do this follow-up on their only suspect, that her boss knew of anyway, David Michaels. She would definitely have to tell the Deputy Sheriff about Peter Martinelli's threats, but first things would have to come first.

The Shore Acres neighborhood in Dunkirk was a stunning lakeside refuge from the commotion of the noisy city. The six-block area was an eclectic mix of sprawling ranches and waterfront mansions. Some of the homes were new construction, but there were many that had been built in the 19th and 20th centuries. Most of the lots were expansive with mature trees and summer gardens resplendent in June with blooming azalea and rhododendron bushes.

"You okay, Merrill?" Farrell asked. He was a bit concerned that the wisecracks they usually exchanged were not happening today.

"Yes. I'm okay. Just lost in thought, that's all," she admitted as the cop pulled his wife's Honda onto Lynn Martinelli's street. She had rarely seen Mike Farrell out of uniform and outside of a squad car, but Johnny didn't want them to display overt police presence in this, until recently, crime-free neighborhood, so today Mike was dressed in cargo shorts and a white button-down shirt.

There were only five houses on Bird Lane, the cul-de-sac where Lynn Martinelli had lived and worked. A thickly wooded area across the street buffered the noise of the city traffic. There were no homes on that side of the street. Merrill wondered if these woods wouldn't have made a good ingress and egress point for a killer. Mike pulled up in front of Dr. Martinelli's driveway. "Very private. Great location for a shrink," Merrill commented.

"Pull that tape, will you, please?" Farrell asked. Merrill got out and untied the yellow crime scene tape from one of the trees at the end of the doctor's driveway, and Farrell pulled up to the three story house. At first look, it appeared to be a classic Victorian Queen Anne, complete with the signature turret at the top, but as Merrill drew nearer, she saw that its shingles were not wooden, but vinyl.

"Oh, cool! This is one of those new homes that utilized the blueprint of an older building. You know, Mike, there are several authentic Queen Annes in Westfield and on the grounds of Chautauqua Institution, too," she called to Farrell as he walked up the driveway. His non-response told her all she needed to know about the extent of interest the man had in local architecture. At the massive front door, he unlocked the security box the department had installed since the break-in, and turning toward her, he waved Merrill in.

The interior of Lynn Martinell's first floor was warm and spacious, painted and decorated in a way that would make any stranger feel welcome. The walls were a beautiful pale blue and the cream-colored couches and chairs were accented with throw pillows that displayed elaborate cross-stitched seascapes and water birds. Merrill had admitted to her friends that she had an unhealthy addiction to throw pillows. She stayed away from the Home aisle in every department store so that she wouldn't be tempted to buy another one to add to her collection of dozens. But in the late Dr. Martinelli's living room, just the right number were tastefully positioned on the plush chairs and couches. A beautiful Persian rug picked up and enhanced the colors and tone of the space.

All along the back of the house, a bank of enormous windows framed a long seawall and beyond it, Lake Erie. Merrill stood still for a moment and stared admiringly. Those windows would have provided the doctor with a breathtaking view all four seasons. The two investigators walked through the ultra-modern chef's kitchen back into the living space with its thirty-foot peak and floor-to-ceiling stone fireplace. Merrill wanted to get closer to the dozen or so paintings that hung on the walls, but Mike stopped that from happening.

"The doctor's office is back here," he said, as he led her past a luxurious master suite. At the end of the narrow hallway was a door. He opened it, and as she stepped into the space, the excitement she had felt moments before in the main part of the house transformed to a calm stillness. She took a deep breath. Just as those in the great room had, the windows faced the lake, but the ceiling and room size were not the same massive scale as the rest of the house. The walls and the small love seat and chair that faced one another were a neutral oatmeal color. A soothing scene of sail boats by a local artist whose name Merrill recognized hung on one wall. A fichus tree stood in the corner. Merrill could see that it needed watering.

"Does this door open to the yard, or to the beach I guess I should say?"

"Yes," Farrell answered. "This was the patient entrance."

She thought about David Michaels coming through that door to give the therapist hell for causing his parents' break-up. Mike unlocked it, and Merrill stepped outside. There was a small brass plate on the door. *Dr. Lynn Martinelli, LMSW.* To the right of the door was a lovely koi pond, the fish surrounded by floating lily pads and irises.

"I think someone needs to feed these fish," she said and jotted that down in her notebook. She glanced at the flagstone path that led from the office door all the way to the front of the house, but the backyard, closest to the lake and the likely crime scene, was her main concern. "What do you think the doctor kept in this baby Queen Anne?" she asked, walking to a storage building, which except for its size, matched and mirrored the main residence, complete with a second story turret. "Not your average backyard She-Shed," Merrill said aloud. A large padlock was on the door. She turned to the policeman and said, "Do you have the key?"

"I don't, but I know a trick." Farrell went beyond the seawall and returned with two fist-sized rocks. Merrill watched as he put one behind the lock and struck the front of it with the second rock. He turned and smiled at the impressed Merrill.

Inside the storage building were all manner of water toys including two jet skis, a rolled up swim pad, and a couple of inflatables for tubing behind a boat. Various sizes of life vests hung on one wall. Two canoes and a couple of very high-end bicycles were stored on racks in the back corner. A shiver crept up her spine as Merrill spotted the empty kayak rack next to the bikes. The sun shone on the silver tanks of two Ducati motorcycles. "Wow! The doctor had expensive taste in toys, I guess," Merrill said. "Interesting that almost all of these recreational amusements come in pairs."

Mike said, "She was married at one time, right? Maybe some of this belonged to the husband."

"Maybe," Merrill answered, picturing Shannon Kramer's frown at the thought of Peter Martinelli sharing ownership of anything her mother had paid for.

"Those stairs must go to the tower," Farrell said, pointing to them.

"The turret room, yes," Merrill agreed. "I'd love to see it."

"No time, Merrill. I'll be back with an evidence team in the morning. We'll check that space out then. Let's head outside."

Placing the lock back on the storage room door, Farrell suggested they walk to the beach and check out the spot where Lynn Martinelli's children had told them that she usually put her kayak in the water. Merrill took off her sandals and walked barefoot around the sea wall to the place where the doctor may have spent her last moments. Overhead, an osprey dove and grabbed a fish out of the water. "Incredible!" she commented. "You can see all the way to Canada from this spot!"

"She had all kinds of privacy here, for sure," Mike said. "Those massive old pines edge both borders of her home." He continued to scan the surroundings, like a robot of some sort, Merrill thought to herself. "The seawall looks like a pretty recent build. The storms over the past few seasons really took their toll on the beaches." Merrill followed Mike as he walked the length of the wall. "A neighbor on either side couldn't see her if she wanted to sunbathe nude, never mind put her kayak in," he commented.

Merrill turned and looked at the back of the beautiful home. "You're right, Mike. Very private and almost impossible for her next door neighbors to see what was happening on her section of beach. We should talk with both of them and see what they might have seen that evening."

"Yeah, and surprisingly, it looks like the doctor didn't believe in security cameras, like the rest of this neighborhood does," Farrell commented.

As Farrell locked the key boxes on the front and back of the house, Merrill felt a sadness wash over her. She wondered what might happen to this lovely place. More than likely, Lynn Martinelli's children, who were California residents now, would sell it to some millionaire or other. All of the doctor's loving attention to details that make a house a home would more than likely be wiped away by new owners.

As the two investigators reached the sidewalk, Mike asked, "Which way, Merrill?"

Merrill pointed in the direction of the two-story stucco home to the right of the Martinelli house. An elderly lady opened the front door before they could ring the bell, in spite of the fact that she was walking with a cane. Mike showed his badge and introduced Merrill to the homeowner. "Oh, yes," she said. "You're the *Deeper Dive* lady. A woman in my bridge group told me about your program. I never miss it."

Mrs. Cleo Mahr introduced herself to them and explained that the cane was temporary. She had had hip surgery recently. "What a horrible tragedy for the whole community!" she said. For a moment, Merrill thought she was referring to her surgery. The woman must have seen the confusion on her face and said, "I mean Lynn Martinelli, murdered!"

"Did you know the doctor very well?" Mike asked.

"Oh, yes. Such a nice lady. She was very pleasant, always,"

"Did you happen to notice any strange cars in the neighborhood on the night of Lynn's disappearance. On June 10th?" Merrill asked.

"Not really. I'm used to hearing cars pulling in and out of her driveway, so I wouldn't know if there were any that day that didn't belong." The woman's face lit up and she pointed to a security camera mounted on her garage. "But I just had these cameras installed in May. My son who lives in Houston insisted on it." Merrill saw that this one was aimed at Mrs. Mahr's front yard, and so she likely wouldn't have a view of her next door neighbor's driveway, or of the garage window that had been the point of entry for whomever broke into Dr. Martinelli's home after her death.

"Where are the other cameras, Mrs. Mahr?" Mike asked.

"There's one other on the back, on the beach side of the house," she said.

"Would it be possible for us to come in and take a look at the lake from your north-facing windows, Mrs. Mahr?" Mike asked.

"Of course," she answered. "Anything you need, officer. After all, none of us is safe until this monster is caught."

Mike and Merrill assured her that they wouldn't take long and that she didn't have to climb the stairs with them. When they reached the second floor, they saw a picture window that framed the lake. "Just as I guessed," Mike said. Because of its position on the lot and the giant pines on the property line, Mrs. Mahr's windows don't give access to even a partial view of Lynn Martinelli's beachfront.

"So that camera on the back of the house is useless to us," Merrill said.

"Looks that way," Mike answered.

Before they thanked her and said goodbye, Mrs. Mahr repeated that she couldn't recall seeing or hearing anything unusual on the evening of June 10th. "But again I want to make it clear that Lynn was a wonderful neighbor. Even though her practice brought all kinds of people into the neighborhood, if you know what I mean. She was a thoughtful and kind person. I knew she was helping folks, so eventually, I stopped worrying about her clients being a problem for the neighborhood, as far as safety goes. I guess I shouldn't have. Stopped worrying I mean," the old lady added.

"Thanks, Mrs. Mahr," Merrill said. "We'll be in touch if we need anything else."

As Mike and Merrill walked around the house and into the yard of the neighbor on the other side of Dr. Martinelli's, they could see that the brick ranch had no security camera on the front. Merrill rang the doorbell, and when no one came after a couple of minutes, they were ready to give up. As they turned to leave, they heard a dog barking followed by light footsteps. A girl of fifteen or sixteen with electric purple hair opened the door. "Back up, Silas," she said to the husky, grabbing his collar to guide him away from the two strangers. "Sorry I took so long. I was sitting out by the pool," the girl said.

Merrill showed the teenager her ID and explained who they were. She asked the girl her name. "I'm Carrie. Carrie Logan. I'm the nanny for the Crandalls. They're not home right now. The baby's napping. I can watch her on my phone," she told them. "You're here about the doctor next door, right?"

"We are," Farrell said. "I'd like to take a look at the backyard, if that's okay."

"Sure," Carrie said, "I think that would be fine with the owners..." Before she could finish her sentence, Mike headed toward the lakeside of the property..

"So, Carrie, did you know Dr. Martinelli?" Merrill asked.

"Not really. She and I would wave if we saw each other on the beach. Sometimes I'll take the baby down there. She loves to play in the sand and chase the gulls. These yards are very private, though. You can't really see anyone on their property. And there's no one on the other side of the Crandalls." As Mike came around the corner of the house, she added, "I do know a kid from my school who saw her. Saw her as a therapist, I mean." Merrill knew who that kid was, but she wasn't about to relay that to this young girl.

Mike returned from the beach and said, "Thanks, Carrie. All set, Merrill?" As they headed back to the car he said, "There's a camera back there, but it shoots straight out from the Crandalls' property to the lake, just like the old lady's. And there's no one across the street, except maybe squirrels and a few deer. No cameras on the Martinelli house either, so it looks like they'll be no video evidence to rely on."

His words helped Merrill to resolve the internal conflict she had been having these last couple of days regarding the thumb drive. After today's investigation, it didn't seem likely that anyone had actually seen David Mi-chaels *or* Peter Martinelli, for that matter, in the doctor's neighborhood that night. She would have to share the ex-husband's messages with Johnny. In the morning, she would call the Sheriff and tell him about the texts. To-night, she needed to delve into the other files on the flash drive. "Maybe we should look at the neighbors' videos, just in case. We'll check with Lovallo, though, to see if he thinks that's necessary," she said to the lieutenant.

After Mike dropped her off at home, she poured herself a glass of wine and sat down at her computer. She inserted the thumb drive and opened up the second folder.

## CHAPTER SEVENTEEN

# VIGILANCE

**D**ON: *How can you do this to me? You know every sordid detail of every rotten thing my family and the others have done to me!! Your cruelty, your coldness, telling me that you can't see me anymore. Why don't you at least return my calls??*

**DON**: *I don't understand. I'm sorry if driving by your house a few times is considered stalking. I'm sorry that I sometimes needed more time than my goddamned allotted hour. And, no, I don't want a fucking referral to some other therapist!*

**DON**: *How can "dismissing" me be ethical? You're my therapist! I should report you to the state medical board. I'll tell them everything. I'll tell them how you led me on. Made me think you cared about me!!*

**DON**: *How can you do this knowing what my mother did to me? I promise you, if it's the last thing I do, I will get even with you, "Dr." Martinelli!!!*

A glance down at her Fitbit confirmed that Merrill's pulse was racing as she read the second file on the flash drive. These and dozens more texts from someone named Don expressed a full range of emotions for Lynn Martinelli. Some proclaimed his admiration and devotion, others his outrage and disgust with her "indifference." The final one was an outright threat.

It was time to tell her boss about the thumb drive. She copied both folders and attached them to an email addressed to Johnny Lovallo. Picking up her phone, she texted him. "Incoming email…URGENT!" she typed.

"Just when were you going to tell me about this?" Johnny shouted over the phone at her the next morning.

"I wasn't sure. I've been pretty busy myself with this Martinelli case, you know," she said.

"Yeah. Well, Alex Sheldon has been on my ass for a day now, trying to get me to question Peter Martinelli. She's convinced he had something to do with the murder of her ex. I sent Farrell over to his place a couple of hours ago for a preliminary chat and the prick refused to let him in."

"Language, please." Merrill wasn't the stereotypical prim and proper librarian, by any stretch of the imagination. As a matter of fact, she had her own cadre of curse words, but she did not want the sheriff to treat her like one of the guys.

"Sorry," Johnny said. "Those toxic messages Martinelli sent his former wife certainly prove that he had an abiding hate for her. I just reached out to Judge DiGeorgio to get the warrant process rolling. It shouldn't take too long. Once I get it, I'd like to have you come to Martinelli's house with me to serve him and search his place."

"Okay. But I have an interview to do for the podcast in an hour. Can you wait for me to finish?" Merrill asked.

"Yes. Hopefully, he hasn't skipped town yet. Text when you're finished."

Merrill walked the four blocks to the Prenderson, trying to organize her thoughts for the interview. She was glad she was already knowledgeable about the Normal School fire in Fredonia that happened in December of 1900. Six female students and a janitor had perished in a holocaust of flames. What self-respecting librarian that worked for the same college where the tragedy took place wouldn't know about it? But her train of thought was interrupted by persistent questions about the three "suspects" in Lynn Martinelli's death, especially Peter Martinelli, who she expected to meet with soon after the podcast. Hopefully, she could pull herself together for this interview. Her guest today had found some never-before-seen evidence regarding one of the victims of the fire that was a sad part of the village of Fredonia and the college's history.

Denise Burton had written to Merrill a couple of weeks before, and although she lived in Connecticut, she had some business in Buffalo this week. She had agreed to take a few hours to do the interview live, and Merrill was relieved when she heard footsteps coming down the stairs to her tiny basement studio. A petite woman in a navy blue suit rounded the corner. "Merrill Connor?" she asked in a confident voice that the podcaster knew was optimal for the subject of an interview.

Extending her hand to her guest and guiding her to a chair she said, "Yes, Denise, so very nice to meet you." Within minutes, Merrill was sitting in front of her microphone introducing the woman to the listeners of *A Deeper Dive*. "Folks, many of you who are residents of Chautauqua County or alumni of Fredonia State may already know about the tragedy that took place at Fredonia College's Normal School in 1900, but for the rest of our audience, I'll do a quick summary. The school on Central Avenue in Fredonia was opened in 1867, and housed teaching candidates, most of them young women, who were studying to become public school teachers. In those early hours of December 14th, with just a few days to go until Christmas vacation, a raging fire lit up the entire sky over the village. The imposing brick building with the magnificent tower above the third story that housed seventy-five students and several staff was decimated that morning, burning to the ground in a matter of two hours. The occupants on the third floor were the most endangered, and six girls and a janitor, who saved many lives before perishing himself, were the fatalities. The story of one of those women, Maude Fizzell, is the focus of *A Deeper Dive* today. Denise, I'll let you take it from there. What is your connection to the Fredonia Normal School Fire?"

"Well, Merrill, I really didn't have a direct connection to the fire or to Maude Fizzell. Not until I went to an estate sale in Hartford last summer. I collect old steamer trunks; you know, the kind that sometimes have a secret panel in the bottom. To my disappointment, the one I bought that day did not appear to have one of those compartments. But when I took it to the man who has refurbished my other trunks, he discovered that it did."

"How exciting!" Merrill said. "Did the trunk belong to Maude Fizzell?"

"That can't be determined for sure, but in the compartment there were letters from Maude to a cousin. A Connecticut cousin," Denise said.

"I think this may be the perfect time for me, with your permission, Denise, to fill our listeners in on Maude's short life and her fate that horrible day."

"I agree, Merrill."

Merrill opened her notebook and read from her research notes. "Maude Prescott Fizzell was born in Dunkirk, New York, just a few miles east of Westfield. She moved with her parents to Bradford, Pennsylvania, and spent her childhood there. She was completing her first semester at Fredonia that terrible December. As a young girl, Maude had been sickly for a good portion of her school years. Her obituary in the *Normal Leader*, the campus newspaper, described her as a good student with outstanding artistic and musical capabilities. In those early morning hours, survivors of the fire said later that they had seen Maude standing at the fire escape exit. She was next in line to climb out to safety when she suddenly turned and told the frantic girls lined up at the window that she had to go back to her room for a diamond ring she had borrowed. Other witnesses that day observed her banging on the doors of girls who might have still been in their rooms as she headed back to hers, yelling for them to get out. They were the last people to see her alive, according to *The Leader*. She was labeled a hero for her actions that day. But my Divers know that when at all possible, I prefer a primary resource. And Denise's findings, Maude's letters, certainly count as primary. Tell us about them, please, Denise."

"There were twenty letters written by Maude to her cousin Emily Fizzell, dating from the time she left her hometown for college in Fredonia until just after Thanksgiving. Most of the letters were about college life, her classes, the many friends she was making, and until that October, several of them were about the Catholic Church she attended. According to other sources I have researched, Maude was a very devout Catholic, but in one of her last letters, she confessed to her cousin that she had left the church and had started to attend an Episcopal Church in the village."

"That was very unusual at the turn of the century. For a young woman to experiment with another religion," Merrill said. "Do any of her letters give a clue as to why she would do that?"

"Yes. I'd like to share that one, if that's okay, Merrill. I think it's the key to Maude Fizzell's actions on the morning of the fire."

"Please do."

Denise took out the delicate parchment paper from an envelope of the same material and started to read.

> "Dear Emily, I am bursting with joy this evening! I must share my news with somebody who loves me, and you are the only one, family or friend, that I can trust.
>
> I've told you that I have left the Church, but I haven't explained why. I feel that I must tell someone, or I will burst. I have fallen in love with a wonderful man, Emily! He is my music professor and from the first day in his classroom sitting at the piano I felt such a rare joy, such as I've never felt before! He is so intelligent, so talented, such an amazing teacher. And very handsome. Of course, there is a gaggle of girls that follow him all over the Normal School building whenever he is there. You know how shy I can be, so I was not one of them. But whenever he sat next to me during my instruction time, I felt like any moment, I would faint. One of my classmates took me aside after class one day, and not in the kindest tone said, 'Professor _____ seems to favor you. You do know he is married, don't you?'
>
> Emily, I was devastated! From that day forward, I tried so hard to ignore the feelings I had for him. I started going to Mass every morning. I prayed that God would help me to be sensible and good. I even went to the registrar's office to get a transfer to another professor's piano studio. When I brought the paperwork and handed it to him after class one day, he looked like I had struck him. He went to the class-

room door and closed it. As he walked toward me, I could see the pain in his eyes. 'Maude,' he said, 'please don't do this.' Emily, when he took me in his arms my world changed from that moment forward.

We began meeting in secret at a park several blocks from the college. He told me that his loveless marriage was a sham, that he was talking with a lawyer about divorcing. Divorce! As a Catholic, of course I could never marry a divorced man. One of the girls from my dormitory is Episcopalian, and I asked her if I could attend church with her that Sunday. I can't tell you, Emily, what relief and solace I feel among that congregation. The Holy Eucharist, (their name for their service), is very similar to our Mass, but their priests are allowed to marry and have children. Most important for me is that they accept the validity of divorce! I am currently receiving instructions so that I can become a convert. It is not easy to leave the faith of my parents and the rest of our family, but I would walk through fire for the man I love!

Dear Cousin, I tell you all this because I love and trust you and I know you will keep this a secret until I tell you it's safe to spread the news. This very afternoon I brought a picnic to our park, and in the oak grove there Professor _____ proposed!!! He took my hand and slipped the most delicate diamond ring on my finger!! I am so happy, Emily! Of course I cannot wear the ring in public, not until his divorce is final. (He is telling his wife about us this evening) I am sorry for her, but it sounds like they were never a good match. Thank God there are no children.

I pray that one day soon I'll be able to share my joy with Mother and Father and my siblings. Until then, dear Emily, be happy for your Maude!"

"Amazing! That ring meant everything to her, but it ended up costing Maude her life," Merrill said. "On behalf of all the Divers out there, let me thank you for your vigilance, Denise. Without your refurbished steamer trunk, more than likely belonging to Emily Fizzell at one time, all these years later we wouldn't know Maude's truth, in life and in death. We will post that letter from her and some others, as well, on our *A Deeper Dive* website."

After her guest had left the studio, Merrill turned on the equipment and recorded an addition to the segment that would air tomorrow. "*Vigilance, Divers, that's the word for today. Without Denise Burton's vigilance, the whole truth of why Maude Fizzell died that day in 1900 would not ever have been told. Today, I'm asking for the same kind of alertness from all of you for the sake of another woman who is gone too soon. Dr. Lynn Martinelli was murdered two weeks ago just miles from this studio, more than likely on her property on the Lake Erie shoreline. The Sheriff's Department has launched an intense investigation and it appears that security cameras in her neighborhood may not have been pointed in such a way as to offer proof of who might have bludgeoned her to death and left her to be carried away during the storm that night. The police are hoping that someone saw something or someone in her Shore Acres neighborhood on the evening of June 10th. If you know anything or saw anything, please reach out to the Sheriff's Department or to me, Merrill Connor, at A Deeper Dive.*"

Merrill turned her microphone off and her cell phone on and saw that Johnny had left her a message. The first line in all caps told her how angry he was. "JUDGE DIGEORGIO HAS GONE FISHING!"

He picked up on her first ring. It didn't surprise her that there was no hello. "I'm trying to get in touch with the judge's stand-in in Dunkirk. I'll let you know if and when I get the search warrant for Peter Martinelli. And then we'll go after David Michaels. See if you can track down this angry Don guy in the meantime." Merrill had no clue how she would go about doing that. She swore that sometimes Johnny forgot that she was a researcher, not a magician.

"Wait! Don't hang up," she said. "Did Farrell tell you we needed to take a look at the security camera footage from Dr. Martinelli's two neighbors?"

"He did. I'm on it." And then of course he hung up.

The click on the other end triggered something in her. She needed to take a break from the Lynn Martinelli case for the sake of her sanity. She needed the kind of therapy that she knew would restore her. She needed her friends.

Sherry answered on the first ring. "Oh my goodness, talk about your psychic abilities! I was just going to call you!" her friend said.

## CHAPTER EIGHTEEN

# ROSÉ ALL DAY

KATE WAS IN New York City, but amazingly both Merrill and Jenna were free to join Sherry in Bemus Point for "linner," the friends' term for a late lunch, early dinner. "Yes, I was thrilled that Jenna accepted my invitation so readily," Sherry told Merrill as they watched her walk toward them from the sidewalk. "I think you're both going to like this place," she said, as Jenna sat down. Only Sherry had eaten at the new wine and tappas bar, *Splash*, whose patio, lush with containers of summer flowers, provided a perfect view of Chautauqua Lake. "After all," Sherry told Merrill and Jenna, "it's my job to find places like this for my clients. So this is my office for the day."

"What an amazing business you've created, Sherry!" Jenna's admiration was sincere. All of the friends marveled at the professional plan she had created and carried out. On one of their Thursday nights at Larry's over wings and beer, she had brainstormed aloud with her three friends about an idea she had. An idea that would mean having to quit her accounting job at the college to realize. Now, *Yellow Brick Road Travel* was in its tenth year, and Sherry was busier than ever creating custom vacations for her clients.

"Aw, thanks, Jenna. How is *Mermaids' Tears* doing these days? I haven't been in the shop for a while."

Jenna's face turned red. She started to answer, but she was interrupted by the sommelier, who was eager to expound on the perfect pairing of the salmon dip Sherry had ordered with a bottle of Conundrum Rosé. It was obvious which one of them at the table was the tourism super star, since the man's entire spiel was directed at Sherry.

As he walked toward the extensive racks to retrieve the wine, Sherry turned back to her friends. "You were saying, Jenna?"

"To tell you the truth, Sherry, business is fine as far as the amount of jewelry I'm selling, but I am definitely low on beach glass."

"Well, the weather has been so pleasant lately. Is the lack of storm action responsible for that?" Sherry asked.

"Not really. I *have* started to collect again." Merrill realized she had been holding her breath while she waited for Jenna's reply. She had been afraid that her friend would stay away from the beach and collecting indefinitely.

"That's terrific, Jenna!" she said.

"My experience at the Stump and also the meeting with Tim and Shannon Kramer were helpful. I know Dr. Martinelli's children are grateful that I was there that day. But," Jenna continued, "I can't bring myself to go back to Boulder Point. Twice now I've pulled into the parking lot and gathered up all my stuff, but I couldn't get out of the car. So until I can conquer this emotional paralysis or whatever it is, I'm stuck collecting from the shorelines of the other two beaches, where finding glass is not easy. All the hobbyists and tourists go to those spots." Her friends nodded, but remained silent. They didn't want to interrupt this flow of candor from their friend. "But I'm determined to get back there. It may take a few tries, but..."

"I'll go with you!" Merrill said. "I'll even put on a mask and fins!"

Jenna and Sherry burst out laughing. Merrill's fear of water was legendary. "*That,* I must see!" Jenna said.

Merrill was thrilled to see Jenna smiling and laughing again. "I'll do it! I mean it!"

"I know you do. Don't worry. I may take you up on that when the time is right," Jenna assured her, as the waiter set the opened bottle of Rosé on the table and asked if he could pour.

"Cheers!" Sherry said, as they clinked their glasses. She waited for the other two to take a sip, and as they did, she decided the time was right for her pitch. "I'm so glad we could get together, girls. I have a proposition for you. Any guesses what it could be?"

Merrill could see Jenna's eyes narrowing with anxiety. *Baby steps, Sherry, baby steps*, she wanted to shout. "Well, Sherry, I've skipped too many of my classes on improving my psychic abilities, so you're going to have to spit it out," Merrill said.

"Well, we've all been under considerable stress lately, what with murdered bodies floating around…"

For Jenna's sake, Merrill interrupted her. "What's your idea, Sherry?"

"I'm proposing that we get the two of you out of Westfield for a couple of days. Kate is playing a sold-out cabaret in New York this weekend. Of course, I scored tickets. The whole trip would be my treat, airfare included. We'll have to stay in a new boutique hotel in Manhattan, since they are comping me for a review they want me to do for *NYC Travel Magazine*." Merrill was certain she detected an eye roll when Sherry said "comping." She looked across the table at Jenna.

A slow smile spread across her friend's face. "Why not?" Jenna said. "I could use a reset button. What about you, Merrill?"

Without even looking at her calendar, Merrill did a quick calculation of what her next week looked like. A podcast to do, security camera footage to look at, not one, but two subpoenas to follow up on in the Martinelli case, and another Psychic Development Class that she had to get to if she wanted to stay on the roster. It would be nearly impossible for her to get away for two hours, never mind two days! But Jenna's look of happy expectation wiped all doubt away. She was going to New York City with her girls. "Why, yes, yes, I could definitely use that, Jenna," she said.

"Fantastic!" Sherry shouted, lifting her glass as the eager waiter returned to her side.

"So glad you like the Rosé Ms. Lawton!" he said.

## CHAPTER NINETEEN

# VIDIOTS

FRANK FOUND A comfortable seat on Merrill's lap and settled in. Johnny's text that morning had requested that his research assistant get to his office at "her convenience" to watch the security camera tapes from Lynn Martinelli's neighbors. Because she was going to New York for a few days, she had some errands to run. And she really needed to catch up on the podcast email before she left, but she knew at this point that these tapes were the only potential evidence in the Martinelli case, so she had resigned herself to being here this morning. Frank's show of devotion was her reward.

Johnny inserted a tape into the VHS player, a useful relic today, since Mrs. Cleo Mahr's security system utilized tape. Merrill and Johnny sat back and watched the grainy video dated *June 10, 6 pm*, on the large screen in the sheriff's office. After fifteen minutes, nothing but swaying trees, birds, and squirrels appeared. Johnny fast-forwarded to the 1a.m. marker, which offered nothing but pitch darkness and the sound of an intense Lake Erie storm. When the sheriff turned off the player, Frank emitted a loud yawn. "I know exactly how you feel, boy!" Merrill said.

"Alright. Let's take a look at the Crandall's camera footage. At least we're moving into the 21st century with them. They sent me footage from their hard drive." Frank jumped off Merrill's lap when Johnny turned the lights off again and headed to the door. "Okay, Frank, I don't blame you. Go see what Linda is doing," his owner said, opening the door to the reception area for him.

"Hmm…who's the master here?" Merrill said under her breath.

"What's that?" Johnny asked.

"Nothing. Let's see what we can see in the Crandalls' back yard." Again, they started at the 6 p.m. spot. At the 6:15 mark, Johnny began fast-forwarding until Merrill shouted, "STOP!"

The image on the screen froze. "What the hell!!?? " Johnny said. "Where did *he* come from? We didn't see anyone going *down* to the Crandall's beach!" The sheriff hit rewind just to make sure, and paused on the image. "No one until right *here.*" Johnny was squinting at the television screen now, the signal that he was thinking deeply. "Is that who I think it is? Jesus, *yes*, he's wearing the same Foo Fighters t-shirt he had on when we brought him in!" Johnny said.

He rewound the video to the 6:30 time stamp and the two of them stood up and moved closer to the screen to take in every detail. At the 6:36 mark, a black shape emerged from the pines that bordered the two properties and began to run toward the Crandall's backyard. By 6:37, David Michaels came into focus. Merrill wondered if the wary look on his face was because he was aware of the camera.

They continued to watch the screen as the boy quickened his pace, skirted the perimeter of the Crandall's swimming pool, and entered the door that was off their back patio. Just as suddenly as he had appeared, David Michaels vanished from Merrill's and Johnny's view.

"What the hell!!??" Johnny repeated.

"Is the judge back from his fishing trip yet?" Merrill asked, as Johnny turned the lights back on.

"Yes, he is. I'll get a warrant and have the kid in here this afternoon. Can you be back by four?"

Merrill said she could, even though she needed to get her podcast prep done and her house ready if she had any hope of being able to enjoy Sherry's generous offer of a getaway weekend. She must call her son Jason, who was also her producer. She knew she could count on him to check *A Deeper Dive's* messages and to go over her research for an upcoming episode. If she promised to leave him some brownies on the kitchen counter, she might get him to water her house plants, too.

Suddenly, the vision of David Michael's cagey stare into the camera intruded upon her thoughts. What was he doing on the Crandalls' beach? Had he been committing a heinous crime at the shoreline moments before he was captured by their security camera? Could the angry teenager whose father boasted about his kindness be capable of murder? Merrill's sense was that he was not, but she had done research on the brain development of adolescent boys for a graduate student's thesis, and the science she had dug up for the project told her that erratic and knee-jerk reactions on the part of young men David's age couldn't be ruled out. As much as her gut persisted in telling her that David Michaels was not that kind of kid, she had to try to remain impartial until the time that she could find solid proof of his innocence.

Merrill parked her Nissan in the staff lot at the Prenderson and took the stairs two at a time. She made plans as she moved. She would check the email, see if a prospective guest had answered her request to be interviewed, and let the ladies at the circulation desk know that she would be out of town until Monday.

Moments later she sat in front of her laptop in the library basement scrolling through a dozen new emails. She had developed the bad habit of not wearing her reading glasses just to challenge herself and her aging eyesight. When she saw the subject line of one of the messages, she grabbed them off the table and put them on and began to read.

**Subject: *Security Camera at Victim's House***
*Dear Merrill Connor,*

*I'm a fan of A Deeper Dive. I just listened to yesterday's episode and what you said about the Martinelli case. About being vigilant. I work for my husband. He installs security systems. I saw the receipt for one he installed in May at the doctor's house. There is a large rock near the pond in back of her house. It's not a rock. Good luck!*

*A loyal fan and Diver*

Merrill's pulse raced as she hurriedly closed her laptop and straightened up the studio. She could get to Shore Acres and back to the Sheriff's Department in time to observe Johnny's interview with David Michaels, but she had to hurry. She reached into her purse for the thumb drive she had intended to look at again, more closely this time. Context, as she thought of it, information about Lynn Martinelli's life, was what she needed to dig for, but that would have to wait until she got back from New York. She didn't want to take the drive with her on the girls' trip and chance losing it, so she locked it in the drawer of her work table.

Being pulled over and ticketed for speeding on Route 5 would not fit into her tight schedule today, so she kept the cruise control on 55 until she reached the Dunkirk city limits. Turning into the Shore Acres neighborhood, she could see that the yellow and black crime scene tape was still strung across Lynn Martinelli's driveway. She didn't want to park on the street. It might raise more questions from the neighbors. Merrill jumped out of the Nissan and took down one end of the tape. Then she pulled in as close as she could to the front door of the beautiful home.

Hurrying around the side of the house, she passed the shattered garage window, noting that someone from the Deputy Sheriff's office had nailed plywood over it. As she got closer to the backyard, Merrill heard the roiling waves on the lake warning that a summer storm was imminent. She moved quickly to the koi pond that she had admired when she and Farrell had been here a couple of days ago. Standing at its edge, Merrill watched as the black and gold fish nibbled on bright pink and pale yellow water lilies. She looked at the layers of flat shale rocks that were placed artfully all around the pond's ledge. They were definitely not large enough to hide a camera, she thought, but at a small distance behind the pond were several larger rocks. Merrill stood in front of them and turned toward the lake. Yes, they were in the perfect position to record any activity at the doctor's office entry and beyond to the sea wall. She picked up three whose heft and weight eliminated them. They were definitely not artificial. The fourth one was light and hollow feeling. "Bingo!" she said aloud. She found a hinged opening at the bottom of the fake rock and pulled it open. Inside, was a tiny camera.

"It's me," Merrill said when Johnny picked up. "I need you to send Farrell back to Dr. Martinelli's house with the evidence kit. I'll explain when I get back there." She hung up before he could ask.

CHAPTER TWENTY

## BETWEEN A ROCK AND A HARD PLACE

CARRYING A SHERIFF'S Department evidence bag in one hand and her shoulder bag in the other, Merrill hurried into Johnny's office. In the waiting area sat the Michaels family with Frank, who was in the process of making sure that all three of them had been licked before he conceded to Johnny's "Frank, come in here." Merrill said hello to David and his parents as Johnny added, "I need you in here, too, Mrs. Connor." He was getting better at interpreting her facial expressions. "Please," he added, politely. "We'll be with you folks soon," he said.

Merrill closed the office door behind her. "What's in there?" he asked, indicating the evidence bag.

She took a deep breath as she tried to conceal the excitement she was feeling. "A tiny camera and the SD card that was inside it. Thanks to one of the Divers, I found it in Lynn Martinelli's backyard," she said, as she held up the compact flash card. "For our viewing pleasure, after we talk to David Michaels."

"Holy Sh...Smokes!" her boss said, the appreciation of her discovery written all over his face.

"Poker-face, Lovallo," she warned him, as he went to the door and invited the Michaels family to come in.

David and his parents sat across from the investigators in the same positions as they had during their earlier interview. Under the table, Merrill quietly removed her flip flops and rested her bare feet on the back of the small dog who had settled there. She opened her notebook and jotted down the date and time.

"So David, I want to thank you and your folks for being here today," the Deputy Sheriff said.

The boy's father responded. "We didn't really have a choice, did we Sheriff?"

Johnny ignored the hostile tone and answered in his professional voice, "That's true, but we appreciate it all the same." From that point on, Lovallo ignored the parents and directed all comments and questions to David Michaels. "You've told us, or rather, your mother has told us that you had an appointment with Dr. Martinelli on the day she was last seen alive. Your music instructor Derrick told Mrs. Connor that you admitted that you were furious with your therapist. You told him that you went back later in that same afternoon to her Shore Acres office."

There was no response from the teen. Johnny waited a few seconds and then asked, "It's also true, as you told Derrick, that you had violent fantasies that included harming the doctor, isn't that right, David?"

The teen maintained a taciturn silence until his mother said, "David. You need to answer his question."

"Yes, I did!" The four adults didn't miss the trembling voice of the teen. "But they were just in my head! Like dreams! I even told her about those thoughts at that last appointment."

Merrill and Johnny exchanged a glance and she could see that her boss wanted her to be directly involved in the questioning of the kid at this point. "That must have been hard for you to admit, David. How did the doctor react?" she asked.

"She didn't freak out or anything. She said she could tell that I wasn't a violent person. That my thoughts were just a way of venting the anger I was feeling about the divorce. And she…" Merrill could see that the boy was close to tears.

"She what, David? Please speak up!" Johnny said, his impatience with the boy obvious.

"She told me to come back, anytime. Anytime I had questions or feelings I didn't understand. And so I went back." he said. "Later that day."

"David!" Bob Michaels shouted, causing Frank to give up his job as Merrill's footstool. They heard his nails clicking on the wooden floor until he reached the spot where David's father's sat. "Sheriff, I want my lawyer in here before we go any further!"

"If David were my son, that would not be a choice that I would make at this juncture, but..."Merrill was startled by Johnny's harsh tone.

"No, Dad! I have nothing to hide! I *was* at her office later that day, but I didn't murder Dr. Martinelli!" David's face was a bright red now, and his eyes were huge.

"You should know, David, and Mr. and Mrs. Michaels, that we've discovered a video from a security camera in Shore Acres from that day. It captures David running up from the shoreline toward and into the neighbor's house. We think it was very close to the time that the doctor most probably put her kayak in the water." Merrill noted the shocked expressions on the faces of the teen's parents.

"The Crandalls' house," David said. "Yes, but I was going to see my friend Carrie, who was babysitting there. I wanted her to know that I had gone back to talk to the doctor, that I was feeling better..."

"Stop talking, David!" his father ordered. The teen heeded his father's words, but he  crossed his arms across his chest and shook his head in disgust.

"The other thing you need to know, perhaps so you can inform your attorney, Mr. and Mrs. Michaels, is that we have discovered another security camera, this one with a motion detector," Johnny said. "We haven't had a chance to view the video from June 10th yet, but if David was at Dr. Martinelli's beach front before running up to the Crandall home, we'll have a digital recording of it." Johnny stood up and went around to the other side of the desk. He leaned down and positioned himself just inches from the teen's face. "It's time for you to tell us exactly what we're going to see, David."

"You'll see me…"

"David, STOP!!!" Bob Michaels shouted.

"…taking the doctor's kayak out of the little storage house," the boy persisted.

"David!!" Lorna Michaels' pallor was ghost-like. "Why? Why would you do that?"

"I'm trying to tell you, Mom! Dr. Martinelli asked me to." Both parents seemed stunned by their son's admission.

"Why would the doctor ask you to do that, David?" Johnny asked, still close to the kid's face.

"When I showed up after her office hours were over, she let me come in. We talked for about a half hour. I felt a lot better, and I told her so. I said that I had to admit that things were better between my parents, even though they had decided definitely to divorce." Lorna Michaels took her son's hand in hers as he continued. "I offered to pay her for the extra session, but she said no. I told her that I was going to go over to see Carrie and she said, 'I don't want you to pay me, but maybe you could do me a favor before you go to the Crandall's. Could you bring my kayak down to the water for me?' She wanted to get a ride in before the storm, she said. And so I did. I wheeled it out of the little house in her backyard and took it down to her beach. I left it there on the sand for her. So that's what you'll see on that video," David said, looking across the desk at Merrill. Johnny walked back to his chair and sat down. Silence filled the small room.

Frank's head appeared from underneath the table as he placed his front paws across the teen's thighs. As usual, he received the ear scratching he deserved. "I never saw Dr. Martinelli again after that," David said. "I hung around with Carrie for about twenty minutes, and then I took off for home."

After thanking them and assuring them that they would be in touch, Johnny walked with the Michaels family to the main door. Merrill counted to twenty and removed the SD card from the little camera. She inserted it into Johnny's laptop and waited anxiously for him to return. Mulling over the kid's explanation regarding his second meeting with Lynn Martinelli that day, her gut told her he was telling the truth.

Moments later Johnny joined her. She pressed play, and they watched together as David Michaels walked toward the little Queen Anne storage shed in Martinelli's back yard. Seconds later the teen wheeled a boat cart out of the shed. It held the large kayak with a paddle in its cradle. "Our guys found the cart and paddle up against the sea wall the day they searched Dr. Martinelli's beach front," Johnny told her. So far the tape was bearing out Merrill's hunch about David's honesty.

The two stared at the screen in silence for a few seconds as the boy moved in the direction of the seawall. Johnny hit the pause button and zoomed in on the kayak. "It's an Oru. I can't see the registration number, but it sure looks like the same model that Alex Sheldon gave Lynn Martinelli."

Moments later, they watched as David ran up from the beach. He veered to his left toward the Crandalls' house, just as he had told them, and disappeared from view.

CHAPTER TWENTY-ONE

# WHAT ELSE CAN WE SEE?

"So AT THIS point, it looks like the kid was telling the truth," Johnny said. "I'll send Farrell to get a statement from the friend, Carrie Logan. Make sure she backs up what David told us. But we have to keep in mind that there's no video of what took place on Dr. Martinelli's beach."

Merrill nodded, in spite of the fact that she believed David was innocent. She turned back to the laptop screen. "Let's see what else we can see."

"Okay. By the way, Merrill, good work on finding the doctor's camera."

"One of my Divers deserves all of the credit for that," she said, as Johnny hit the play arrow on the screen.

A shiver crawled up Merrill's spine as she watched a figure walk toward the seawall as the sun was beginning its slow descent toward the water. It was Lynn Martinelli. The camera time stamp said 7:05 p.m. In the doctor's hand, she held the neon yellow life vest that Merrill knew would eventually anchor her lifeless body to The Table at Boulder Point. The woman's long dark hair was pulled into a pony tail and she was wearing the black track suit that she had had on when Jenna discovered her. As the therapist disappeared behind the break wall, the camera footage stopped. "Oh, shit!" Johnny said, and before Merrill could admonish him, the tape began to play again.

"Who is *that*??" Merrill shouted and stood up. According to the time stamp, it was 7:08 p.m., when a tall man wearing a Yankees cap, jeans, and a denim jacket opened the door to the doctor's storage shed. Seconds later, his head down and his face, except for his dark sunglasses, obscured from their view, he walked out of the miniature Queen Anne storage building carrying a kayak paddle. When he disappeared around the seawall, the camera halted again.

"*Come on, come on!*" Johnny shouted as the two of them waited for some motion to activate the camera. Merrill gasped when the man appeared again, this time walking toward the device. The time stamp read 7:20 p.m. as the figure walked, head still bent, toward the pine border of Dr. Martinelli's home. In his hand, he carried a kayak paddle. The camera shut off then and the screen remained dark, as Johnny fast-forwarded to the end of the tape.

Merrill sat down again and pulled up Peter Martinelli's Facebook and Instagram profiles. Tall and ginger-haired, in a lot of his photos he displayed his well-tended abs on a beach, domestic or foreign. In most of them he was surrounded by other smiling and under-clad people. In many of the pictures, the two investigators recognized the Shore Acres seawall behind Martinelli. In only two photos, Lynn Martinelli stood by his side at the shore, squinting into the sun. In one, the couple sat, unsmiling, in separate canoes close to the shoreline. In nearly all of the pictures, Peter Martinelli wore a Yankees cap. It could have been the one they had just seen on the man in the security camera video. "Linda!" Johnny opened the door and yelled into the reception area, "Get me Judge DiGeorgio, NOW!"

Two hours after she assured Johnny, a diehard Cleveland fan, that there were thousands of Yankee devotees in Western New York besides Peter Martinelli, he phoned her. He had calmed down somewhat, but Merrill imagined that Frank would have his work cut out for him that night. "Martinelli is nowhere to be found. Farrell and a couple of his guys have been watching his house. Newspapers from three days back are on the doormat and his mailbox is bulging. According to a neighbor across the street, his porch light has been on for days."

"Okay, well that is interesting," she said when he paused to catch his breath.

"And get this! DiGeorgio is fishing alright…in *Alaska*! The justice of the peace in Dunkirk begged off and says, since there's *no hurry*, his words, he would prefer to have our magistrate handle this. So, enjoy your weekend away, Merrill, and think of me. While you're gone, to top off my agenda, Alex Sheldon has requested another interview with me after I told her there was some new evidence in the case. I'm Zooming with Tim and Shannon Kramer tomorrow morning and then Ms. Sheldon will come in the afternoon."

"I'm sorry to have to miss that," Merrill said.

"You won't," her boss replied. "I'll have you watch the tape when you get back on Monday. I'll ask Alex Sheldon if I can record our interview, so you won't miss that either. So much for my having a much-deserved day off." There was that familiar sarcasm tinged with anxiety in his voice, and before she could respond, there was the click.

Two hours later, carry-on in tow, Merrill got into the first class line at the airport behind Jenna and Sherry.

## Chapter Twenty-Two

# WHIRLWIND

BY THE TIME Merrill pulled out of the parking lot at the Buffalo airport on Sunday after returning from the weekend in the City, it was 11:30 p.m. and she had a forty-five minute drive in front of her. Jenna and Sherry had decided to hang out another day in New York with Kate, but Merrill couldn't afford the time to stay on, not with Lynn Martinelli's killer still at large. As she pulled onto the Thruway, she turned up the volume on the radio so that she wouldn't give in to the exhaustion that was creeping up on her.

The quick trip with the women had been a whirlwind, but it was an excursion each one of the friends had needed. It had been the perfect combination of excitement and relaxation. The hotel that Sherry had been contracted to review was located in Chelsea near Madison Square Garden and the Flatiron Building, and it was just a mile-and-a-half from the High Line.

On Saturday morning, knowing her friends rarely had time in their busy lives for self-care, Sherry booked the three of them for facials and massages at a spa she frequented when she was in the City. From there, it was a quick walk to the New York Public Library. Merrill couldn't resist spending a portion of Saturday afternoon wandering through the vast collections while the other women shopped. Memories flooded back as she roamed from one floor of the august space to another. Once they could afford it, she and Richard traveled into the City at least three times a year, often taking Amtrak into Grand Central and grabbing a cab from there. They usually began their adventure at the Metropolitan Museum of Art and ended it at the Library.

On Saturday night, after an amazing meal at Babbo Ristorante, the three women walked to the small nightclub in the heart of the Village to attend Kate's cabaret. "Oh my God, what are you guys doing here?" she called out as her three friends entered the cozy room.

"Surprise!" was the unanimous response. Sherry had reserved a table close to the stage, and after hugging each of them, Kate walked to her place behind the baby grand. Every seat in the place was taken by the time she played the opening chords. The main part of the show featured Kate's original compositions and her virtuoso piano playing and signature vocals. Merrill was so glad she had come. She knew her friend was talented, but it was great to look around this room full of strangers and see the looks of admiration and hear the applause for her.

When the set ended, Kate sat down and ordered a bottle of champagne for the four of them. "You all look wonderful!" she said. "The City agrees with you. Jenna. You look like your old self! I'm so glad you came!" Merrill wasn't always appreciative of Kate's candor, but her encouraging words tonight seemed to land exactly right. Jenna was beaming. On Sunday morning Kate joined her friends again as they wrapped up the trip with brunch and a matinee performance of the Broadway revival of *Funny Girl*.

All in all, it had been an exciting, jam-packed weekend. The bonus for Jenna's friends was that she had been more like her old self, just as Kate had said. She had seemed to truly enjoy their company and sharing the city adventure with them.

As she drove west on the Thruway, Merrill could feel her eyelids growing heavy, but she took comfort in the fact that she was almost home. Johnny had scheduled a busy Monday morning for her. She would watch the tape of his interview with the Kramers and listen to Alex Sheldon as each person answered Johnny's questions about Peter Martinelli. She knew that the sheriff wouldn't express any of his own opinions about these meetings until she, his research assistant, had observed, taken notes, and come up with her own conclusions. But still, as was always the case with Johnny, he was a lot. Merrill knew it, and Frank knew it. She tried not to think of the stamina it would take to be in that small office tomorrow morning, Johnny's hyperbolic energy spilling out and filling the room. She took comfort in the fact that, tonight, she was just a short car ride away from her bed.

Forty minutes later, as she began the climb to the upper deck that led to her kitchen door, the motion light was triggered. Merrill was glad that she had only taken a carry-on on the trip and not her large suitcase. And although she was a dedicated walker and sometimes-runner, her legs ached from the miles of walking they had done these past couple of days in the city.

Halfway up the stairs, she stopped and dug into her purse for her keys. Head down and still digging, she reached the top step. As she stepped onto the deck, Merrill's psychic sensibility, her intrinsic alarm system, was suddenly alerted. Something wasn't right. She looked down at the deck planks and there it was - broken glass scattered from one end to the other. She looked up and saw its source. The shattered kitchen window. "*What the hell*?" she said aloud.

Merrill stopped digging in her purse. She wouldn't be needing her keys. The back door was wide open.

## Chapter Twenty-Three

# INVASION

Merrill sat in the dark on the front porch swing, her carry-on at her feet, as she waited for Johnny and Frank to arrive. She held her key ring in her hand, but she couldn't bring herself to go inside the house. Besides, the sheriff had told her very firmly that she should wait for him before she attempted to take an inventory of damage or stolen property.

It didn't take much convincing. Merrill was freaked out to think some-one had broken into her house. She kept very little cash there and her jewelry consisted mainly of Jenna's lake glass designs, precious to her, but probably not to the creep who had broken in. She was sure the s.o.b. had stolen some of Richard's paintings and sculptures, but she just wasn't ca-pable of walking into the Shed or any other room in her home by herself. Thankfully, she didn't have to wait long for Johnny. His headlights lit up her driveway within minutes of her call.

As he ran up the front steps with Frank galloping in front of him, he didn't bother with a greeting. "What do you mean, you *don't* have a *secu-rity system*?" he shouted. "What kind of moron..." When he drew closer and saw her face, he stopped the diatribe that he had been practicing in the Bronco on his way to her house and lowered his voice. "Merrill, am I wrong? Or did you not let a murderer and a want-to-be murderer into your house a couple of years ago?"

"Yes." Her answer was just above a whisper, but Frank reacted to the fear in her voice. He jumped up on the swing and leaned his warm body into hers. She was trembling. Johnny's reminder of how close she had come to being murdered while investigating the Grace Phillip's disappearance made her feel nauseous. Maybe she didn't have the brains or the guts to be a criminologist.

As the porch light shone down on her face, Johnny decided that this was not the time to lecture her. "I'll send the security company that the department uses to install a system tomorrow," he said, carefully lowering his voice. "Let's take a walk through the house, starting at the intruder's point of entry on the deck, and see if there's anything missing."

A squad car had followed Johnny into the driveway, and Mike Farrell waved to her before heading to the backyard. "Going to do some print dusting, Merrill," he said, as if he was used to having his colleagues' homes burgled.

Merrill carried Frank as she and Johnny stepped gingerly around the broken glass lying on the deck. Before they crossed the threshold into the house, Farrell handed them booties to put over their shoes. "I'll dust for prints inside before I leave," he told them.

Lovallo reached for the light switch just inside the door, and Merrill held her breath as she looked around the room. Nothing was out of place or missing from the kitchen as far as she could see. She stepped over some pieces of glass, and as they left the kitchen, she set Frank down on the floor. Though it was not his usual inclination or position, he proceeded to follow the two humans from one room in Merrill's house to the next. The bathrooms, the three bedrooms, the dining room, her small study, none of those spaces showed signs of an intruder. "Have you been to the beach lately?" Johnny asked Merrill.

Incredulous, she tried not to shout. "No! Why?"

"Have you noticed the sand on the floor? From the kitchen all the way down this hallway," he said, dragging his bootie covered sandal across the oak floorboard to demonstrate. Merrill did the same, and she agreed that she could feel the grittiness, too.

As they drew closer to the Shed, Merrill was filled with a kind of trepidation, the type of fear induced by nightmares. She said nothing, but with an obvious gesture, indicated that Johnny should lead the way into her husband's art studio, the place where she still felt his presence the most. She had moved her favorite chair and her small desk in there several months ago so that she would be close to his art, as well as Richard's essence, as she read or worked.

Following Johnny into the room, she resisted the temptation to close her eyes. He turned on the overhead light and then the switch that turned on all the art lights that had been installed above Richard's works. At first glance, Merrill thought everything looked like it was in its place, including the painting she cherished, *A Deeper Dive*, which remained in the center of the room on a tripod. "So," Johnny said, "what do you think? Everything here?"

"I think so, but let me check the inventory list I made to be sure. I'm so nervous, I might not have noticed if something isn't in its place. The list is on my laptop." Merrill walked to the far corner of the Shed to her small desk with Frank at her heels. "What the...my *laptop*! It's *gone*!!" The little dog yelped in sympathy with his friend's troubled tone as Johnny came running from the far side of the studio.

"What do you mean..." The sheriff stopped in his tracks. All the desk drawers had been overturned and the contents were scattered on the floor. "Your laptop...are you sure you left it here?"

"Yes!" I'm sure!" Merrill shouted. "This is where I work when I'm not at the library." Johnny said nothing, but his disbelief showed all over his face. "I *know*, I *know*," she said. "A laptop is a *mobile* device, as my kids tell me all the time. But I like having a fixed station for it, just like my old PC days. I even bought another one to keep at the Prendersen so that I wouldn't have to take this one when I needed to work in the studio."

"Merrill, who the hell would want whatever was in your desk?" Johnny said, picking through the miscellaneous office supplies that had been dumped on the floor. "Or whatever was on your laptop?"

"I have no effing...WAIT!!! I do have an effing idea!! The thumb drive! Lynn Martinelli's thumb drive!! But who knew I had that???"

"Is it here? The thumb drive??" Johnny yelled, rooting through the spilled contents of her desk.

"It's not!" Merrill shouted.

"*Where is it*?" Johnny hollered.

A look of triumph broke out on Merrill's face. "The loser can look at every file on that laptop he stole! I never downloaded the stuff that was on Lynn Martinelli's flash drive! It's locked inside my work table at the library!"she yelled.

With a backward glance at the boisterous humans, Frank whined and walked out of the room.

## Chapter Twenty-Four

## KRAMER VS MARTINELLI

Monday morning came way too soon for Merrill. The quick trip to New York City and the shock of the break-in had exhausted her. Thanks to Johnny's order that Mike Farrell remain in her driveway all night, she had slept soundly without fear of being victimized twice in one weekend. She typically didn't need to set an alarm, but she was glad she had thought to do that after Johnny left. This morning he wanted her input on the two interviews he had done while she had been away. He had to leave for a meeting in Albany at eleven, so Merrill recognized that they would have to work efficiently if he was going to make his appointment on time.

Juggling a cardboard tray containing a cup of coffee and a bagel in one hand and her work bag in the other, she swept into the Sheriff's Department with a minute to spare. Johnny sat in front of his computer and didn't look up when she came in. "How are you this morning, Merrill? Did you manage to get some sleep?" he asked.

"Surprisingly, yes. I am a bit shaky this morning, though," she confessed.

"It's no wonder. You had a horrible welcome back from NYC. Burglary is a violation, for sure. Anyone who has been victimized that way knows how it levels you emotionally. We've got the evidence team looking at those footprints. They dusted the place for fingerprints, too. Don't worry, Merrill. We're on it."

She appreciated Johnny's concern, but she didn't want to talk about it. At least not yet. "Where's Frank?" she asked Johnny, as she sat down in the chair next to his.

"At the groomer's," he said.

"Why?" She just couldn't resist the urge to needle her boss. She wasn't used to the empathy he was showing her. It made her uncomfortable. "You mean to tell me that you can't manage to give that little guy a bath by yourself?"

"He hates water," Johnny replied. She watched as he got his laptop set up to play the Kramer tape. "I don't want him to hate me." He turned off the overhead light and Lynn Martinelli's children appeared in two separate Zoom boxes on the large screen. "It's bad enough I have to leave him at Doggie Daycare for the night."

"So what's going on in Albany?" He ignored her question and pressed play.

Shannon spoke first. "Where is Mrs. Connor?" she asked.

Johnny had not taken video of himself on the Zoom meeting, so off-camera he said, "She had to be out of town this weekend. I'll share this video with her, so feel free to address any questions or comments you might have for her. I'd like to start by asking you to share your memories of the time when Peter Martinelli came into your mother's life."

"Sure. I was just starting grad school and Shannon was in her first semester at Cal State," Tim said, "so that would have been ten years ago. Our dad had passed a couple of years before that. Mom had a very difficult time with his death for many reasons. They were very much in love from the time they had met during college. His death was sudden and unexpected." Johnny tried not to be obvious as he glanced at Merrill. He was sure she could relate to Dr. Martinelli's loss of a beloved husband.

"So at the time she met Martinelli, she was just starting to socialize a bit. She met him at a party her tennis partner was throwing at the country club," Tim said.

"Was your mom a member?" Johnny asked.

"Yes," Shannon said, "but except for the tennis courts, it was not Mom's usual scene."

"Our mother hated pretense above all else, but she decided she should at least make the attempt to have a life beyond her professional one," her son added.

"Pretty ironic, right, Sheriff Lovallo?" Shannon said. "Our mother hated inauthenticity and yet she ended up marrying a raging, creepy narcissist!"

"Another irony that can't escape us is that Martinelli was selling insurance at the time he met Mom. And now that she's been murdered, he's going to try to sue her estate for survivor's benefits, according to our attorney!" Tim Kramer said, his contempt for the man obvious. "Of course, he didn't stick with the insurance profession for long. He tried all kinds of schemes… er, jobs in those years he was married to our mom."

"Jobs?" Johnny asked, "Plural?"

"Oh, yes. Let's see, first it was insurance. Then he became a financial planner." He looked at his sister for confirmation.

"That's right. Then he got into being credentialed for various careers. He went to an "*institute*" in Florida to become a golf pro. When he couldn't get hired at any country clubs or golf academies, he decided to go to culinary school. He fancied himself a great cook…"

"*Chef!*" her brother interjected. "Please use the correct term, Shannon." It was obvious that these two had never had any use for Peter Martinelli, no matter what his occupation. "What was his last thing, Sis? Do you recall?"

"Real estate. That's what he's doing now, as far as I know."

"Right," Tim said. "And in every one of those endeavors, he tried to use our mother's connections and her bank accounts to reach success. I'm sure that's why he stole her email contact list. So he could reach out to her friends and clients and sell them an expensive piece of property."

"Would you say that Martinelli was good to your mother?" Johnny asked.

"It depends on what you mean by good," Shannon said. "Peter loved being married to our mother. She was gorgeous. And she had a beautiful home on the lake. She was a respected professional with connections all over Western New York that he tried to parlay into sales and profits with one scheme or another."

"And her two skeptical adult children were thousands of miles away," Tim said. "That was a definite bonus for him."

"What do you think your mother saw in him?" Johnny asked.

"That is an excellent question, Sherriff, and I'm damned if I know," Shannon said. "Of course he love-bombed the hell out of her that year before their wedding."

"Love-bombed?" Johnny asked. "I'm afraid I'm not sure what that is."

"My brother the shrink is better qualified to answer that, I think."

"This isn't exactly professional terminology, but love-bombing is the act of overwhelming someone with lavish amounts of attention, affection, and material generosity," Tim said. "That's what Peter Martinelli did within weeks of meeting our mother. He bought her seasons tickets for her beloved Buffalo Bills, he took her scuba diving in Aruba, knowing how much she loved anything to do with the water. He even bought her a Porsche, which she immediately sent back to the dealer. By then, she was beginning to recognize how excessive it all was, but his over-the-top behavior continued in torrents up to and including a honeymoon in Tuscany. Of course, he slipped up a bit, as narcissists often do, when he booked a flight for them to see the Yankees play the Red Sox. He's a rabid New York fan. Our mother had never watched an inning of baseball in her life."

Merrill couldn't see Johnny's expression, but she heard the excitement in his voice. "I'd like to show you something. It's a video from a security camera of a person in your mother's backyard the evening she was murdered." A screenshot from the tape appeared in a separate box on the Zoom screen. Merrill recognized the figure in the Yankees cap from her first viewing of the tape. Brother and sister stared at both segments of the video - the one of the man going to the storage shed and then down to the beach, and the second one that showed him coming back toward the house carrying the kayak paddle.

"That's got to be him. I think." Shannon didn't sound sure.

"I'm not certain. Martinelli might be taller," Tim Kramer said.

"But he's hunkered down, obviously, so his face can't be seen. That may be why he looks shorter," his sister said.

"The guy does tend to wear that Yankees cap in every picture I've seen of him. He's self-conscious about losing his hair, for one thing. I guess it could be him," Tim said.

"Okay," Johnny said, leaving the still photo of the Yankee fan on the screen. "At least in the beginning, your mother seemed to be happy with Peter Martinelli. What happened? In your opinions, why did they divorce?"

"Well, after the smoke from the love-bombing cleared, Mom started to see some things and to figure some other things out," Tim said. "Her credit card bills were exorbitant three months after the wedding. This is about the time he got out of the insurance business and was '*in between*' gigs. Mom had been billed for all those thoughtful and extravagant gifts."

"So he was defrauding her, but that wasn't enough. He started to undermine her relationships, with us, as well as with some of her life-long friends. When a friend's daughter came to her and told her that Martinelli had tried to kiss her at her parents' party one night, Mom kicked him out the next day. They had a pre-nup, thank God, but she still gave him the down payment for the house he lives in to this day," Shannon said.

"True to the profile of a narcissist, he couldn't believe that she wanted to divorce him," Tim added. "He was sure she would change her mind. He dragged his feet for a year, but eventually he had to get a lawyer."

Merrill heard Johnny's cautious tone as he asked the Kramers, "Was it during that year that your mother discovered that she was attracted to women?"

"I believe it was," Shannon said, a hint of surprise in her voice. "I didn't know you were aware of that, Sheriff."

"I am. Only because the kayak that washed ashore soon after your mother's body was recovered was registered to Alexandra Sheldon. She explained that they had been together for a time. Did you know her?" Johnny asked.

"Mom never mentioned her specifically, but she did talk about her own growing awareness of her bisexuality," Shannon said, "and that she thought she might try dating soon."

"If it *was* a relationship, it couldn't have lasted very long, right Shannon?" her brother asked.

"I don't think so. Mom hadn't mentioned any particular love interests to me in the months before her death. She and I talked at least once a week. Maybe our mother wasn't as emotionally invested as Alex Sheldon was, Sheriff Lovallo. She didn't want to lead her on, is my guess," she said, "so she ended it."

"Maybe that rat of an ex-husband of hers knew about the relationship. I say that because Martinelli thought it would be to his benefit to "out" our mother in court, but I understand his lawyer advised against it if he hoped to get the amount of maintenance he wanted," Tim said.

"That being the case, what do you believe could have been Peter Martinelli's motive to kill your mother?" he asked.

"Let me put on my shrink hat for a moment, Sheriff," Tim Kramer said. "A narcissist, or someone with narcissistic tendencies, has the need for control, for dominance. He or she can have a super-ego and an unrealistic sense of entitlement. They can be very charming, but they often don't have the emotional capacity for real intimacy and connection with others. They may have a self-righteous belief that they are always right, so they often shift blame on someone beside themselves. They never feel that they are responsible for anything that goes wrong. They can often rage when they are frustrated, and if Mrs. Connor has shared with you some of his texts to my mother, I'm sure you can see that his level of anger with her was irrational."

"And you believe that Peter Martinelli could possess that kind of fury? Do you think he harbored so much rage that he could have murdered your mother?" Johnny asked.

Merrill felt the shock creep up her spine when Shannon Kramer answered Johnny's question with Martinelli's own words. "' *I suggest you do us both a favor and climb into that kayak of yours and drown!*'" Obviously, Lynn's children had a copy of the files that Tim had passed on to her.

Johnny paused for a moment and then asked, "Did your mother ever mention someone named Don?"

"No," Tim said. "But I've read the angry texts he sent her, and it sounds like he was obsessed with her. That unfortunately can happen sometimes with a client. My mother did the ethical thing when she referred him to another therapist."

With this last comment by Tim Kramer, Johnny turned off the tape. "Well, what do you think?" he asked Merrill.

"I think you should find out where in the process Judge DiGeorgio is in filing that search warrant for Peter Martinelli," she said.

CHAPTER TWENTY-FIVE

# OFFICE HOURS

On his way to Albany, Johnny managed to reach the judge. He texted Merrill while she was still in his office to let her know a subpoena for Peter Martinelli would be prepared and delivered to him in the morning. Also, he wrote that the crime lab was analyzing the fingerprints and footprints that had left their impressions in Merrill's home over the weekend. Lovallo would be back from Albany tomorrow before noon. "I'd like you and Farrell to go with me to Martinelli's home in Dunkirk," he wrote.

"I'll be there," she replied. "Hey! Stop texting while you're driving," she added, even though she doubted that he was.

"I'm at a rest stop, for your information!" he wrote. Just then her phone buzzed and Frank's wise eyes and long nose appeared on her screen. Except for official communications, Johnny had started using his beloved canine's photo for every one of his profile pictures.

"Yes, Sheriff?" she said.

"Too much on my mind to text," he explained. "Any comments regarding my meeting with Alexandra Sheldon?" he asked.

"Nothing noteworthy," she said, putting him on speaker so that she could pack up her notebook and coffee mug. "Although I noticed that she was pretty disappointed when you told her that I wouldn't be joining you for the interview."

After viewing the Kramers' session, Merrill had sat alone in the Deputy Sheriff's office with the lights out and her notebook opened in front of her.

As soon as she pressed the play button, she was startled by the rare beauty of the woman sitting in Johnny's office. Alex Sheldon's auburn hair, cut very short, offset her heart-shaped face and stunning green eyes. Beautiful, sad eyes, Merrill thought. Even though the woman sat across from Johnny in a worn chair that took inches off Merrill whenever she sat in it, Alex's height was obvious. In spite of the track suit she wore, she had a model's posture and demeanor. She was wearing the rare red sea glass earrings that Jenna had created, the ones that she had bought for Lynn Martinelli.

A pang of sorrow hit Merrill. She looked down at her garnet wedding ring, the one Richard had designed. The five year anniversary of his death was approaching. Her grief for the first couple of years had been insular and isolating. It was self-centered in the most definitive way. In those early months she felt it in her heart, her lungs, her gut and she carried it with her wherever she went, day or night, awake or asleep. As time passed, she had slowly begun to open her eyes and her heart to the feelings of others. She grew stronger, and her empathy had expanded and extended to fellow sufferers. Like the one she watched on the screen in Johnny's office. Like Johnny himself.

"Yes, she did look disappointed when I told her you were in New York for the weekend," he said.

"I wasn't shocked to hear that she has the same negative opinion as the Kramers when it comes to Martinelli. She was very convincing, I must say. I think we may be able to cross David Michaels off our list as a possible suspect."

"Not so fast," Johnny said. "After all, it's the kid's word alone that he had nothing to do with bludgeoning his therapist to death. Dead victims can't talk."

Merrill resisted arguing the point for the time being. "I was somewhat surprised when you asked Alex about Don and his angry texts," Merrill said. "She didn't seem to know him or anything about his messages to Lynn."

"That might give us a timeline of sorts. Lynn and Alex broke up in the spring, right?" Johnny asked, not pausing for an answer. "So Don must have come into Martinelli's practice after her break-up with Alex."

"I have to look at my notes from that first interview, but I think that's right," Merrill said. Just before she hung up she asked, "So what's going on in Albany?"

"See you tomorrow," he said. Merrill understood that no answer from Johnny was actually an answer. It usually meant, *none of your damn business.* Maybe she could get something out of his receptionist regarding his secret mission to Albany.

After jotting down a few more observations in her notebook and turning on the lights, she waved at Linda, who was busy talking to someone at her desk. Merrill didn't have time to wait and question her. She resolved to ask her about Albany the next time she had to be in the office, and hurried out the main entrance of the Sheriff's department. Turning left onto Main Street, Merrill headed toward the Prenderson Library. The thumb drive texts were waiting for her to dive into them, and now that she finally had the time, she was eager to read them more closely.

Her studio was definitely a preferable workspace compared to her home at the moment. The alarm installers had shown up around the time she was pouring her first cup of coffee and the glass service that would replace her shattered kitchen window had come soon after. She tried her best to concentrate on those repairs instead of thinking about the shocking breach of her home by someone who most likely knew about, and desperately wanted, that thumb drive.

The library was alive with patrons this morning. Toddler story time always drew dozens of littles and their parents. Several high school kids, shepherded by their summer school teacher, were on a mission to accomplish a research project, one they likely didn't turn in during the year. Merrill waved to the volunteers and the librarians she passed and headed down the stairs to her studio.

Unlocking the work table drawer, she felt a sudden jolt of anxiety. Was the drive still here? She fumbled around in the shallow space until her fingers grasped it. As she held the thumb drive in her hand, she tried to analyze her sudden sense of disquiet. Was it because, she asked herself, she was about to delve into the mind and words of the person who had invaded Merrill's home and killed Lynn Martinelli?

## Chapter Twenty-Six

# A CLOSER LOOK

"*Did you actually think you could get rid of me by divorcing me? I'm very persistent, Lynn. I always get what I want!*"

"*Why can't you see that you are so much better when you're with me? A better shrink, a better mother. A better person. I'm telling you Lynn, you will have hell to pay without me!*"

"*You made a promise to support me, to invest in me, as I did you. What happened to your sense of fairness?*"

"*You'll never find anyone better than me, Lynn, man OR woman. You say you want to cut ties for good, but I'll always have a hold on you! I know more about you than anyone else on the planet!*"

Merrill read each of these cryptic accusations and warnings from Lynn Martinell's ex-husband and was convinced that the therapist's children were right. He was a terrible person. Still, none of the texts contained an outright threat. Martinelli sounded more like a whining child than a violent narcissist. Except for that last one – the one where he said she should "*climb into your kayak and drown.*"

The Don folder contained a series of texts that were much more hyperbolic than Peter Martinelli's messages. Merrill had done some preliminary research on clients who were "fired" by their shrinks for sound therapeutic reasons. Some of Don's texts proved that he had an obsessive need for Dr. Martinelli, and that he couldn't accept the fact that she had dismissed him from her practice.

*"You were supposed to fix me!!! Now you're abandoning me???"*

*"Your regard for me in the beginning meant the world to me! Your good opinion of me and the work I was doing on myself kept me going!"*

*"I trusted you with my deepest secrets! And you betrayed me!"*

The last and longest message was the only one that went beyond a list of accusations to an actual threat. The final line especially gave Merrill the creeps, even though she was reading it for the second time.

*"You're my therapist! I should report you to the medical board. I'll tell them everything. I'll tell them how you led me on. Made me think you cared deeply for me!! I promise you, if it's the last thing I do, I will get even with you! I will ruin you! I will make you sorry, "Dr."Martinelli!!!"*

Merrill opened Facebook and clicked on the memorial page dedicated to Lynn Martinelli. She needed to readjust her thinking about the woman. As she read the posts, she was struck by how the hate-filled texts from the two men were in direct opposition to the testimonies of dozens of people who had posted here. Each one praised Lynn Martinelli, not only as a wonderful friend, an involved citizen in the community, but especially as a mental health professional who helped so many. The same sentiment was repeated over and over again. The doctor would be terribly missed and did not deserve to die.

It seemed likely to Merrill that near the premature end of her life, Dr. Martinelli had wanted to terminate two relationships, one personal and one professional. Her decision to do so had brought the wrath of two men upon her. The texts proved that. One was her ex-husband and the other was a former client, yet to be identified. Merrill wondered which one of them was actually capable of bludgeoning her to death?

Her phone buzzed with a text from Johnny. *"I'll pick you up at 10 tomorrow for our meeting with Peter Martinelli,"* it read.

## Chapter Twenty-Seven

# YANKEE FAN

"Good morning, Mr. Martinelli. I'm Deputy Sheriff Johnny Lovallo, and this is Merrill Connor, a member of our criminology team, and Assistant Deputy Sheriff Farrell, who will be conducting a search of the premises. And this guy is Frank," he added, pointing at the tail-wagging dachshund at his feet, "the Department's service dog." Johnny showed Martinelli his badge and handed the shirtless and shoeless man the official document that granted the team access to his house. The guy looked like he had just woken up, and Merrill was glad he had at least had time to put jeans on.

"My lawyer told me you'd be coming. Yeah, that guy has got connections," he explained when Sheriff Lovallo shot him a wary look. Merrill knew what her boss must have been thinking. Crime suspects were not typically warned of an impending search warrant. "Didn't expect you this early, though," Martinelli added pleasantly. When he spoke, Merrill was reminded of every local weatherman's amiable voice and manner. "I had a showing of a house in Brocton last night. It went later than I expected, but I'm pretty sure I'll be getting an offer today, so it's all good. Come on in, folks. Let me put a shirt on first, and I'll be right with you." Merrill, Johnny, Frank, and Mike stepped into the foyer, and Martinelli disappeared from their view at the end of a long hallway.

"What did he mean by 'connections'?" Johnny asked in a loud whisper, turning toward Mike Farrell, who shrugged and said nothing. "This guy is obviously a wiseass. There's no way his lawyer could have given him a heads up about the subpoena." The sound of drawers being opened and closed in a bedroom off the hall silenced the disgruntled Sheriff.

When the investigators pulled up to Martinelli's home moments before, the three of them had had a conversation about what a nice place Lynn had bought for her ex. The mature trees and landscaping were lovely. The backyard, Mike reported after he followed Frank there, was spacious, complete with a large utility shed and an outdoor entertainment center. Although it was miles away from the beach and from Dr. Martinelli's deluxe Shore Acres place, it was a pleasant neighborhood, walkable to the Dunkirk Pier, as well as to the city center.

"So how do we do this?" Martinelli asked Johnny as he emerged from the bedroom, grinning cordially and wearing a Yankees t-shirt. He squatted down to give Frank a somewhat reticent pat on the head.

"We'd like you to guide us through the house, Mr. Martinelli. If we need to take anything, we'll photograph it and catalogue it and make sure we give you a copy," Johnny assured him.

Martinelli led them down the hallway. The first room on the right was obviously dedicated to the man's rabid Yankee fandom. "I wanted to do this in the lake house, but Lynn put her foot down," he explained. He certainly seemed like an agreeable person, Merrill thought, not one capable of writing the vitriol she had read recently. But in her second year as Deputy Sheriff Lovallo's research assistant, Merrill knew very well how an evil person was capable of masking his true self. They followed him into an 8X10 space whose four walls were covered with posters and autographed pictures of famous Yankees through the years, as well as a multitude of balls, bats, and gloves set inside framed shadow boxes.

The usually straight-faced Mike Farrell couldn't help himself. "Wow!" he exclaimed, standing in front of an 11X14 picture of a smiling Peter Martinelli with his arm around Aaron Judge.

"You like that?" Martinelli asked Mike. He was beaming with enthusiasm. "Lynn and I flew down to Port Charlotte during spring training. That was Judge's rookie year. I've been part of the Jury ever since!" he said. "Do you follow baseball, Merrill?' he asked.

"I don't," she said, resisting his attempt to charm her.

"The Jury. They're Aaron Judge's biggest fans. They actually wear black robes to the games to cheer him on. Get it? Judge? Jury?" Merrill could tell he was delighted with himself. The guy seemed acutely aware of his own likeability.

"Did Dr. Martinelli share this love of the Yankees with you?" Johnny asked.

"At first, yes," he said, still staring at the photo, "but Lynn didn't believe in leisure time. She was very busy with her practice." Merrill could not detect an iota of judgement or anger in his tone. "Unless, of course," Martinelli added, "she could spend that time on or in the water. The irony of the way she died…it's just horrible, isn't it?" The three investigators did not respond. "So is there anything in here you'd want to take?" he asked the sheriff.

Johnny did a 180 turn around the room. "As a matter of fact, Mr. Martinelli, I'd like to take one of the hats from this display," Johnny said, pointing to a case that held a chronological collection of Yankees caps, starting with 1909, all with the interlocking NY logo. "This one." Johnny pointed to it and turned to Mike Farrell, who pulled a pair of blue vinyl gloves from his pocket.

Merrill watched Martinelli's reaction. He seemed displeased with Johnny's official tone, or perhaps he resented the power the Deputy Sheriff had to take one of his beloved Yankee artifacts. For the first time since the team's arrival, he showed a different side of himself. He narrowed his eyes and wiped the smile off his face. "Well, you're the Man, Sherriff, so I guess I can't do anything about it."

"I can assure you, Mr. Martinelli, everything we take will be handled with upmost care by our people," Johnny said.

During the rest of their search throughout the two main floors, the basement, and the attic, Martinelli reverted to his pleasant demeanor, pointing out architectural features of the house built in the 1940's, "when most of the boys from Dunkirk were coming home from one of the two fronts."

He explained that he was a history buff, as well as a successful realtor, and that he often researched the origin of a home before he showed it. "Here's my card, if you should ever need to buy or sell," he said, passing one out to each of them.

Merrill noticed that, except for the Yankee room and the kitchen, the rest of the house was sparsely furnished. There were dozens of cardboard boxes stacked in the corners of rooms, taped closed and labeled. Martinelli glanced at Merrill as she stared down at a couple of the boxes in a bedroom devoid of furniture. "Since Lynn and I broke up, I haven't decided on an exact look for the place," he said, in spite of the fact that she hadn't asked. Knowing that he had been trying to sue Lynn for more maintenance money, Merrill suspected he simply wanted to be prepared when the cash started to flow and he could move to the type of home and neighborhood he felt that he deserved. A house on the lake, perhaps.

When they reached the second floor study, Johnny explained that Martinelli would have to surrender all of his electronics, including his phone. Merrill felt the tension in the air as each of the team members awaited Martinelli's explosion. But it didn't come. He said nothing as Mike began to disconnect wires and chargers and headed down the stairs with the devices. "Let me know when you finish, Sheriff," he said evenly, following behind Farrell and then disappearing into his kitchen.

Johnny stood looking out the window at the yard below. "Hey, Mike," he called over the bannister. "Don't forget the shed." As Merrill, Johnny, and Frank joined Mike in the backyard, Johnny turned to her. "What do you think?"

"I think he doesn't behave like the miserable bastard who threatened his ex-wife," she said. "But then again, Tim Kramer says he's a narcissist, capable of putting on a pretty convincing act. He couldn't hide the fact that he didn't like you taking his precious Yankee cap, that's for sure," she said.

Merrill watched Peter Martinelli's long-legged stride as he came toward them. She noticed that he had changed into a pair of khakis and a sports jacket. Could this be the same person as the one they had watched on the doctor's security camera? Maybe. He had a very thin alibi regarding his whereabouts on the early evening of June 10th. He had had a bad summer cold, he told the Sheriff, and had cancelled all his calls after noon so that he could go home and rest.

"I'm sorry, folks, but I have another showing in a half-an-hour. I'll just leave you with the key and you can put it in the mailbox when you're done," he said.

"Thanks for your time and cooperation," Johnny said. "If we need to take anything from the shed, we'll get ahold of you."

"I don't think there's anything in there that you'll want, but sure, you can call the realty company if you need to reach me, since I don't have my cell phone at this time," Martinelli said, once again kneeling down to pet Frank. "So long, pup," he said. Merrill would say later that she had seen Frank give the man the side-eye in response to the stranger's disrespectful term for him.

"Mike can handle this," Johnny said to Merrill. "I'm going to sit in the car and fill out some paperwork."

"And I'm going to sit under this tree and make some notes while everything is still fresh in my head," Merrill said, sitting down at a picnic table. Fifteen minutes later, she was running to Lovallo's squad car. "You're going to need to get ahold of Martinelli! Farrell has hit the jackpot!"

"What? What is it?" Johnny demanded, trying to keep up with her as she jogged back to the yard.

Standing next to the picnic table, Mike Farrell, with a huge grin on his face, held in his gloved right hand a kayak paddle. As Johnny and Merrill drew closer, they simultaneously read out loud the word inscribed on the paddle. "Oru!" The blades had originally been white, but they were streaked with a dark substance. Merrill felt a wave of vertigo sweep over her, as she realized that the vermilion stain was more than likely Dr. Lynn Martinelli's blood.

"Hold on," Farrell said, as he leaned the paddle up against the table. Johnny and Merrill watched as he headed back to the storage shed. A minute later he emerged. "I found these balled up inside a deck box in the back corner." He held up a pair of jeans with one hand and a denim jacket with the other. "There's a pair of boots in there too. I have to get a bigger evidence bag from the car for them. The soles are caked with sand."

## CHAPTER TWENTY-EIGHT

# WAITING FOR THE PROOF

WHEN JOHNNY AND Mike Farrell showed up at the open house he was hosting with an arrest warrant for the murder of Dr. Lynn Martinelli, her ex-husband said nothing, but his jaw slackened and the blood drained from his tanned face. He did not resist as the sheriff read him his rights and cuffed him. "I want my lawyer," was all he said. The potential home buyers who had been milling around throughout the house were totally freaked out, however. When Johnny called Merrill, he told her that they couldn't get out of the place fast enough.

"They scattered like rats jumping ship," he said.

"So David Michaels is off the hook, correct?" Merrill asked.

"Not so fast. The kid is still a suspect, Merrill. It's a shame that the only one who could clear him is a dead woman. Once the lab reports come back, they'll be able to confirm if Martinelli is or is not our man," he said. "You'll have to hold your horses until then."

"It's just that David is so young. He has no arrest record, Johnny. It could ruin his life if he's a suspect in a murder investigation. The kid has been devastated by his parents' break-up. He doesn't need to have another trauma added to the list."

"I'm sorry, Merrill, but he's still on my radar. Until the crime lab proves that Peter Martinelli's DNA is on that paddle, David Michaels is not in the clear. On June 10th, he had motive and means, and he admitted he was in close proximity to where Dr. Martinelli was killed, and we have him on video pulling the kayak to the water."

"But she asked him to…"

"That's what he says. Just be patient. Let the science clear him. Or not," Johnny said, and hung up.

Merrill, as an analytic thinker, was all for empirical proof when it came to the solving of a heinous crime like the therapist's murder. But her experience with the powers of the paranormal had opened her mind up to other possibilities. She had dropped out of the *Expanding Your Psychic Powers* class mainly because of the schedule conflicts caused by the Lynn Martinelli case. Although she had been told in her first reading at Lily Dale that she possessed the gift of an intuitive nature, she knew she couldn't rely on her own psychic energy to solve this case. But she was fairly sure she had other options.

Merrill had done hours of research on psychics who assist police agencies and private detectives in solving crimes, and even though they had been used by kings, military chieftains, and religious leaders through the ages for purposes of fortunetelling and predicting future events, until 1845, their use in criminal investigations was not documented. It was only lately that popular culture, mainly in movies and on television shows, portrayed the utilization of mediums in assisting police agencies in the investigation of crimes. And except in those creative renditions, the track record of psychics who were successful was about 30% of the time. Merrill was forewarned by the facts, but her intuition told her to take a chance on the powers of the spirit world. What harm could come from at least trying?

"Hello, Merrill! How wonderful to hear from you!" Victoria Erikson said. Merrill felt prickles erupt on her scalp. She hadn't spoken a word yet. Could she be in the medium's contact list, or was Victoria showing off her psychic talents? Merrill decided she wouldn't give her the satisfaction of asking, "*How did you know it was me?*"

"Hello, Victoria. It's been a long time." She saw no need to mention that the medium had seemed fine at the Stump a couple of weeks ago. Merrill crossed her fingers to ward off the bad luck that lying could bring. "I was wondering if I could get an appointment with you sometime in the next twenty-four hours?"

"Let me check my book," Victoria said. A minute later came the response Merrill had hoped for. "Tomorrow looks good. Would sometime in the morning work for you?"

"It will. But this isn't exactly about me."

"Why doesn't this surprise me?" she said. Did Merrill detect a bit of snarkiness in the medium's tone?

"It's about…"

"Dr. Lynn Martinelli?" Victoria said.

"How did you know?" Merrill asked, feeling foolish the second after the words came out of her mouth.

"I've told you before. I don't miss an episode of *A Deeper Dive*. And I read about Peter Martinelli's arrest in the *Dunkirk Express* this morning."

"Yes, you're right. It does concern the murder investigation." Merrill had another thought in that moment. "Hold on! I just thought of something. Maybe we could do this over the phone," Merrill said.

"ABSOLUTELY NOT!" the medium shouted.

"Okay, okay," Merrill said. "What time do you want me in Lily Dale?"

"I don't want you here. I want to meet you at Boulder Point," Victoria said.

Merrill said nothing for a few seconds. "You want to meet at the beach? I didn't know you went on remote assignments."

"Yes, I do when the situation calls for it," Victoria said. "If the police reports are correct about the time of death, Lynn Martinelli entered the spirit world a few hours before Jenna Berlin found her. When her body reached Boulder Point, she would have just recently crossed over."

Merrill bit her tongue. She knew that Victoria had been instrumental in helping her solve two cases last year: one of a missing girl and the other of a vanished woman. She didn't want to offend her or her religious beliefs. "Of course I can be at Boulder Point tomorrow," she said now, attempting a humble tone.

"Let's make it 9 a.m.," Victoria said. "And if you have anything belonging to Peter Martinelli, bring it, please."

She didn't have anything, but she thought Johnny could help her with that. And, with Derrick the Drummer's assistance, she might be able to get her hands on something belonging to David Michaels, too. "I'll do my best, Victoria," she said. "I'll see you tomorrow morning."

Before Merrill could hang up the medium spoke again. "And Jenna. Bring Jenna, too."

## CHAPTER TWENTY-NINE

# LADIES AT THE LAKE

"I CAN PICK you up," Merrill said, in an attempt to convince Jenna to accompany her to Boulder Point. Yesterday, after she had made the appointment with Victoria, Merrill gathered her courage and stopped in to see her friend at *Mermaids' Tears*.

"Let me think about it," Jenna had answered. An hour later she got back to Merrill. "I'm still thinking. No need to pick me up. If I decide to come, I'll meet you there."

The two friends had yet to have a conversation about what had taken place at The Stump. Merrill hadn't wanted to bring it up on their trip to New York City, and she hadn't seen Jenna since their return to Westfield. Had her friend thought about the message Victoria delivered that day? It was obvious to Merrill that the person who had "*saved*" someone, who would have been "*lost*" otherwise, was Jenna.

As far as Merrill knew, Jenna had not been on the Boulder Point beach since discovering Lynn Martinelli's body, except for their failed outing with Kate and Sherry. As much as she wanted to call her this morning and find out for certain if she was coming, she decided not to take the chance of alienating her friend.

Victoria was already at Boulder Point when Merrill arrived. A perfect June day in Western New York had been predicted, and the medium was dressed for it. By the time that Merrill entered her sophomore year in college, she stopped praying for a couple of more inches of height and made peace with her "petite" frame. But as she walked toward the statuesque figure standing at the water's edge, she felt a spark of jealousy. Victoria was dressed in a gauzy pale blue caftan, her hair pinned away from her classic features. As she grew closer to her, Merrill thought about how Richard might have found Victoria Erikson a perfect sculpture model. The movement of the dress in the light offshore wind was reminiscent of the garment a Greek goddess might wear. After a very long night of interrupted sleep, during which she thought of dozens of disastrous scenarios that could possibly take place at the beach the next day, Merrill had pulled on shorts, a tank top, and flip-flops. Her hair in a hurry-up pony tail, she was dressed for work. But so, she realized, was Victoria Erikson.

"Hello, Merrill!" Victoria said. "It's so good to see you again."

Merrill wondered if she should greet the woman with a hug, but decided that would not be a good idea. This was a business meeting, after all. "Thanks for agreeing to this, Victoria," she said as she held up a small evidence bag marked Sheriff's Department. "Do you want to look at…hold on to these objects that belonged to the suspects?"

"No. Not yet," the medium said. For several moments the two women stood together at the sunlit shoreline and stared at the horizon. The morning sky was postcard blue, and the contrasting white of the clouds reminded Merrill of one of Richard's paintings that hung in her bedroom.

Neither of the women spoke a word to one another, but after several seconds, Merrill could tell that Victoria was praying. Suddenly the medium broke her silence. "Ah, here's Jenna," she said, still staring ahead at the lake. Merrill turned toward the parking lot and saw only her Murano and Victoria's Subaru. Seconds later, she watched as Jenna's panel truck with the *Mermaids' Tears* logo on its side pulled into the lot.

Merrill did her best not to appear in the least impressed with this first sign of Victoria's psychic gift. Instead, she got busy removing from her bag the two objects she had brought. She laid them on top of the towel she had set on the sand. The Yankees cap had been easily accessible from the crime lab, but yesterday she had had to interrupt David Michael's drum lesson at

Derrick's studio. When she called Derrick, the teacher had told her that his student would be there that afternoon. Wearing the lanyard with her Sheriff's Department ID and a blue glove, she had shown up in time to take one of his sticks from the very annoyed David.

Both women watched as Jenna walked slowly toward the water's edge. When she reached them, Merrill smiled and extended her arms to her friend. She resisted holding her as long as she wanted for fear of freaking Jenna out. "Victoria Erikson, this is Jenna Berlin," she said, trying not to sound as foolish as she felt. Jenna had been with her at Victoria's home that winter day that had changed everything in the Grace Phillip's case, although there had been no formal introductions then. And although the medium had not named her at The Stump, Merrill was fairly sure Victoria knew that the message she delivered that day was meant for Jenna.

"I'm very glad to meet you, Jenna," Victoria said, extending her hand.

"I'm not sure what I'm doing here, but I know how much you've helped Merrill in the past," she said. She took Victoria's hand, but her eyes seemed to be tracking something at a distance in the lake. "I was further down the shore that day, closer to the lighthouse," she said.

"It would be best, then, if we moved there," Victoria said.

Merrill picked up the Yankee cap and Derrick's drumstick and shook the sand off the towel. She followed the two women as they moved toward the spot where she and Johnny had stood with Jenna that day in early June. "I walked out to The Table, there," Jenna explained to Victoria, pointing to the huge boulder. "I was looking for glass that morning, but then I noticed something unusual in the water." Merrill heard the confidence in her friend's voice and she was proud of how far she had come since that terrible day.

"Alright, good," Victoria said. "Let's begin with a prayer, and then I'll ask Spirit to join us."

Jenna and Merrill stared straight ahead at The Table as Victoria prayed for Spirit to guide them today. When she finished, she turned to Jenna and spoke very gently. "I'm going to ask you to do something that may be painful for you, Jenna. I'd like you to close your eyes and picture yourself on top of the boulder, as you were that day." Jenna looked at Merrill and then back at Victoria. She nodded and closed her eyes.

Except for the sound of children playing farther up the beach and the gentle waves lapping the shore, there was silence at Boulder Point. Merrill grew anxious, but the other two women seemed oblivious to her discomfort. The stillness was finally broken when the medium said, "I see a woman standing there next to you, Jenna, on top of the boulder." Merrill squinted into the sun, struggling to see what Victoria saw. An enormous flock of gulls appeared from seemingly out of nowhere; dozens of the shrieking birds landed on and completely covered The Table. The rest remained aloft above the boulder. Her eyes still closed, Jenna reached for Merrill's hand.

Victoria spoke again. "The woman is turning to you, Jenna... She says, 'Thank you for finding me.' She says she wasn't ready to leave this world... Before her children were settled...before she had grandchildren... before she was through helping people." Without changing her position or opening her eyes, Victoria said, "Merrill, please hand me one of the objects you brought." Merrill released Jenna's hand and picked up David Michael's drumstick. She placed it in Victoria's outstretched hand.

The medium spoke, this time directly to Lynn Martinelli. "Lynn, please help the police find the person who is responsible for ending your earthly life. Tell us who hurt you, Lynn." The medium raised her hand and held the stick above her head. Later, Merrill would say to Jenna that it must have been that movement that caused the birds that had been circling the boulder to take flight. Victoria, eyes still closed, shook her head slowly and handed the stick back to Merrill. A sense of relief washed over her. She knew David Michaels wasn't capable of murder.

"The other item, please." Victoria gestured for Merrill to place the Yankees cap in her hand. The medium held it over her head as far as her arm would reach. Merrill stood stock still and held her breath as the rest of the gulls, screeching loudly, rose from The Table and flew up to the clouds.

Victoria shook her head again and opened her eyes as she turned and faced Merrill and Jenna. "She's gone," she whispered.

## Chapter Thirty

# SERENITY

"So what does that mean? Why did Lynn Martinelli leave?" Merrill tried to keep her voice even and non-accusatory, but she was frustrated. She had expected so much more from this session with Victoria.

"I believe it means that neither of these two suspects was responsible for the doctor's death," Victoria said. The medium had told her that she had an appointment at 11a.m. in Lily Dale, and she was obviously not going to stay around and dissect what had just happened with Merrill and Jenna, or rather, what had *not* happened at the Point this morning. Victoria said goodbye to both women and took her sandals off so that she could move faster over the sand. Just before she left the beach and headed to her car, she turned and called, "Good luck, Merrill."

Merrill was crushed with disappointment. She had had high hopes that the killer of Lynn Martinelli would be revealed today. She could kick herself! She should have relied on logic and reason, instead of paranormal mumbo jumbo. Her research had borne out that it was a lot less likely that a crime would be solved by a psychic, compared to the results gained with standard police procedures. Merrill tried to reassure herself by saying so to Jenna after Victoria had left them staring out at the lake. "The good news is that Peter Martinelli is in custody because of solid police work. Hopefully, the crime lab can tell us more about his part in Lynn's murder than our 'expert' from Lily Dale did. I'm sorry I dragged you into this, Jenna."

"I wanted to help, Merrill, even though it didn't turn out the way you hoped it would," Jenna said. "Come on, let's walk."

The two friends were in no hurry to resume their regular routines. If observed from afar, they appeared to be casual beachcombers, taking advantage of the lovely summer day. Merrill asked her friend, "How are you feeling about being back here at the Point?"

"Not as bad as I thought I would feel. I'm sorry I've been so difficult..."

Merrill interrupted her. "You haven't been difficult. You're entitled to take your time to heal. You've been through something horrible."

"This beach used to be the place where, no matter what was going on in my life, I could find peace. I could be restored and become balanced again, the same way there is a balance in Nature. It's all around us here at the lake. I want to find my way back to that feeling," Jenna said. "Truthfully, Merrill, imagining myself next to Lynn Martinelli on The Table wasn't disturbing at all. As a matter of fact, I felt that same serenity, that equilibrium that Boulder Point used to bring me."

Merrill was relieved to hear this revelation from Jenna. As they walked shoulder to shoulder, she glanced at her friend's face. It appeared that the session with Victoria had not been a waste of time or damaging to Jenna's battered psyche. As a matter of fact, judging by the smile of contentment she wore, Merrill dared to hope that the experience had been therapeutic for her friend.

The day was warming up as they ambled along the shoreline, each woman with her head down, looking for lake glass treasures. Suddenly, Merrill stopped and dropped to her knees next to a huge tree root that had washed up on the beach. "What are these? Is this some kind of lake glass?" she asked Jenna as she stood up again and held her palm out to her friend. In it were two small, pure white squares. Before Jenna could respond, Merrill answered her own question. "Wow! This isn't glass at all. It almost looks like porcelain, or ivory."

"It's neither. You found two Lake Erie Lucky Stones, Merrill!" Jenna said, obviously thrilled for her friend. "They're fairly rare, and to find two at the same time is amazing!"

Raising her hand closer to her eyes, Merrill said, "Look, they're monogrammed! They have tiny *L's* etched into them!" Jenna recognized the childish delight on her friend's face. She had worn that same expression over and over again, each time she discovered a treasure on the beach. "Wow! These are stones?" Merrill asked her.

"No, they're not really made of stone. They're actually a part of the sheepshead fish. The technical term for them is otoliths. They're a part of the fish's ear," Jenna said, her voice echoing the delight she heard in Merrill's.

"Wait. Fish have ears?"

This question provoked a sound from Jenna that her friend had not heard in a long while. She was roaring with laughter. "No, they don't have ears, Merrill! It's really a balancing organ, kind of like our own inner ear. The fish, even in dark and murky water, is able to swim on a straight course because of these organs, like a pilot who can fly inside a cloud without being able to see. When the fish wash up on shore and decompose, they leave these little 'stones' behind."

"Amazing!" Merrill said, looking down at the nearly identical objects in her palm. As the sun shone down on them, she thought the finish resembled mother of pearl. "Why are they called Lucky Stones?"

"Well, beyond the fact that they have the first letter of the word luck carved into them, they actually have a very long history of bringing luck," Jenna said, taking the treasures from Merrill and tracing the tiny letters etched into each of them with her fingernail. "They've been found over many years on archeological digs. It's believed that aboriginal people carried them as tokens that would bring them good fortune."

"Really?" Merrill responded, already planning to do some of her own "digging" on line to find out as much as she could about these stones.

"Yes. And sailors and fishermen throughout the decades have kept them in their pockets to ward off storms, or to bring them luck in cards or love." Jenna recognized the sudden look of intense curiosity on her friend's face.

"Can you make a piece of jewelry using these?" Merrill asked her.

Jenna examined them. "Absolutely. I've done it before. These two are plenty thick enough. What are you thinking? Earrings, a necklace?"

"I'm not sure. Let me think about it."

Jenna handed the little "stones" back to her friend. "You keep them, Merrill. You spotted them first. I've found dozens over my many years of beachcombing, so when you decide what you want to do with them, I can certainly supplement them with the ones I've collected, if need be."

As she took the little stones from Jenna and put them in her bag, Merrill realized that she couldn't stop smiling. If she had been asked to describe this feeling of elation she would have to say it was pure joy, like the kind a child might experience. And it had come on the heels of frustrating disappointment, which made it all the more magical.

Walking back to their cars an hour later, she turned to Jenna. "Wow! No wonder you love it here. Suddenly, I feel so much better, in spite of our failed medium experience. Can we do this again sometime?"

"Yes," Jenna answered without hesitating, "I would love that."

## CHAPTER THIRTY-ONE

# BACK TO WORK

On her drive back into town from the beach, Merrill spotted The Chautauqua County Deputy Sheriff patrol car parked in front of the Prendersen. What was Johnny doing at the library, she wondered, as she pulled into her parking spot. As far as Merrill knew, Johnny's reading life was mainly limited to reports from the State Attorney General or the New York State Sheriffs' Association, although he had mentioned that he read memoirs when he had the time. He told her he especially liked *Unbroken* 'because Louie Zamperini was from Olean.'

She pulled open the heavy oak door of the Prendersen and stepped into the three story high foyer. Scanning the reading rooms on either side of the spacious lobby, she saw no sign of Johnny on the main floor. Doris Breonski was working the circulation desk this morning and Merrill stopped to say hello. "Your boyfriend and his hound dog are looking for you," she said.

"Always the wiseass, aren't you, Doris?" Merrill said. She was almost used to this wistful thinking on the part of her friends and acquaintances, and she was no longer infuriated by their silly comments. Only mildly pissed off. It was the twenty-first century, for God's sake! Why couldn't a man and woman work together and have a friendship without adults making a romantic "thing" of it?

At her work table the in the dark studio space, Merrill could see the outline of man and dog sitting on the chair where her guests usually sat during interviews. She turned on the harsh fluorescent light and asked, "To what do I owe the pleasure of your company, Frank?" She bent down to pet the dog who now sat at Johnny's feet. "And Deputy Sheriff Lovallo?" she added.

"Hey," Johnny said. "Sorry to show up with no notice, but you didn't answer your phone."

"Oh, yeah, sorry, I had the volume turned all the way down. Jenna and I were at the beach." She couldn't possibly tell Johnny that she had turned her phone off so as not to disturb a medium's raising the dead for a chat about the murder case they were working on. "What's up?"

"It's not good news, Merrill. Lynn Martinelli's blood *was* on the kayak paddle, just as we had assumed. It was present both on the power face and the back face, as well as on the stock. The crime lab has concluded that the paddle *was* the murder weapon. But Peter Martinelli's fingerprints were not found anywhere on it."

Merrill shouldn't have been shocked to hear this, since within the past hour she and Jenna had witnessed her mystical source clearing Martinelli of murder. As a skeptic, though, Merrill was reluctant to give Victoria credit for knowing the truth. "But what about the clothes and shoes? They belonged to Martinelli, right?" she asked.

"They could have, but that's inconclusive and probably irrelevant, because his prints did not match another set that was found on the kayak's stock. More than likely those prints belong to the killer. But the lab couldn't identify them." Johnny's tone of resignation was unusual for the determined deputy, Merrill thought. Under this cruel light, she noticed that he looked pale and that the lines around his eyes were deeper than usual. "And I know you're not going to like this," he said, "but we need to bring David Michaels back in. For fingerprinting."

"But we saw him on the security footage going back to the Crandall's place *before* Lynn Martinelli walked onto the beach." Merrill tried very hard not to sound as desperate as she felt.

"He still could have come back minutes later, out of the range of any of the security cameras. He could have crushed her skull with that paddle. That sea wall is our biggest enemy, since it blocks our view of the actual murder."

"But the clothes…"

"A Yankees cap, jeans, and a denim jacket. We saw on the video that Michaels had on a t-shirt and jeans that day. He could have put on a ball cap and grabbed a jacket before he went to the shoreline to commit murder."

"And then stashed everything in Peter Martinelli's storage shed? That doesn't make any sense, Johnny," she argued.

"Doesn't it? His friend Carrie told him that the doctor was divorced. It wouldn't take a genius to find out her ex-husband's address," Johnny said. "He's a bright kid, Merrill. Pinning it on Martinelli would have kept us off David's tail."

"I just don't believe the kid could have done it." She felt her eyes welling up with tears of frustration. She couldn't tell Johnny that Victoria Erikson's Spirit messenger didn't believe it either.

"I know that, Merrill, and I get it." He handed her a tissue from the box on the table. "I'll try to go easy on him. I'm going to appeal to his parents to bring him in for a voluntary sit-down again. I want to avoid having to get an arrest warrant. But we need his fingerprints to clear him."

"Okay. Once he's cleared, and I'm almost positive he will be, we move on from there," Merrill blew her nose. "We've still got those nasty texts from Don to look into, right? And eventually the court will approve of our petition to examine Dr. Martinelli's clients' treatment plans, don't you think?" When he didn't respond, Merrill asked, "Are you okay, boss?"

"Not really," he said, getting to his feet. He reached down and picked up Frank. "It's not a good day for me, Merrill."

"We'll figure this out, don't worry. We'll start over from Square One," she said.

"It's not the Martinelli case."

"What is it, then?" she asked.

"This is June 20th. Rosie's birthday," he said. "She would have been twenty years old today."

"Oh, Johnny. I'm so sorry." As someone who had lost a loved one, Merrill recognized that there was nothing she could say that would assuage her friend's grief. All she could do was listen.

"Everything she could have been and done, all of the times, good and bad, we should have shared. Gone forever." He stood and his sadness was palpable. Frank could feel it, too, and did his job, even though Johnny was attempting to avoid the dog's wet tongue on his face.

"Where are you going?" Merrill asked as Johnny turned toward the staircase.

"Back to work," he said, turning to face her. "Linda says that Alex Sheldon has called twice already this morning wanting to know about Peter Martinelli, *her* prime suspect. I think she's going to be very disappointed when she hears the news that he's pretty much off the hook." He started to climb the stairs with Frank in his arms, but he turned toward her before he got very far. "What do you do when one of these milestones punches you in the gut?"

Merrill didn't have to think the question over for long. On every major holiday, on their kids' birthdays and Richard's, as well as their wedding anniversary and the anniversary of her husband's death, she experienced the crush of grief as though it were brand new. And the thought of her first grandchild, who would be here soon, never meeting Richard brought her to tears whenever she allowed herself to think about it.

"I go back to work," she said. She listened as Johnny's footsteps echoed on the stairs and faded away.

## CHAPTER THIRTY-TWO

# WIPED

MERRILL SAT IN front of her laptop in the basement of the Prender-son, her pulse racing. She knew that her brain was on overload, and a rare panic attack might be on the horizon. Johnny had texted her shortly after leaving the library and told her that he had contacted the Michaels. He let them know that they needed to bring their son into the office to be fingerprinted on Monday, and although she and Victoria knew he wasn't a murderer, she prayed that they were right. Partly to keep her mind off the alternative, she had to find a more viable murder suspect. In Merrill's mind, the only candidate that she knew of at this point was Don, Dr. Martinelli's obsessed and angry client.

As a librarian, Merrill had been a dogged researcher, hunting through complicated data for instructors in every department at the college. Most of them were working on publishing papers that would guarantee their positions for another year or help them attain the tenure they sought to extend their teaching careers. Students, too, knew they could count on her keen and thorough investigative techniques when they most needed her. Unfortunately, some of them were already on academic probation by the time they came to the library to write the paper that they expected would save them. She did what she could in those circumstances, too, so she was used to the pressure that came from finding a needle in the haystack.

On the flash drive that Tim Kramer had given Merrill, Dr. Martinelli had copied messages from two people who wished her evil. She must have wanted her son to see them, perhaps in the eventuality that she wouldn't be around to tell anyone about these threats. Merrill was grateful for the flash drive containing the two files.

Investigating case studies about therapist-client relationships that took an unhealthy turn fascinated Merrill. Her research informed her that Don's obsession with his therapist was hardly unusual. Merrill had taken notes on twenty or so of these cases, and the clients, like Don, were bitter and accusatory toward these professionals. But once she got into reading about New York State HIPPA laws as they applied to a therapist's treatment notes, she knew she was in over her head. Thank God the subpoena for Dr. Martinelli's notes was being filtered through the Sheriff Department's legal advisors. Johnny had told her they would be filing the summons soon, but the legal red tape could delay it indefinitely.

She said a silent prayer that David Michaels would be cleared. Between her strong intuition that the kid was innocent and her affinity for people David's age because of the college students she had guided through the years, she had been his champion from the beginning. If he was cleared, she knew that Johnny would join her in her pursuit of Don, once they found out who he was.

Merrill shut down her laptop and stood and stretched. The library had closed two hours before and the summer sun was on its way down. She needed a glass of wine and a sandwich, but she didn't want to go home. Ever since the break-in at her house, it didn't feel like the place she had known as a refuge from the world for so many years. It struck her that this was the way Jenna felt about Boulder Point after the beach had become polluted by a murder. Maybe she would ask Jenna to join her at Larry's. Merrill felt like her friend was finally strong enough to commiserate with her.

She climbed into the Murano and as soon as she started the engine, her phone rang and Johnny Lovallo's face appeared on the screen. Had he brought the Michaels family in already? She felt the muscles in her face tighten as she pressed Answer.

"Sorry to call so late, Merrill," he said.

"What's up?" she asked. She knew he could hear the dread in her voice.

"Bad news on Dr. Martinelli's treatment notes," he said.

"The court denied the subpoena request?" Merrill held her breath as she waited for his answer.

"No. There's been no action at all on the request," Johnny said.

Merrill exhaled. "So what's the problem?"

"Our IT guy just called me. Dr. Martinelli's computer, all the files, anyway, have been wiped."

"Wiped?"

"Erased. Gone," Johnny said.

She knew that this had been a very bad day for the Deputy Sheriff, personally and professionally. She wanted to say something comforting in this moment. A month before when she thought she had lost the transcript of an interview for *A Deeper Dive* episode, Jason had recovered it. "What about the Cloud?" she asked Johnny. "The treatment notes would be there…"

"Not if she didn't back them up. And according to our computer guys, she didn't."

"Why would Dr. Martinelli wipe her computer?" she asked him.

"She didn't. It was done remotely. The day after Jenna discovered her body at Boulder Point."

"A hacker?"

"Maybe a hacker who was working for a killer," Johnny said. "Or an ex-husband who was savvy enough to sabotage her private email addresses and put a tracker device on her car."

"So does this eliminate David Michaels as a suspect?" she asked.

"No. Hopefully, his fingerprints will, though. Where are you anyway?" he asked. "I hear your engine running."

"On my way home," she replied.

"Well, have a good evening, Merrill," he said. "We'll have to start all over again tomorrow."

Typically, this would be the time during a phone conversation with

Johnny to squeeze in one more smart remark, a satirical quip that would give her that little boost of *"gotcha"* triumph. It was harmless, of course. It was a part of their relationship banter, and each one of them enjoyed playing the game. But tonight, she stopped herself. Throughout the day she had been thinking about his confiding in her this morning about this being his child's birthday. So tonight she would say the one thing that she had resisted saying in the years they had known each other. "Goodbye, Johnny," she said, and hung up.

## Chapter Thirty-Three

# EDITING

Merrill sat down across the table from her son and put her headphones on. The interview that would air tomorrow had been recorded this morning. She hoped this editing session wouldn't take up too much of her son's time this evening. Jason's boyfriend Craig had just moved into her son's condo and they had been busy all week trying to merge two households into one. From the look on his face, she guessed it might not being going smoothly. She hoped she could count on his technical skills, as she typically could. This episode in particular was very important to her. Jason nodded, signifying that he was ready for her to begin.

*"Hello, listeners, and welcome to A Deeper Dive. I'm your host, Merrill Connor, and I'm so happy to introduce you to today's guest and my good friend, Jenna Berlin."*

*"Hello, Divers! Hi, Merrill."*

*"Jenna was on an earlier show, Episode Four to be exact, which was about women reinventing themselves later in life. Listen to it, if you didn't catch it the first time, Divers. So I'd like to welcome my guest for a second time. Many of you may actually own some of the beautiful jewelry that Jenna creates from the sea glass that she gathers from the coves, shorelines, and waters of Lake Erie. Her business, Mermaids' Tears, has been lauded all over the country for Jenna's unique designs and beautiful craftsmanship. But today's interview with her is on another, more somber, topic.*

After the twenty-year cold case of Grace Phillips was solved with the help of our fans, I decided that the theme of *A Deeper Dive* should continue to be 'finding what's lost.' In this season's episodes so far, we've explored the discovery of an Irish ancestor, whose paper trail seemed to have disappeared. We've heard about the missing piece of the puzzle in the life of one of the young women who died in the Fredonia Normal School Fire, and we interviewed the children of a Vietnam War vet who, according to his service records survived the war, but has never come home or been heard from since. My guest today will talk about her own loss and recovery. Jenna, please."

"Thank you, Merrill. I never intended to talk so openly about my glass seeking or divulging the beaches where I find the best samples for my jewelry, but fate has intervened and I'm going public on this podcast because of that. A month ago, while combing Boulder Point for glass, as I do on most summer days, I made a horrible discovery in Lake Erie: the battered and lifeless body of a woman. From one of the boulders where I have often times contemplated the beauty of those natural surroundings, I held onto a lifeless stranger until the police arrived. Of course, everyone knows now that the victim was Dr. Lynn Martinelli.

From that day forward, until just recently, that traumatic event caused me to lose so much. The searching and collecting of beach glass has always been a restorative activity for my body and my soul. There is something about being close to the water, about the beauty of the rocks, the sun, the driftwood, the birds...there is a synchronicity that nature provides at the beach. Even on days when glass is scarce or the weather isn't ideal, I find there, what some people might label, a spiritual connection. But on June 10$^{th}$, that connection was broken."

"Can you talk about what that severing felt like?"

"I'll try, Merrill. I'm able to describe the response my body had to the trauma very easily. I couldn't sleep, I couldn't eat. My blood pressure went up and my appetite decreased. I vacillated between feeling frozen with depression to being shaky with anxiety. I avoided talking to my husband, my kids, my friends. I couldn't concentrate on making jewelry, and worse yet, I couldn't get up the nerve to return to my favorite glass gathering beach, Boulder Point. I truly lost my sense of purpose, my sense of self."

"How awful, Jenna! Can you please tell our listeners where you are in your journey to recover from this traumatic event?"

"I've come very far, Merrill. Tim and Shannon Kramer, Lynn Martinelli's children, reached out to me early on. They were grateful for my part in recovering their mother's body, and that meant so much. The support and understanding of my husband and friends, even when I outwardly rejected it, was constant. With some therapy, as well as some input from a Lily Dale medium, I have begun to face the pain and deal with it."

"And have you been able to return to Boulder Point?"

"I actually have a date with a friend to do some glass hunting very soon. I'm almost 100% sure that finding my way back from trauma means finding my way back to Boulder Point."

"Wonderful!"

"And something else I wanted to say to your listeners, Merrill. Dr. Martinelli's life was taken from her and from her children, her community, her clients. She was a therapist, a helper, someone who dedicated her life to serving the needs of others. And she was a very private person, too. She *did not have much of a social media presence, according to the police. I want to rally all of your wonderful Divers out there to join me in trying to discover who took that life. The investigation of two possible suspects seems to be heading toward a dead end, according to the news reports. I'd like to invite all of Lynn Martinelli's friends, acquaintances, neighbors, and clients who may know something or suspect something that could lead the police to find her murderer, to please contact Deputy Sheriff Lovallo's Office. Of course, you can choose to contact Merrill at ADeeperDive.com as well."*

When the interview concluded, Jason took off his headphones, avoiding eye contact with his mother. Merrill set her headphones on the table. "I think that was near to perfect. How about you?" she asked. When he didn't respond she said, "I'm happy you don't need to spend a lot of time editing, especially when you're in the middle of rearranging your entire household." Had Jason and Craig had a fight, she wondered. Moving could be so stressful, she wouldn't be surprised. She was not the kind of parent who probed into her kids' personal lives, but something was definitely wrong with her son today. "You look tired, honey."

"Nope. Not tired," he said.

"Angry?" she asked.

"I guess you could say that."

"What's going on?" He continued to wrap up wires and ignored her question.

"Jason. Talk to me, please," she said.

Jason stopped what he was doing and turned to face her. "Yes, I guess you could say I am angry. Whenever my mother, who is supposed to be an *assistant* for the Deputy Sheriff's office, who is supposed to use her vast academic experience to *research* books, documents, online sources, to *assist* the police, when my mother broadcasts all over the internet that she's personally attempting to draw a murderer into her net, into her life…when she does this for a second time, after narrowly escaping death after using that tactic before…Yes, it pisses me off, Mom! You are about to become a grandmother in the next couple of months. Your family wants you here when that baby arrives!"

The last thing Merrill wanted was for her children, especially Dina, eight months into her pregnancy, to be anxious about her work. But that's what it was. Work. It was her job, her career, not a post-retirement hobby. Her three children had not seen that coming when she had started *A Deeper Dive,* but then, neither had she. "Jason, you and your sisters have nothing to worry about," she said, trying to sound consoling.

"Okay, so we're not supposed to worry about your house being broken into? What if you had been there that night? He could have taken more than a laptop…"

"I have a security system now, honey, and we don't know if that incident had anything to do with the Martinelli case." Merrill felt a flash of guilt as she lied to her son. More than likely the attempted theft of the flash drive had everything to do with the break-in.

Jason didn't respond and continued to clean up his workspace. Merrill hoped she had said something that would reassure him. He turned his back to shelve the headphones, but his mother heard him mutter, "And you don't even carry a weapon."

---

## Chapter Thirty-Four

# BABY SHOWER

Merrill had thought she would have Dina's baby shower at her house, but the mother-to-be had agreed with Sherry. It would be so much less stressful to have it at the beautiful Harbor Hotel on Chautauqua Lake. As she walked around the sunlit room greeting guests, Merrill felt happy and grateful for so many blessings.

On this day she was especially appreciative to have Sherry in her life. It was wonderful to have a friend who was capable of making all of the arrangements for this celebration. Details like the menu, whether or not to have games (not), setting up the gift registry, attaining the most lovely room for the gathering, the seating arrangements, deciding on favors for the guests, having to make all of these choices would have driven Merrill crazy. Sherry handled them all with expertise and grace.

Jenna and Kate had cleared their schedules, too; they wouldn't have missed the celebration. Merrill was going to be the first grandmother in their circle of friends. After everyone was seated, Kate stood and made a toast. "Here's to Dina, who some of us have known since she was a child. May she revel in the joys of motherhood. And to the guest of honor, baby Lucy, Dina and Patrick's daughter, who will be here before we know it. May she have a life full of love and adventure. And music. Always, music." Everyone in the room raised their glasses.

Merrill was typically resistant to attending, never mind giving, these rites of passage, but as she looked around the room and listened to the laughter, she was glad she had decided to do this. Her two daughters, Dina and Merrill's youngest, Mickey, were seated together at the next table. She watched as each of them leaned in and smiled, as one of their childhood friends delivered a punchline. Merrill wondered if they had talked to their brother lately. Did they know about Jason's disapproval of her role in the Lynn Martinelli case?

Two hours later, after dozens of presents had been opened and cake had been served and eaten, the baby shower was over. Merrill hugged her daughters and told them she would see them at the house. "We'll wait for you in the car," Jenna said to Merrill, as the grandmother-to-be walked into the hotel manager's office, her credit card in her hand.

The young woman behind the desk stood to shake her hand. "Hello. I'm Hannah Reese, the events coordinator here at the Harbor Hotel. Please have a seat, Mrs. Connor."

"Thanks, Hannah," she said.

"How did it go today? I hope everything met up to your expectations?"

"Everything was wonderful," Merrill answered.

"Oh, I'm glad to hear that! Please check this out and make sure it's correct."

As she scanned the itemized receipt, Merrill could feel Hannah Reese's eyes on her. "I'm a fan of *A Deeper Dive*, Mrs. Connor," the young woman said.

"Thank you. That's good to hear." Merrill looked up from the paper and smiled. "Call me Merrill, please."

"Merrill."

"Yes, this looks right, Hannah…"

"I listened to the latest episode, the one with Jenna Berlin," she said. Merrill wondered why the woman's tone had changed from the pleasant customer service voice to a more serious one.

"Oh. Did you enjoy it?"

Hannah ignored the question. "Dr. Martinelli was my therapist," she said. Merrill looked up into the manager's eyes. "For a short while," the woman continued. "I had an issue after my baby was born. Post-partum depression. My doctor suggested that I make an appointment with a counselor. I looked at some reviews on line and I called her office the next day."

"I see."

"Dr. Martinelli helped me so much. I was devastated when I heard that she had..." Merrill saw tears forming in the young woman's eyes. "I can't imagine what kind of...monster would want to murder her."

"I understand, Hannah. It had to be quite a shock, especially for her patients," Merrill said. "Did you notice anything unusual, anything out of the ordinary, at your appointments with the doctor?"

"Not really. I only had a few sessions with her, like I said. Her office was in her house, you know. The only thing that was a bit unusual was that almost every time I had an appointment, which was typically after five when my husband got home from work, there would be packages in front of the office door."

"Packages?" Merrill asked. "Like Amazon or Fed Ex packages?"

"I didn't think to pay attention to the labels at first, but then when there were three or four at a time, I checked," the young woman said.

"And?" Merrill was trying to sound calm, but she could feel her heart racing. She wondered what these packages might tell her about Lynn Martinelli's personal life.

"No. They weren't from Amazon or Fed Ex. They *were* all the same though," Hannah said.

"The same? How so?"

"They were all wrapped in brown paper, with a handwritten label that had only "Dr. Lynn Martinelli" printed on it. I thought it was odd that she didn't pick the packages up to bring them inside. One day I asked her if she had a secret admirer. I felt bad because my silly joke seemed to fluster her. I only had two more appointments with her after that, and there were no packages at either of those."

Merrill's hand was shaking a bit as she handed Hannah Reese her Visa card. "Would you be willing to repeat this information about the packages, should the Deputy Sheriff want to speak with you, Hannah?"

The young woman reached across the desk for her business card and handed it to Merrill. "Yes, I would," she said.

Merrill walked through the beautiful lobby of the hotel. The artifacts and photographs from the original Celeron Amusement Park were on display everywhere. The Harbor House had been built on the lakeside where the popular nineteenth and twentieth century attraction once stood. The owners utilized its decor to commemorate the amusement park's place in the region's history. Merrill barely noticed any of it. Stopping for a moment in front of the large sepia colored picture of the Ferris wheel that had stood several stories above the lake, she tried to make sense of what Hannah Reese had just shared about the mysterious packages in front of Lynn Martinelli's office door. She jumped when her phone buzzed inside her purse.

"What's up, Johnny?" she asked, attempting to pull herself together. She walked toward the main entrance of the hotel.

"I'm sorry to bother you on your weekend," he said. "I want to fill you in on a couple of developments."

"Okay," she said, "but please make it snappy. I'm going to be left at the Harbor Hotel without a ride if I don't leave soon."

"Sure. I'll make it fast. I actually have two pieces of good news. Frank got his service animal certification today. He's officially your colleague at the department."

"Oh, that's great, Johnny!" Why could she never turn down an opportunity to tease this man? "Did he have to take the same civil service test you made me take?" When he ignored the jab, she said. "What else?"

"David Michaels' prints. They were not the ones on the kayak paddle."

"I knew it! Thanks, Johnny, I've…"

"Hold on! One more thing," he said. "The footprints at your place, they were the same size and pattern as the boots Farrell found in Peter Martinelli's shed."

"What??" Merrill exclaimed as she pushed the lobby door open. "Peter Martinelli broke into my house?"

"Maybe. Or maybe it was somebody who had his sandy boots on," Johnny said.

As Merrill walked toward her friend's Jeep she said to her boss, "Let's touch base later. I've got something else that might be a lead."

"Oh, yeah? Where did it come from?"

"A faithful Diver, of course," she said.

CHAPTER THIRTY-FIVE

# THE COVE

WHEN MERRILL ACCEPTED Jenna's invitation to return to Boulder Point for a day of beachcombing, she had not expected her friend to bring a canoe for the excursion, but there it was strapped on top of her Jeep in Merrill's driveway. In response to her friend's shocked expression Jenna said, "Just in case we decide we'd like to explore a cove or two." That information didn't erase the look of horror on Merrill's face. "Don't worry," Jenna added, "It's going to be very calm out there according to the weather report, and of course we'll wear life vests."

Merrill fervently wished she had not carried her fear of the water with her from childhood, but her father had instilled it in all three of his children. She was sure it had not been his intention, but when he told them the story of being flown back to the states after he had been wounded in Germany at the end of the war, his kids felt every rattle and shake of that aircraft carrier in its turbulent flight over the ocean. "The cast on my broken leg weighed a ton, and I never learned to swim. So I knew that if we had to bail into the sea, I'd sink like a cannon ball," their father had told them. "That scared me as much as anything that happened to me over there."

"As kids, whenever we went to the beach," she explained to her friend, "our dad paced the shoreline and yelled at us not to go in over our knees. It got so bad, as tweens we begged our mother to take us to the lake when he was at work." As Jenna pulled out of her driveway and headed toward Boulder Point, Merrill crossed the fingers on her right hand and wished very hard for a no boating day.

"So what's new with you, Merrill?" Jenna asked, handing her a cup of drive-through-window coffee. "I haven't seen you since the baby shower."

"Well, I was going to share this with all of you at Larry's on Thursday, but something has been bothering me."

"Oh?" Jenna said. "I'm listening, Merrrill."

"When I got back to the house after the party, there was a stand-off in my kitchen."

"What? A stand-off?" Jenna said. "With who?"

"With my three adult children and their partners."

"I can't imagine that. Your kids adore you, Merrill," Jenna said.

"And therein lies the problem, I guess," Merrill said. "The six of them are united in their cause."

"Which is?" Jenna asked.

"The kids believe that I'm endangering myself by inviting my Divers into certain cases."

"What kind of cases?" Jenna asked, although Merrill could tell her friend was baiting her with the question.

"Murder investigations. My family thinks that publicizing my need for information on the podcast makes me a target."

"Hmm...as it did in the Grace Phillip's case?"

"Yes," Merrill answered.

"So, I assume you ended the stand-off without blood being shed, since you're here with me today," Jenna said.

"Well, as with any good diplomacy session, after the shouting was over, we compromised. Craig, Jason's wonderful partner, made a solid suggestion, which seemed to have settled everyone down, at least for now," Merrill said. "I'm signed up for a self-defense class through the Sheriffs' Academy, which the department will pay for, and Johnny is looking into getting me a Taser. In the meantime, he gave me a case with pepper spray and mace to keep in my car."

"Wow! I don't think there are many librarians that have that kind of training, or those types of work supplies," Jenna said.

"I suppose not," Merrill said, as her friend pulled onto the beach access road. "But I love my new life, Jenna, at least my new job. Although I think the kids are right. I need to be able to protect myself, even though it's highly unlikely that I will have to do that, but just in case."

Merrill reached into the back seat to grab her bag. As she stepped out of the Jeep, her heart sank. Jenna was unfastening the straps that secured the canoe to the roof rack. Taking a deep breath, she reached up and released the straps on her side. If Jenna was strong enough to face down her trauma here at Boulder Point, Merrill would try to overcome her water phobia, if just for a day. "Help me drag it down to the beach, in case we decide to paddle to a cove or two, will you? Yesterday's storm may have left a few treasures in the little inlets we'll come across," Jenna said. "And look how calm the water is," she added, hoping to reassure her friend.

Leaving the canoe on the sand, the two women began their glass-gathering trek, heading east on the shore toward the lighthouse. Before long, the friends were in a steady rhythm, both lost in quiet exploration. "Oh, Jenna, look at these," Merrill cried, picking up four amber pieces, all similar in size and shape and worn smooth over time by the motion of the waves.

"Nice!" Jenna said, and held out her hand to show Merrill the aqua and olive green treasures she had found. The women opened their bags and placed their bounty in the tennis cans Jenna had brought. By the time they had walked the two miles up the shore and back to their starting point, they had filled the cans with sea glass in an array of colors and shapes.

Merrill stretched and the wind on her face felt like a kiss. "No wonder you love this," she said. "It's an amazing combination of yoga, meditation, and a treasure hunt! I haven't felt this relaxed and peaceful in forever. Thank you for inviting me to come with you, Jenna."

"You're welcome! I'll put our glass in the car and grab our lunch," Jenna said.

The women sat together on an enormous piece of driftwood and ate their veggie wraps that Jenna had made. They stared out to the horizon and were silent in the way old friends can be. The two felt no need for small talk or useless commentary in the presence of Nature's perfection.

The roar of a school bus pulling into the parking lot was their cue to dispose of their trash and head to the Jeep. At least that's where Merrill thought she was going. "You wait here," Jenna said. "I'll be right back."

In the meantime, thirty or so little preschoolers were filing off the bus, squealing with delight. They had escaped the daycare center on this perfect sunny day. "Alright boys and girls, grab your partner's hand and line up behind Mrs. Morrow." Merrill knew she had a silly grin on her face as she watched them. She couldn't help but feel the joy that was radiating off the children. With a jolt of pleasure, she thought about her own granddaughter, who soon would be having a day like this. Maybe she would be sharing it with Merrill.

"Okay, perfect timing," Jenna said, as she approached her friend.

"To leave?" Merrill asked, even though the life vests Jenna carried gave her the answer.

"No. To escape these rug rats and paddle to a couple of coves. You'll be amazed at some of the gems that may be lying in and around those little puddles, especially after the windy day and night we had yesterday."

The excitement in Jenna's voice was wonderful to hear. Merrill took a deep breath as she stood, and reminded herself of the commitment she had made. If Jenna could return to Boulder Point after what she had been through a month ago, she should be able to paddle a canoe without having a nervous breakdown.

Jenna's instructions were very easy to follow. The fact that her voice stayed at a calm register helped too. "Okay, Merrill, I'm in charge of keeping the boat steady. You step in and hold on to each gunnel until you get seated in the front." Within minutes of securely positioning themselves in the canoe, they established a steady pattern of rowing. Fifteen minutes into their quest, Merrill began to breathe in and out in an almost normal pattern while Jenna explained where they were headed. "There is a cove east of here, almost to the state park. It's at the base of the cliffs, and if I'm correct, yesterday's winds and waves may have sent some treasures there." The lake was as smooth as glass and Merrill started to feel a sense of accomplishment as they rowed. Within the hour, they were paddling the canoe around a couple of massive boulders toward Van Buren Cliffs.

"I see it, Jenna!" Merrill was surprised to hear the childish delight in her voice. "That's the cove, right?"

They maneuvered the canoe until it faced the cliffs, and within minutes, the women were stepping out into the knee-deep water and pulling the canoe onto the narrow shore. Jenna took Ziplocs from her shoulder bag in anticipation of a successful hunt, and handed her one. Merrill's upper body had definitely had more of a workout than she was used to, but she felt wonderfully exhilarated at the same time. The two friends began their hunt, again, in silence.

Jenna had been right about the amount of glass the wind had brought here. Merrill had filled a quart sized bag in minutes with cobalt blue, green, white, brown, and turquoise pieces. Like a child on Christmas morning, Merrill's attention was totally focused on the search.

When Jenna cried out, Merrill was so startled; she dropped the pale blue pieces she had been imagining as earrings. "What is it, Jenna?" There was no answer.

Merrill waded toward her friend, who stood staring down at her open palm. "Oh my goodness, Jenna, you found red glass!"

Jenna's mouth was open, but still she said nothing. Merrill could see that the hand that held the glass was shaking. "Yes," she finally said. "I found it just now, but the *first* time I discovered it wasn't today." Merrill moved closer and suddenly understood what her friend meant. The red glass was attached to a broken silver chain. A silver ball on each side of the beautiful piece of glass held it in place. Jenna flipped the pendant over and looked down. "*MT*," she read. "Merrill, this is the pendant that Alexandra Sheldon bought for Lynn Martinelli, but kept for herself. It's the one Alex told me she never took off."

A gleam of sunshine reflected off the cliffs and shone on the red glass. Jenna handed the necklace to Merrill and asked her friend a question. "Why would someone break this beautiful silver chain?"

## CHAPTER THIRTY-SIX

# HEROICS

MERRILL STARED DOWN at the red glass pendant and the broken silver chain that lay on her kitchen table. She reached for her phone and redialed Alex Sheldon's office number, and for a second time no one picked up. Setting her phone down, she poured a cup of coffee, and listened again to the professional sounding voice coming from the speaker. *"Hello. This is the office of Alexandra Sheldon, IT Solutions. I'll be out of the office for the July 4th holiday. If you need to get a hold of me before Monday, the 7th, please leave a message after the beep, or drop me an email on my website."*

Merrill was not about to leave a voice message, one that that would surely sound unhinged. Instead, she hung up and spoke to her empty kitchen. *"Hello Alex. This is Merrill Connor from the Deputy Sheriff's office. I wanted to let you know that I have your beautiful necklace. You know, the one you bought for Lynn Martinelli, but kept for yourself? The one you never take off? I just have a few questions regarding the necklace. Mainly, how did the chain get broken and how did it end up in a cove near the Van Buren Cliffs?"*

Merrill had lain awake for the better part of last night, disturbed by the fact that in the four weeks since her body had been found, Lynn Martinelli's personal life remained a mystery to Merrill and the rest of the Deputy Sheriff's investigation team. She had solved the Grace Phillips case twenty years after the woman disappeared by scrutinizing the people who surrounded her while she was alive, friend *and* foe. That tactic had led the guilty parties to Merrill. But in Dr. Martinelli's case, even her children didn't seem to know much about her private life, including her dating habits, if those even existed after the break-up of her marriage. Their mother had revealed to Tim and Shannon that she was bisexual. She had been on a gay dating site for a short time, but so far the Sheriff's department had failed to verify it. The Kramers didn't seem to know who Alex Sheldon was, never mind that their mother had been in a relationship with her. That seemed weird to Merrill, given how close her children were to their mother. Weirder yet, Merrill thought, was that Alex seemed to know a lot about Tim and Shannon, their addresses and phone numbers, as well as their aversion for their mother's ex-husband.

Merrill looked at her watch and did a quick calculation. She decided against trying to call Shannon Kramer before 9 a.m. Pacific Time. Besides, she had a meeting scheduled with Johnny this morning. The two of them had decided to take some conservative measures to meet her children's demands that she protect herself. Beyond that, Merrill wanted to summarize where they were at this point in time with the Martinelli case.

When she walked into Lovallo's office at 10, she saw a bright pink device, no bigger than a cell phone on his desk. "Very delicate," she said, picking it up to examine it more closely.

"Looks can be deceiving," Johnny said. "This thing can dissuade an attacker pretty effectively." He pulled down a wall chart displaying a bare-chested torso of a man. He pointed to the three spots on a would-be attacker's body where the jolt would do the most damage. "Place the end on the hip, shoulder, or below the bad guy's rib cage, although the shoulder would be the most effective spot. Like this," he said, taking the stun gun from her and demonstrating. "And pull the trigger. The shock will keep him incapacitated for the seconds you would need to get away."

"Seems pretty simple," she said. He watched as Merrill put the device in her bag.

"Tell your kids not to worry. We're getting you enrolled in that Sheriff's Academy self-defense class this fall."

"Okay," she said. She reached into her pocket and pulled out the Ziploc bag that held the red glass pendant on the broken chain. "I wanted to show you this."

"What is it?" Johnny asked, taking the bag from her.

"It's the necklace that Alexandra Sheldon gave to Lynn Martinelli. After they broke up, I'm guessing Dr. Martinelli gave it back to her. Alex bumped into Jenna at a craft fair in May, and she was wearing the necklace and earrings. She told Jenna that she never took them off. But here it is. Jenna and I found it in a cove near the Cliffs this weekend."

"That's strange," Johnny said, as he stared at the necklace. "How do you think it ended up there? Alex told us she wasn't into water sports, so…"

"I'm not sure. I tried calling her this morning, but apparently she's away for the Fourth," Merrill said. "I'll keep trying. I'm also going to call the West Coast today. I need to find someone who was close to Dr. Martinelli, someone she may have confided in about her personal life. I'm hoping Shannon or Tim may be able to give us a name, someone from her past who might have known her for years. That's another reason I want to talk to Alex Sheldon. They were a romantic couple for a year. She must know some of Lynn's friends."

"Good idea. Thanks for touching base this morning, Merrill. I appreciate it," he said.

"It's my job, right?" she said. She hesitated for a moment. There was something she wasn't ready to tell Johnny, something that had bothered her since Dina's baby shower. The hotel manager, Lynn Martinelli's client, had seen several unopened packages at the therapist's office door. Merrill's hunch, or "gift," as Victoria would call it, told her that the obsessive Don may have had something to do with them.

Johnny handed her the bag with the pendant and chain. "I'll give this back to you, in case you reach Alex. Until last week, she and I talked on a daily basis. She kind of dropped me like a hot potato, once she heard that the case against Peter Martinelli is much weaker than we first believed."

"Okay," she said, taking the bag from him. "I'm sure Alex will want this back. Jenna says she can repair the chain, and this large piece of red glass is pretty rare. I'll let you know if the Kramers give me any leads on who their mother's friends and associates were," Merrill said, opening Johnny's door. Frank was sitting like a perfect gentleman waiting to give her a goodbye lick on his way into the office.

"Hold on a minute, Merrill," Johnny said. "I have a favor to ask you. Close the door again, please." Frank and Merrill came in and stood in front of the Deputy Sheriff's desk.

"What is it?" she asked.

Johnny's demeanor had changed in the last few seconds. "Could you sit down, please?" Frank, obedient as ever, beat Merrill to a sitting position, and she would have laughed at the dog's reaction if her boss hadn't looked so serious. Oh, God, she thought to herself. Please don't let him be sick. This sense of dread was her default mode ever since Richard had shared his diagnosis with her. She sat down in front of Johnny.

"What do you need?" she asked.

"A dog sitter. Just for one night. I don't want to leave Frank at a kennel. Kennel cough is real, you know. And when he went to Doggie Day Care, well, it wasn't his cup of tea. They told me he barked pretty much the whole time I was gone. And he loves you. I know he'll be absolutely no bother."

Merrill breathed a sigh of relief. "Of course Frank can stay with me. But I'm curious," she said, reaching down to give the dachshund some ear scratches. "You take him everywhere, to department meetings, into inter-rogation rooms. Where are you going that you can't bring him? Another secret mission to Albany?" Frank was looking up at her as though she was representing him in a court of law.

"New Jersey," Johnny said, as if that explained everything. When she didn't respond, he continued. "You know I've been going to therapy, don't you, Merrill?"

"Yes," she said, "for your anxiety."

"Yes, definitely for that. But also because we, Melissa and I that is, lost Rosie. And our marriage." Merrill waited while he carefully chose his words. "Even though it happened a long time ago, I haven't been able to talk about it until recently. My therapist thinks that Melissa and I should have a hard conversation, even though it's been twenty years since Rosie passed. Melissa has agreed to it, which I can hardly believe. I'm meeting her at her parents' house next weekend. As much as I'd love to have Frank by my side, I think it would complicate things."

"Of course Frank can stay with me," she said. Her eyes were welling up. She needed to get out of this office before Johnny saw her tears.

"Thanks, Merrill," Johnny said as she stood up and opened the door. "I'll bring his bed and food and toys. He'll be no problem at all, I promise. I've even got a tracker collar for him, in case he decides to take a walk by himself," he added.

"Okay, sounds good," Merrill said, and quickly closed the door behind her. *Why the tears*, she asked herself, relieved that she had escaped before Johnny saw them.

As she walked to her car, she had an epiphany. What she had discovered and reacted to moments before was that Johnny Lovallo was one brave man. Sure, in his professional life, courage was required. In the face of all kinds of odds, including violence, he had to stand up to real danger. But Merrill thought that this challenge of returning to his past was something even more difficult than those physical risks. He was willing to make himself emotionally vulnerable in order to gain some understanding. He would once again face the worst tragedy of his life. And the fact that he had the courage to do this made him heroic in Merrill's eyes. It was that realization that had made her cry.

## CHAPTER THIRTY-SEVEN

# CALIFORNIA CALLS

MERRILL LOOKED UP at the kitchen clock and decided to pour a glass of wine before calling Shannon Kramer. She had gathered tomatoes, basil, rosemary, and oregano from her little backyard garden to make a primavera sauce, and Kate would be joining her for dinner. It had been a busy summer for both of them. Kate had been on the road nearly every weekend and Merrill had her hands full with the Martinelli case. This would be a chance for them to catch up. She stirred the sauce, making sure that nothing was sticking to the bottom of the pan. When she finished, she picked up her phone and pressed Shannon's number.

"That's a tall order, Merrill," Shannon Kramer said in answer to her question about needing to speak with Lynn Martinelli's friends. "In case you haven't figured it out, our mother was a workaholic. Her clients were the main people in her world."

"How about someone from her past, like a childhood friend or a college roommate?" Merrill asked. "A lot of people keep those friendships throughout their lives."

"No. No friends from childhood, that I know of. As far as roommates, Mom commuted to UB from her home in Lockport for undergraduate school. Even though she had a couple of scholarships, money was scarce for her family. She couldn't afford to live on campus. After our father died, Mom went back to school. She was in her thirties then, raising two kids while she was doing research for her dissertation," Shannon said. "I can't remember her having time for anything or anyone else besides school and Tim and me. That's why, when Peter Martinelli came into her life, I imagine she was pretty susceptible to his particular brand of *charm*." The young woman's sarcasm could not be missed.

Merrill thought about her own circle of friends and silently counted her blessings. They always had her back. She could and would confide in Kate, Sherry, and Jenna, about almost anything. Unlike her own, she imagined that Dr. Martinelli's life was a lonely one. Except perhaps for her relationship with Alex Sheldon, and she had decided to end that. Merrill would reach out to Alex on Monday when she returned from her vacation. Certainly she would know essential facts about her former lover's private life. And perhaps, Merrill hoped, Lynn would have told her about a client who was obsessed with her.

"Our mother was a very private person, Merrill. I can't think of anyone in her life that she would trust enough to confide in, except for possibly Tim or me. But on the other hand, she wouldn't have wanted to burden us with her problems," Shannon said.

*Or tell you about a client that was leaving her threatening texts or mysterious packages*, Merrill thought. At least she wouldn't tell her children about that disturbing part of her life. Not until she was found dead in Lake Erie. Not until she left a flash drive behind as their legacy.

"I understand that the case against Peter Martinelli is weakening, which amazes my brother and me. And Sheriff Lovallo contacted us and said Mom's treatment notes were wiped from her computer, so except for those ugly texts, there's no proof that she was threatened by any of her clients, either." Merrill wondered if Shannon was reading her mind. "I'll talk to my brother and have him give you a call if he can think of any of Mom's associates that you might talk to," Shannon said before hanging up.

Two hours later, after she and Kate had had dinner and were catching up, her phone vibrated on the table. A California area code appeared on the screen. When she picked it up, Tim Kramer did share something with Merrill, something she had never seen coming. Like his sister, he couldn't name one friend of his mother's. But although he couldn't prove it or name the person, he was fairly sure she could have had one confidante in her life.

"Who would that be?" Merrill asked.

"Her therapist," he said.

"Wait a minute!" Merrill said. "Therapists have therapists?"

"Yes. Most do, in fact, including me. Mine had been my supervisor when I was fulfilling my clinical hour obligations for my licensure. But I still see him from time to time to get his input on my more difficult cases. And, of course, when I need some guidance in my personal life, I go to him."

Merrill could feel the excitement that came whenever she got that jolt of energy that told her she was at the threshold of a discovery. She picked up her phone and began to pace back and forth in her kitchen and then all the way to the study at the front of the house, leaving Kate at the table. "Who was your mother's therapist, Tim?"

"No idea. She never mentioned that she had one, but I assumed she did. First as a young widow and single parent, then as the victim of a narcissist in her second try at marriage, then as a gay woman coming out in her fifties, I'm sure she could have used the therapeutic support for any one of those reasons. But, no, I'm sorry Merrill. I don't have a name for you."

"Tim, this could be a big help to us, especially if your mother shared with her therapist some of the threats she was receiving," Merrill said.

"It would seem that way, wouldn't it? But I happen to know, even if we found the individual, he or she couldn't share any information from my mother's therapy sessions. Not without some very complicated legal maneuvers. You can thank the HIPPA Laws for that," Tim Kramer said. "I've got a client coming in soon, Merrill. I've got to go. Let's touch base in a few days."

"Will do," Merrill said.

"Uh-oh," Kate said when her friend came back into the kitchen. "You have that expression of rabid curiosity on your face. What's up?"

"Can you give me a ride to Lily Dale tomorrow? I'd like some company and I'll pay for the gas," Merrill said, as she searched for Victoria Erikson's number in her contact list.

## Chapter Thirty-Eight

# ANNIE

As she stepped over the threshold from the living room into Victoria Erikson's sunroom, Kate was positively glowing. "So I take it from the look of elation on your face that Spirit told you it *is* wise to go on that European tour," Merrill said.

"How did you know, Merrill?" Although she hadn't completed the *Expanding Your Own Psychic Powers* course, on their ride to Lily Dale Merrill *had* heard Kate's euphoric description of the major cities and venues her agent had outlined in his proposal. She was just drawing a logical conclusion, but still her friend seemed impressed.

"I've got the gift, too, remember?" Merrill said jokingly, carefully stretching out her legs to signal to Victoria's tabby cat that it was time to vacate her lap.

"Welcome, Merrill." Victoria Erikson stood smiling in the doorway, a vision in her usual gauzy and gorgeous caftan. The medium never disappointed when it came to dressing the part, Merrill thought. *Get your tongue out of your cheek* she silently chided herself. *This reading was your idea. Face it, woman, you're desperate. Until you find Lynn Martinelli's therapist, if there is such a person, you're at a dead end.*

"I'm going to walk around the grounds, Merrill. Maybe do a little shopping. I'll see you at the Beamer when you're done. And I'll see *you* when I return to the states, Victoria. And thank you again," Kate said.

Merrill hadn't been in Victoria's home for over a year, but she could have found her way to the reading room blindfolded, if she had to. As she entered the small space, she saw that the shades were already drawn and the overhead light was off. She sat down across from the medium, and focused on the little blue lamp that sat on the corner table. She tried to breathe naturally. "Well, here we are again," she said, "I've got something…"

"Let's pray first," Victoria said, as Merrill fumbled silently in her purse, her fingers searching for the Ziploc bag.

"Amen," Merrill echoed when Victoria had finished. "I have an item I'd like to give you for this session." Taking the red glass pendant out of the bag, she passed it to the medium. Lynn Martinelli, according to Alexandra Sheldon, had worn this at least once before she gave it back to her lover. Her hope was that Victoria could, through Spirit, contact the dead woman. Merrill had some questions for her.

Victoria took the necklace from her and examined it closely, holding it in her right hand between her index finger and thumb, just as she had done with Merrill's wedding ring the first time Kate had nagged her into getting a reading. What a difference a year could make, Merrill thought. The skeptic inside her was still there, that was true. After the Spiritualist's failure to identify if either of the suspects, Peter Martinelli or David Michaels, was guilty of the therapist's murder, her doubts had returned. But because of the role the medium had played in finding Grace Phillips, as well as Victoria's message of hope to Jenna at the Stump, the criminal investigator was open to receiving any help the she could give her regarding the Lynn Martinelli mystery.

The medium bowed her head and closed her eyes tightly. Merrill tried to do the same, but she found that it was impossible. Instead, she stared at the illuminated dial on her Fitbit. A minute, then three, then four passed in silence. All the hairs on Merrill's arms stood up when Victoria finally spoke. "*Someone is coming through…It's the man in the art gallery… It's Richard. He's here. He's so glad to see you,…*"

Merrill felt like she might faint. "*He wants you to know… that he's always with you, Merrill, but he's worried about what the pendant…*" Victoria began to whisper something. Merrill leaned in, trying to make out the words, but they were unintelligible. The medium's final words, however, were as clear as they could be. *"'Many tears are trapped inside the glass,' Richard says...he wants you to stay safe for your granddaughter's sake... Oh! He's leaving..."* For several seconds Victoria was silent until she said, *"He's turning back toward us. 'Trust your gut, Merrill, but be careful'...he says."*

Richard. Merrill hadn't expected that her husband would make an appearance today. And his last words contained a foreboding that truly rattled her. Merrill felt like grabbing the necklace and fleeing, but she willed herself to stay. It was so quiet in the little room, she could hear Victoria's calm respirations. She tried to match her own ragged inhalations to those of the medium, whose eyes had remained closed. Merrill shut her eyes and Victoria spoke again. *"A little girl is coming in, Merrill...Amy... or... Annie. Annie, she tells me. She is wearing a little crown. She is carrying gifts...she says they are for you, Merrill..."*

Although she had been taken aback by his appearance, Merrill had been entirely open to Richard and whatever message he might have for her. She had always trusted him, even after he had left this life behind. But the appearance of the little girl with the crown was freaking her out. She didn't know any little girls, alive or not. Her mind and her pulse raced as she tried to make a connection. Was it her future granddaughter? What presents would *Lucy*, not Annie, want to give her grandmother? Did Victoria somehow know about the baby shower? Had she gotten her psychic lines crossed? And then another thought hit Merrill in her gut. *Oh my God, had the medium misheard the name? Could the little girl be Johnny's baby, Rosie?*

Merrill's gasp filled the small space. She snatched the pendant from the medium's fingers. "Gotta go, Victoria! I'll Venmo you."

CHAPTER THIRTY-NINE

# FIREWORKS

"WHERE ARE YOU going?" Kate demanded as Merrill stepped over the candy-grabbers sitting on the curb. The Fourth of July was the best day of the summer for just about everyone, but especially for these little people. Their day began with begging folks on the parade floats or in the fancy sports cars to toss some tootsie rolls their way, and it ended many hours later with a thrilling fireworks display. "The Westfield High School Marching Band is coming down the street! You'll miss them!" Kate shouted.

"I have to make a call," Merrill yelled back as the band played the opening measures of *Up Town Funk You Up*. "Watch my Bloody Mary, please, and if Sherry asks, tell her I'll be right back."

Vodka before noon had done little to soothe the anxiety Merrill had felt ever since the mysterious little girl had come to her in Lily Dale. She was nervous and jumpy, as if there were something vital she was forgetting to do. She was hoping today's celebration would supersede her worry, possibly erase it. But before she could throw herself into the celebration, she had some business to attend to.

Sherry's travel agency on Main Street was the perfect spot to watch the Fourth of July parade. Her annual party on the side lawn of the building was one that no one in Westfield wanted to miss, but even before the band stood and played in front of Sherry's business, Merrill couldn't hear herself think. Every fire truck in the county was there, their sirens blaring excruciating decibels up and down Main Street. She threaded her way through the partiers to the back door of *The Yellow Brick Road Travel Agency* and let herself in. Sherry's office was in the back of the building, and when Merrill closed the door, like magic, all of the noise and fanfare from the street ceased.

Even though she had shut out the deafening sound, Merrill was close to frantic. She pulled her phone from her back pocket and pressed the icon next to Alexandra Sheldon's name, as she had done dozens of times in the past week. Lynn Martinelli's battered body had been found four weeks ago and the Deputy Sheriff's Office had zero leads, mainly, Merrill believed, because they couldn't find anyone who really *knew* the victim. Certainly after a year-long romantic relationship, the woman had to have revealed something about herself that could lead to the arrest of her killer. Merrill desperately needed to talk to Lynn's ex.

> *"Hello. This is the office of Alexandra Sheldon, IT Solutions. I'll be out of the office for the July 4th holiday. If you need to get a hold of me before Monday, the 7th, please leave a message after the beep, or drop me an email on my website."*

Merrill hung up and texted what must have been her tenth message.

> *"Hi Alex. It's Merrill Connor from the Deputy Sheriff's Office trying to reach you once again. It would be very helpful if you would get in touch so we can make a date to speak about Lynn Martinelli. I'm available all day and night. Thank you, Alex."*

Merrill went into the bathroom and splashed some cold water onto her face. The weather was hot and humid, perfect conditions for the Fourth, but Sherry had apparently turned her AC off. Merrill looked in the mirror and observed that whenever her curiosity went unsated, it seemed to add a few years to her face. She pulled a comb through her hair and resolved to go back to the party and forget about work for a few hours.

Sherry had arranged for the Parkview Cafe to cater lunch for her guests, and afterward Kate and Derrick and his band were set to play for them.

Merrill was happy to see that David Michaels had taken off his Westfield High Marching Band uniform and was standing next to Derrick and The No *Names* with a set of percussion instruments in front of him. His parents stood close to Kate and her keyboard, and Mrs. Michaels returned Merrill's wave with a smile.

The afternoon was filled with good food and great music, and Merrill attempted to calm her nerves with a quick meditation on the gratitude she felt for this day. As the band played their last number, Jenna, her husband Steve, and Merrill began clearing Sherry's lawn of garbage, leftovers, and chairs. Kate helped Derrick and his band break down their gear as the party crowd drifted away.

"Do you think you might ever reach an age when your plans included *too much fun* packed into one day, Sherry?" Jenna asked, as the five of them headed to Sherry's Audi and their next stop. There was a Christmas in July craft fair on the Boardwalk in Dunkirk, and Sherry had happily put it on their agenda.

"I've told you before, Jenna, it is fun, but fun *is* my work. I'm writing an article for next year's county tourism magazine. The title is: *Twelve Things to See and Do on the Fourth of July - Chautauqua County Style.* You should all think of yourselves as valuable research assistants," she added.

Steve Berlin said out loud what everyone else was thinking. "*Twelve things,* Sherry? I won't make it through four!"

"That's okay. I've done some of the preliminary activities earlier this week by myself. Don't worry, Steve, I promise not to kill you with too much fun!" Sherry said.

A few hours later, as the sun began its long July descent over the lake, the group loaded their craft fair purchases into the Audi. They had unanimously voted for bar food for dinner before they would head to the fireworks display at the Dunkirk Pier. Leaving the car at the boardwalk, the five of them joined the throng of revelers heading to the new Dunkirk Brewery on Central Avenue.

This street was the only business section of the city that had escaped the devastation of urban renewal in the 60's and 70's. The stately brick buildings, most of which were built in the previous two centuries, were three or four stories high. They were reminders of the thriving commercial center of the county that the city had once been.

Merrill hung back from her friends, studying the business names and logos painted on the doors and windows of the buildings. As a college student, she and her freshman roommate had hitchhiked to downtown Dunkirk from their Fredonia campus. The thought of sticking her thumb out and jumping into a stranger's car made her stomach queasy now, but it had been such an innocent time back then. She was thankful always that her own children had not been as naïve as she had been in her early years. But the trade-off made her uneasy when she thought about it. Her kids had not felt as free, as secure, as she had felt in the world of her youth.

Merrill turned from the street into a narrow alley where a Polish bakery had once stood. She and Richard would sometimes treat the kids to the punchkes that were freshly baked here each Saturday morning. A stab of nostalgia brought the start of tears to her eyes as she drew closer to the little shop. Looking up, she read the sign that hung above the doorway. *George Downey, D.D.S.* She sighed and walked back to Central Avenue.

The buildings on the main street of the city were very dark on this Fourth of July evening. At the end of the block, next to City Hall, Merrill could see little white lights strung on the trees in the brewery's beer garden, but she decided that she wasn't ready yet to join her friends.

She stopped in front of one of the largest buildings on the block. This had been Sidey's, a wonderful department store that had first opened in the 20's and closed just before the millennium. She and her college roommate could never resist the offers of cologne sprayed on their necks and wrists in the cosmetic department before they headed to the second floor where the clothes were. The two would spend a whole Saturday afternoon trying things on, and even though they could rarely afford to buy anything, the sales ladies, back when that was actually a job title, would share their honest opinions when each of them emerged from the dressing room. When her parents visited her at college, after a couple of hours of shopping, her father had to drag her mother out of Sidey's. Years later, the old department store had been converted to multiple office spaces. Merrill read the names of attorneys and accountants and other enterprises that were housed in the beautiful building: *Acme Tax Preparation, Chautauqua County Veterans' Administration, Alexandra Sheldon, IT Consultant.*

Merrill sucked in her breath. Backing away to the curb, she looked up at the building. On the second floor, a light was on. Her heart rate sped up. She couldn't be sure that this was Alex's office. There had been no physical address listed on the business website. But when she tried the heavy oak door and it opened, her psychic alarm went off. Without hesitating to think about her actions, she climbed the steep marble stairs that used to lead to the women's clothing section of Sidey's. She was shocked at the racket her echoing footsteps made, but she didn't slow down until she reached the second floor landing.

A dim light from the interior of an office down the hallway cast its light on the beautiful mosaic floor tile that Merrill remembered. She walked toward the light and stopped at the office door. The sign plate to the left of it read *Alexandra Sheldon, IT Consultant.* Merrill could feel her pulse quicken. It was more than likely that a cleaning service was in the office, but on July 4th? She doubted it. Merrill decided she had to find out. She tried the door. It was locked. She rapped lightly on the window. Nothing. So she pounded on the glass. At last, coming from a back office space, a tall woman emerged.

"Mrs. Connor! What are you doing here?" Alex Sheldon asked, as she unlocked the door. She was obviously taken aback. Merrill was rattled, too. She had the weird impression that this woman couldn't be Alex. The first time Merrill had met with her, as well as when she had seen her on the Zoom interview, she had been in business attire, every hair in place, the same way she appeared on her company website. Tonight, she wore ragged cutoffs and a tank top. One black bra strap slid down on her shoulder. On her ears were the exquisite red glass earrings, but they looked peculiar with this sloppy outfit.

"I came with friends," Merrill said. "To watch the fireworks on the Pier. I saw the light on in your office, and I've been trying to reach you for days, so I decided to…"

"I put my phone and email on vacation mode. I'm so sorry about not getting your messages. Come in," the woman said, holding the door open and locking it behind them. Merrill followed Alex as she moved toward the back of the building. They walked through a reception area that contained only a desk and chair. A philodendron in the corner was suffering badly from neglect. Merrill followed the woman to an office that she assumed was Alex's space. She was surprised to see a dozen or so clear plastic bins stacked against the walls in the room. Some were packed full of computer equipment, others filled with manila file folders. A large oak desk stood in the middle of the room, its drawers open and empty. "Have a seat," Alex said, pointing to one of the two office chairs.

"Are you moving, Alex?" she asked as she sat down. Merrill's phone buzzed in her back pocket, but she ignored it.

"I am."

"Where are you going?" Merrill asked.

"Back to Cleveland. My trip back these last few days…well, it made me realize that I never should have left. I walked away from a business partnership that was a successful one, until it wasn't. It's for sale now, and I've decided to buy it. There's nothing here for me now. Just business, and that's not enough."

"I see." Merrill didn't see, but it looked like Alex was about to cry, so she didn't probe. "Do you have family there, in Cleveland?" she asked in her most gentle voice.

"No, Mrs. Connor. I actually don't have family anywhere. I was in the foster care system from the time I was three years old. I'm in touch with no one from those miserable placements. My only family was here, with Lynn." She put her head in her hands. Her sobs erupted and reverberated from the thirty-foot-high ceiling.

"I'm so sorry, Alex," Merrill said. She saw a box of Kleenex in one of the half-filled bins and grabbed it. Passing a tissue to her, she continued to try to offer some comfort. "Grief is such a personal thing, but I can assure you that someday…"

The woman's face twisted into a strange grimace. "Are you going to tell me that someday I'll get over losing the only person who ever loved me?"

"Oh, no!" Merrill said, "I know from experience that you never get over that loss. But at some point in the future you'll be able to live your life once more." The phone in her pocket buzzed again, and she pressed the Do Not Disturb button before putting it back. "I think it will help you very much to move forward, to eventually heal, if you could answer some questions about Lynn. Answers that might help us to find her murderer."

"I've told you, Mrs. Connor, Peter Martinelli…"

"Alex, Martinelli has been cleared. His alibi was weak, but there is no evidence to prove that he was in the Shore Acres neighborhood or on the beach that night. He is no longer a suspect. But you may know some things about Lynn's life that we haven't discovered yet. Things that might lead us to her killer."

Alex blew her nose, and began to pace around the empty office. "What kind of things are you talking about?"

"Well, for instance, was she close to anyone, beside you, of course? Her children weren't a part of her daily life in the past few years, since they live so far away. Do you know if she had any friends that she may have spent time with? Did she have anyone that you know of that she would have confided in?"

"Confided? About what?"

"Well, specifically facts that might help us understand what was going on in her practice with a client that may have been problematic," Merrill explained. "Her computer with her treatment notes has been hacked and wiped clean, so there's no way of knowing about a client that may have had malicious intent, unless she told someone about him."

"What do you mean? Malicious intent?"

"Did you know that Lynn had received a series of threatening texts?"

"No! She never told me about that! Who…?" Merrill watched, fascinated, as a bright red flush spread across Alex's neck and cleavage. "Or that she was receiving some mysterious packages on a daily basis up until the week before she was murdered?"

"No!" Alex shouted. "But we weren't in touch at that point." She took a deep breath, obviously trying to compose herself. "She had ended our relationship weeks before," she said. The woman slowly lowered her long body into the other chair. It rolled a few inches closer to the window that overlooked Central Avenue. Merrill looked across the desk and recognized devastation when she saw it.

"Alex," she asked gently, "do you know if Lynn Martinelli was seeing a therapist?"

Alexandra Sheldon looked stunned. "What do you mean? You're asking if Lynn was in therapy?"

"Not exactly. Are you aware that most therapists do have a person that they see, sometimes for professional supervision?  For input and advice regarding their clients."

"I wasn't aware of that. And, no, Lynn never told me that she was seeing anyone like that!" she said. Merrill was aware of a defensiveness creeping into the woman's tone. "Her therapy was the lake, her kayak, and me!" Alex Sheldon stood up suddenly and stared down at her from her six foot height. "Look, Merrill, I'd like you to leave. I want to finish packing before I lock up tonight. It's been an exhausting week."

"Of course." Merrill stood and followed Lynn to the office door. "Well, I wish you luck in your new venture, Alex. The Deputy Sheriff will want your new address, of course. In case we have any questions or make any new discoveries."

"I'll email him in the morning," she said as she led Merrill from her office to the top of the marble stairs.

"Oh! I almost forgot!" Merrill said, turning back to face her. "My friend Jenna found your red lake glass pendant! The one you said you never took off…"

"What?" the young woman looked shocked. "Where?" It was a demand, not a question.

"In a cove east of Boulder Point, in Van Buren by the cliffs. Just a mile down shore from Lynn's beachfront at Shore Acres. In a shallow puddle. The chain was broken..."

The woman took three steps forward until she was in her face. Instinctively, Merrill grabbed on to the bannister. "I want that necklace back!" the woman shouted. The echo ricocheted throughout the building as Alex's tall frame loomed over her.

"I'm sure after the case is closed, you can have it back, but it's evidence at this point, so..." Merrill wasn't sure why she was telling this lie.

"No! Now! I want it now!" Merrill took two backward steps down the staircase, and Alex followed. "Before I leave town! I want it back!" Merrill held on to the heavy wooden bannister as the woman shouted down at her.

Suddenly, from the lobby below, someone spoke. "Merrill, are you up there?" Jenna called. Merrill watched Alex Sheldon as she turned away from the staircase and rushed back to her office.

"Yes, I'm up here, Jenna. I'm coming," she said, holding on to the bannister for dear life as she descended. "How did you know I was here?" she asked her friend when she reached the bottom step.

"We got to the brewery and realized you weren't with us. I remembered that I had been tracking you on Maps that day that we went glass hunting, just in case we got separated. I texted you a couple of times tonight, but you didn't answer, so I checked your location on the GPS. We didn't want you to miss the fireworks," Jenna said, opening the door of the Sidey's building for her friend.

"No," Merrill said, "I didn't want to miss the fireworks, either!"

## CHAPTER FORTY

# SLEEP IS OVERRATED

MERRILL HAD NOT been sleeping well since her conversation a few days before with her oldest child. "I'm not so sure these cramps are just practice pains. Did you have Braxton-Hicks contractions with any of us, Mom?" Dina had asked.

"I honestly don't remember," Merrill said. "But if your doctor says that's what they are, she's probably right. How's your appetite?"

"Okay. I'm 90% nausea-free, finally. Sleeping isn't what it used to be, though. I never make it to morning without having to get up to pee at least three times." Merrill resisted sharing her nerdy librarian insight at that moment. She was thinking that Dina's observations and complaints regarding her pregnancy were almost certainly universal ones, shared from daughter to mother throughout time and cultures. But she knew at this moment Dina would not appreciate that particular insightful commentary. Her good-natured child had become understandably grouchy during her last trimester.

"Well, once you start your maternity leave, you can catch up on your sleep," Merrill lied. All these decades later, she could still remember the turmoil an infant in the house could cause its parents, disrupting eating, sleeping, and all other bodily needs. "Call me whenever you feel like talking. My bag is packed and I'm ready to come whenever you need me. I love you, honey. Sleep tight."

Since the Fourth of July, Merrill had been having her own issues with sleep. As she explained to Johnny the details of her encounter with Alex Sheldon in the Sidey's Building, she tried to remain objective. But when she was alone, she replayed the incident in her mind over and over again. Had Jenna saved her from being thrown over that beautiful bannister? No. More than likely, that was not Alex's intention, she reasoned; Alex Sheldon's anger at not being given her necklace back had obviously made her extremely upset. Still, in the middle of the night, reliving those moments from the evening of the Fourth made it impossible for Merrill to get back to sleep. The fact that the woman had not yet forwarded her new address to the Deputy Sheriff wasn't helping to quell her anxiety either.

Dina's contractions, Braxton Hicks or not, were on her mind, too. She realized that she needed to move her thoughts away from the real world if she wanted to get some sleep tonight. The hot shower she decided to take did help, even though she often did her best thinking and planning while warm water cascaded over her. Merrill managed to keep those inspirations out of the shower tonight, and by the time she was toweling off, she felt more relaxed than she had in a long while.

She put on her pajamas and settled into bed with Stephen King's new murder mystery. Three chapters in she felt her eyelids getting heavy, and she reached over and turned off the reading lamp. When her phone buzzed on the bedside table, she had been dreaming that she was holding a baby, and she startled awake.

"Oh, thank God, Merrill!" the man on the other end said. "You finally answered. I know it's almost midnight there, but I had to call you!"

"Who…Tim?" she stammered as she propped herself up against her reading pillow. "What's wrong?"

"For the first time in months, I believe something is right!" Tim Kramer said.

"What's going on?" she asked, swinging her legs over the side of the bed. She stood, hoping she could shake off her grogginess more effectively in this position.

"Shannon and I just got off a two-and-a-half-hour Zoom meeting with

Mom's attorney. He was a personal friend of our mother, so he kindly agreed to delay it until after my last client, even though it was 9 p.m. there by the time we got started. Mr. Morgan read us her will and also revealed the contents of a safe deposit box that she had at her bank," Tim said.

"Okay." Merrill was fuzzy headed from being awakened in the middle of REM sleep. She couldn't follow Tim Kramer's line of reasoning. Why call *her* with this information?

"Beyond her final wishes for the distribution of her estate, he shared a document in her safe deposit box she had left for my sister and me."

"What kind of document, Tim?"

"Do you know what a HIPAA form is, Merrill?"

"Of course, I've signed dozens of them in every medical office my husband… I've ever been in. It guarantees that your health details will remain private, right?" she said.

"Basically. But did you know that a patient can actually waive those rights to privacy?" She was mystified by his tone of voice. It sounded like he had won the California Lottery.

"How can a patient do that?" she asked.

"With another form, of course!"

"Forgive me Tim, but I'm not following…"

"Our mother signed a HIPAA waiver form, giving her *psychiatrist* permission to share the details of her health record with Shannon and me in the event of her becoming physically or mentally incapacitated. Or in the event of her death." Tim was breathless by the time he finished his sentence.

"What? Her psychiatrist? Your mother *did* have a psychiatrist?" Merrill was finally wide-awake.

"Yes, just as we speculated, she *was* seeing a counselor, perhaps for professional advice, maybe to seek help for personal reasons. Possibly for both. I have the therapist's name and address here. I'll text it to you right now."

Merrill opened Tim's text and read it out loud. "Dr. Maureen Colby, Forest Place, Fredonia, New York."

"Mom's attorney will send Dr. Colby a notice mandating her to release all treatment notes to Shannon and me. I've already signed a document verifying that I want a copy of those notes sent to Chautauqua County Deputy Sheriff Johnny Lovallo and to C. I. Merrill Connor," he said. "It will be mailed overnight to the office."

After thanking him and hanging up with Tim Kramer, Merrill began her pacing pilgrimage from her bedroom to the kitchen to the Shed and back again. She was wide awake now and her thoughts were racing. This could be the break they needed! Hopefully, Lynn Martinelli's therapy with Dr. Colby would reveal who had killed her.

When Merrill entered the kitchen, her eyes traveled from the clock to the coffee maker. So what if it was 3:15 AM? She was wide awake now. She would take a mug of Columbian Select out to the front porch swing and watch the sun come up. Maybe she would make a few notes to gather her thoughts before she received Dr. Colby's treatment document. Coffee in hand, she walked out to the porch, and before she could sit down, her phone rang.

"Mom. I'm in labor!" Dina said. "Please come!"

## CHAPTER FORTY-ONE

# SPECIAL DELIVERIES

Lucy Jane O'Hara was born on her grandfather Richard's July birthday. For the three days that the new grandmother stayed at Lucy's house, mainly to shop and cook for the infant's parents, Merrill thought there was never a more perfect baby born. Her Uncle Jason and Aunt Mickey visited for a day and concurred. Lucy's paternal grandparents were coming for the rest of the week, and so she would return to Westfield. On the morning she was to leave, Merrill took dozens of pictures of the infant. She was packing her suitcase when her phone rang.

"When are you getting back, Merrill?" No hello, of course, she thought.

"I should be back late this afternoon, Johnny," she told him. "Have you received the document from the psychiatrist yet?"

"Yes, it came last night. That's why I'm calling." Johnny paused for a second. She could hear him flipping through pages. "It's interesting that Lynn Martinelli signed the health waiver to include everything that took place in her visits to the shrink from March 1st on and not the appointments that took place before that. Still, it's a pretty thick document."

"Have you read through it?" she asked, putting him on speaker. Merrill closed her suitcase and set it on the floor.

"I have," Johnny said. "There's a lot of stuff in Dr. Colby's notes that doesn't apply to the case. I'm going to do you a favor and make another copy and highlight only the things that could pertain to our investigation."

"I'd like both of them, Sheriff," she said, "the original and your redacted copy."

"Of course," he said. "The Prendersen is open until 8 p.m. tonight. How about if I drop the folder off at your studio?"

"That should work," Merrill said. "Are you free to meet in the morning?"

"Yes, I am." She was about to hang up when Johnny said, "How's the baby?"

"Beautiful! Thanks for asking."

After she hung up, Merrill could feel her face flush with excitement. The thrill of making a potential discovery, as she did for years as a researcher in her professional role at the college, excited her like nothing else. The documents from Dr. Colby were a primary resource. Lynn Martinelli could possibly tell them in her own words about a client who may have wished her harm and worse. She couldn't wait to read the notes and confer with Johnny. The two of them worked so well together lately, and Merrill had to admit, their relationship had evolved this summer. He had asked her about her grief and confided to her about his own, something only real friends would do. They still enjoyed pulling each other's legs, but underneath that teasing, Merrill knew that there was a true appreciation and bond.

Merrill kissed Lucy and her parents goodbye before heading west on 90. She had intended to listen to one of her favorite true crime podcasts, *My Favorite Murder,* while she drove, but Johnny's phone call had changed that plan. She didn't want to be distracted by the hosts' bantering about other homicides. Instead, she passed the three hours ruminating over everything she knew and didn't know about Lynn Martinelli's demise. As she pulled into her parking spot at the library, she had come up with the two questions that would serve as the compass that would guide her through Dr. Colby's notes. *Who would want to end Dr. Martinelli's life,* and *why in such a vicious way?*

Merrill had picked up a salad at Wendy's and was in her basement office by 6 p.m., a thick envelope sitting in the middle of the table. A yellow Post-it note containing Johnny's scrawl read: "Enjoy. See you in the morning. JL."

She was glad the wonky AC in the library had finally been fixed. It was 80 degrees out, in spite of the sun beginning to set. Merrill had the creature comforts she needed to settle down to what looked like, by the size of the document in the envelope, a long evening.

She read over the HIPAA authorization form first.

"I, Lynn Martinelli, hereby authorize the use or disclosure of my protected health information as described below

AUTHORIZED PERSONS TO USE AND DISCLOSE PROTECTED HEALTH INFORMATION

Maureen Colby, PsyD, is authorized to disclose the following protected health information to Dr. Timothy Kramer and Ms. Shannon Kramer of Los Angeles, California, to be shared with other parties and agencies as they deem necessary

DESCRIPTION OF INFORMATION TO BE DISCLOSED

All treatment notes of Dr. Maureen Colby for Lynn Martinelli from March 1st, 2019, forward

PURPOSE OR USE OF DISCLOSURE

The purpose or use of disclosure is in the event of my physical or mental incapacitation or in the event of my death"

The rest of the page included an authorization clause signed by Lynn and her psychiatrist. A notary's stamp appeared to legitimize the document and because of this, the Sheriff's office could avoid the quagmire of the subpoena process.

Merrill turned to the next page and saw another Post-It note with a message in Johnny's handwriting: "*Dr. Maureen Colby recorded these sessions with Lynn and converted them to text. In the margins she has labeled her words and Lynn Martinelli's with their respective initials: MC and LM. The entire transcript is here, but I've highlighted the passages that are most pertinent to our investigation.*"

Merrill decided she would need sustenance before she dug into the fifty pages or so of yellow highlighted text. She hadn't eaten a thing since breakfast at Dina's. She opened the Styrofoam container and ate every bite of the salad. Clearing everything off the table but the document, her notebook, and a pen, she took a deep breath and turned to page 1.

# CHAPTER FORTY-TWO

## WAIVER

**March 20, 8 AM:**

**LM:** *I saw a client last week for the first time. I'll not use her given name in our conversations, but instead I'm going to refer to her as Don. What I'm looking for, Maureen, is your opinion regarding going forward with her treatment plan. Don suffered severe trauma as a three-year-old when her mother abandoned her at a church daycare. The mother disappeared and was never heard from again. My client was initially given to relatives who weren't in a position to raise a child. From there, she was placed in foster care. She endured physical and emotional abuse throughout her childhood and teen years up until she aged out of the system. It's no surprise that she suffers from attachment disorder brought on by the initial abandonment by her mother, along with several traumatic incidents that followed.*

**MC:** *Given these details of her early years, I would agree with that as a likely diagnosis.*

**LM:** *The client herself resists any kind of diagnosis, even when I've pointed out that some of her negative thoughts and behaviors stem from this fear of abandonment.*

**MC:** *What are these specific thoughts and behaviors?*

**LM:** *I'm not clear on the thoughts so far, but she has manifested some extreme behavior. She moved to Western New York from Florida after a bad fight with her roommate. The police were called. The roommate ac-*

cused Don of reading her emails and rooting through her stuff when she wasn't home, which my client denies.

**MC:** *Why were the police called?*

**LM:** *Apparently, the disagreement became physical. Although up until her move to Florida she had spent most of her life in the Cleveland area, Don packed her car the next day and headed to Chautauqua County. She had no connection to the place. She had read an article in a tourism magazine she found in a waiting room about "Dunkirk, the Lakeside Gem of a City" and decided to come to the area. Within a week of arriving, she found an apartment and office space for her business. What are your thoughts about treating her?*

**MC:** *I would say that Trauma-Focused Cognitive Behavior Therapy is the right direction to go in with Don. But be careful, Lynn. A client with this disorder is more likely to project and seek a personal relationship with her therapist.*

**LM:** *I think that could be true. She has already asked several questions about my personal life.*

**MC:** *What specific questions?*

**LM:** *At her first visit, Don asked if I was gay. Of course, I told her that the answer to that question did not belong in our therapeutic relationship.*

**April 2, 8 AM:**

**MC:** *How is your client Don doing?*

**LM:** *I wanted to talk about her today, so thanks for asking. After two more sessions, she's accepted the Attachment Disorder diagnosis. But when I explained that Trauma-Focused Cognitive Behavior Therapy must be done in a specific time frame of 12 to 16 weeks, she became very anxious.*

**MC:** *Her issues probably make her hypersensitive to the idea of a time limit. She doesn't want to have an end date for therapy. It means she'll be "abandoned" by you when the treatment is concluded.*

**LM:** *Exactly. She stormed out of the session yelling, "You're trying to get rid of me." She wrote me an apology email that evening and said she* *was getting so much from the reading I had given her about the effects of trauma. She promised she would work harder on understanding the connection between her thoughts, her emotions, and her behaviors.*

**MC**: *If that attitude is genuine, Don should make great strides in therapy.*

### April 22, 8 AM:

**LM**: *I do believe that Don is benefitting from our sessions and the therapy, in spite of her erratic bouts of temper. I wanted to share with you specific techniques I'm trying to incorporate. Although she hasn't been completely cooperative, she is following through on some of my suggestions. She bought a small journal and wrote pages about her traumatic experiences in foster care. She said it helps her to understand herself more. She feels less anxious.*

**MC**: *Good.*

**LM**: *Except that along with the journal that she wanted me to read, she tried to hand me a small box wrapped in tissue paper. I gently moved her hand away and I told her that the journal should be for her use only. And as far as the box went, that I couldn't accept a gift from a client.*

**MC**: *She didn't take that well?*

**LM**: *No. Not at all. She tore the box open and showed me a set of lake glass jewelry she bought. "This was for you!" she shouted, and then for the second time, she stormed out of the office.*

As Merrill read these words, prickles spread from the base of her neck to the top of her head. "Oh my God!" she said. The AC was on, but she was suddenly sweating. She got to her feet and walked to the end of the work table. Unlocking the drawer, she picked up the red pendant. "Oh my God," she repeated. Concentrating on slowing her breathing down, she went back to the other end of the table and began to read where she had left off.

**MC**: *Did you give her the jewelry back?*

**LM**: *Yes, I chased after her, and managed to convince her to take it. Shortly after she left though, I got an email telling me I was the worst person in the world for rejecting her and the gift. And that she felt sorry* for Tim and Shannon, having a rotten mother like me.

MC: *You told her about your kids?*

LM: *Of course not. I didn't tell her about Peter either, but in the same message, she wrote, 'no wonder he wanted a divorce.' That I was not only a gay woman, but a cold gay woman.*

MC: *Hopefully, she is done with you, but if she isn't...Lynn, this is serious. She's obviously been prying into your personal life. You need to refer her to another therapist.*

LM: *Yes, I agree. I'm looking into several options before I let her know once and for all that our association is not beneficial to her healing.*

### May 16, 8 AM:

MC: *How are things going with Don?*

LM: *If you had asked me that two weeks ago, I would have said pretty well. Once again, after the hate email she sent, I had not heard from her for a while. In the meantime, I looked for and found a couple of practitioners in the area who are experts in T-F CBT so that I could refer her if she did come back to see me. When she called for an appointment, I was ready to share the names with her.*

MC: *How did that appointment go?*

LM: *Surprisingly, she was very calm. After I told her I had a list of possible referrals to give her, she said she understood. She had been feeling great lately, she told me. She had been running every day and eating better. She was writing in her journal and looking into finding group therapy for trauma and abandonment. I was relieved to see she was wearing the earrings and necklace she had tried to gift me. She seemed appreciative when I handed her the paper with the referrals on it. She asked if we could meet one last time. Against my better judgement, I agreed.*

MC: *How was that last meeting?*

LM: *Awful.*

MC: *What happened?*

LM: *When I opened the door to the office that day, she stood there beaming at me. Behind her on my lawn was a very expensive kayak.*

MC: *A kayak?*

LM: *Yes, she said it was a farewell gift. She told me I had saved her life and that she wanted to show her gratitude this way.*

MC: *How did she know that you were a kayaker?*

LM: *No idea. I never shared that with her. When I look back on our time together, I see signs that she may have been using her technical expertise to spy on me, especially after I dismissed her from treatment. For one thing, she started signing her messages, which were becoming increasingly more anger-filled and distraught, Don. I hadn't told her that I had used that as a code name for her in my treatment notes, something I do for privacy purposes with all my clients. I use the last three letters of their surname.*

"Of course! DON!!!" Merrill shouted. "The last three letters of Sheldon!"

MC: *So what did you do when she came with the gift that day?*

LM: *I told her she had to take the kayak back. She refused and stormed off. I decided it would make the most sense and cause me the least trouble to keep the kayak. I looked up its value and that evening I Venmoed her twice as much as the retail price.*

MC: *I'm concerned that she may continue to try to see you, Lynn.*

LM: *Yeah. I'll have to get the police involved if she does. A few of the texts I shared with you were threatening.*

MC: *Yes, I agree, they were.*

**June 1, 8AM:**

MC: *Have you had any contact with Don?*

LM: *Not in person, but my security camera catches her several times a week at the office door.*

MC: *Again, Lynn, the police need to be called. She's no longer your client. She's trespassing.*

LM: *You're right, of course. I'm trying not to make her life more complicated than it already is.*

MC: *What is she doing on your property?*

LM: *Leaving packages. Gifts for me, it seems. I've opened only the first one and inside with the nice bottle of cologne was a heartfelt message... to be honest, it was a love letter. Or a love/hate letter would be a better description.*

**MC**: *That's a problem. How many packages has she left?*

**LM**: *One or two a week for the past three weeks. I've not opened any of them. There was quite a pile on the threshold. I left a voice mail for her and asked her to come and take them, but she didn't answer and she didn't come again. I moved them, so my clients wouldn't have to step over them.*

**MC**: *Let's look at this from Don's distorted sense of reality. She loves you, but you are rejecting her gifts and abandoning her. I'm worried, Lynn. It sounds like she left Florida in a hurry. Maybe she is not above using physical force when she is in pain.*

**LM**: *I don't take any of Don's behavior lightly, Maureen. I will call the police if she gives me any more reason to do that. But my messy divorce has made the newspapers, thanks to Peter's histrionics. Having a client arrested for trespassing is the last thing I need right now.*

"Oh, my God!" Merrill shouted again into the empty room. She had stopped sweating and was suddenly freezing. She stood up and crossed her arms across her chest in an effort to warm up. As she paced around the small space, she thought she might be experiencing some mild symptoms of shock. It was no wonder, she told herself. Last week she had stood at the top of a two-story staircase with a violent murderer angrily shouting in her face. "Oh, my God!" she repeated again as she began another lap around her work space. Suddenly her phone vibrated on the table, breaking the spell. It was Johnny.

"Have you read it?" he asked.

"I've just finished reading the highlighted portions," Merrill said, trying to pull herself together so her boss wouldn't suspect that she was freaking out. "So where do we go from here?"

"I've reached out to all police agencies in and around Cleveland, including the F.B.I. They have released an all-points bulletin to find and bring Alexandra Sheldon back to New York for questioning in the murder of Dr. Lynn Martinelli."

## CHAPTER FORTY-THREE

# QUESTIONS AND ANSWERS

Two weeks after the Sheriff's Department had received Maureen Colby's treatment notes for Lynn Martinelli, Johnny stood in Merrill's kitchen with Frank is his arms. "What's the latest on the hunt for Alex Sheldon?" she asked him as Johnny set Frank down on the floor. "Are there any leads from the Ohio agencies?"

"There's nothing new. At least not from the Cleveland area police and the FBI, who have been called in now that she has warrants in New York, Ohio, and Florida."

"Florida?"

"Yes. Apparently she beat that roommate within an inch of her life. So far, though, the trail is ice cold everywhere. That's why I've decided that the time is right for me to make that trip to Jersey." Frank padded across the kitchen floor to his bed that Merrill had placed next to her chair at the kitchen table. "And it looks like someone isn't going to miss me at all," Johnny said, kneeling down to pet Frank.

"We're going to have fun. Don't worry about us," she said as a timer dinged on the stove. Merrill put on oven mitts and pulled out the peanut butter treats she had baked for Frank. "The weather is supposed to be beautiful all weekend. We'll take advantage of it and spend a lot of time outside. Your drive should be pretty easy today."

"Yeah. The one thing I'm not worried about is the drive," Johnny said. The lines on his forehead were deeper than usual, Merrill thought. "But I'll be back Sunday evening. Frank's food and water dishes are in this bag. His leash is in there too, but he's pretty reliable off-leash. If he should happen to go off on his own, just use the tracker app I sent you."

Merrill had been wanting to tell him something, but compliments didn't come easy to her when it came to her boss. She took a deep breath. "I admire what you're doing, this weekend, I mean. It's not going to be easy, Johnny, but it's essential. For you *and* Melissa," she said. The two could not sustain the raw emotion that was flowing between them in that moment. It was just not their style. "So go, already," she added. Johnny said nothing more and was gone before Frank could emit one faint goodbye whine.

Merrill touched the dog treat shaped like a policeman as Frank made meaningful eye contact with her. "Yup. It's cool, buddy," she said.

After a walk in the neighborhood, followed by a half-hour in the backyard playing catch and retrieve the Frisbee, Frank was ready for his lunch and a nap. While he snored softly in the kitchen, Merrill went to her desk in the Shed and pulled out her notebook. She wanted to look over the observations she had made on the Lynn Martinelli case from the time of discovery and identification of the body up to the questioning of David Michaels and the arrest of Peter Martinelli. Her notes ended there. Now she could add the murder victim's own words from her psychiatrist's treatment notes.

Once she made that addition to her summary, Merrill wrote a list of pertinent questions regarding the case. The challenge she made for herself was to be able to answer each of them with only one name.

Who had the technical expertise to gain access to the details of Lynn's personal life?

Who had purchased the red glass pendant from Jenna's shop for the victim?

Who had purchased the kayak for Lynn Martinelli?

Who had left unopened gifts for the therapist, at least one containing a love letter from the giver?

Who might the figure in the Yankee cap be that walked toward the sea wall with the oar in hand?

Who could have put the bloodied oar in Peter Martinelli's storage shed?

Who had worn the red pendant before it ended up with a torn chain in the Van Buren cove, one mile from Lynn Martinelli's shoreline?

Who had shown a propensity for violence in the face of rejection?

Merrill felt a calm resolve come over her as she wrote the last question. After a summer of mystery, Dr. Colby's notes had given her the key to unlock the puzzle. She could answer the final question with the same answer as all of the others on her list.

*Who killed Dr. Lynn Martinelli?*

## CHAPTER FORTY-FOUR

# SKY PICTURE

SITTING ACROSS FROM Jenna on Larry's patio, Merrill took a last sip of beer. Frank lay at her feet, stretched to his maximum wiener dog length on the sun-warmed bricks. "So you think that those plans will work, right?" Merrill asked her friend.

"I think so, and I think it's a great idea, Merrill." Jenna closed the notebook on the sketches she had made. "I'll keep you in the loop as I work on them."

"I've got this," Merrill said, as the waiter laid their tab on the table.

"No, you don't. We were talking about jewelry design. I can write this off as a business expense," Jenna said, grabbing it from the table.

"So can I," Merrill said, taking the bill from her friend. Reaching for her wallet, she noticed the pink stun gun case in her purse. It made her a bit uneasy, but Johnny had asked her to carry it with her this weekend.

As the women stood to leave, Frank was on his own four feet in no time. Jenna reached over to give Merrill a hug and looked down at the dachshund. "How's your little house guest been?"

"He's such a good boy and so smart. I think I might have to get a puppy one of these days soon. I've been without a dog for several years and I'm going to miss the company after Johnny picks him up tonight," Merrill said. "Before he gets here to reclaim him though, Frank and I are going to take a walk on the beach. It's supposed to be a wonderful sunset." The two friends hugged goodbye and promised to get together soon.

Merrill had Frank's leash in her shoulder bag, but as he had all weekend, the dog heeled beautifully at her side as they left the village and walked toward the beach at Boulder Point. It had been another glorious July day and Merrill wanted to get some photos in this light. Looking toward the horizon, she marveled at a massive cloud bank. Its many layers of pink were backlit and edged in gold by the setting sun. It would make a wondrous backdrop for her pictures.

As she and Frank walked in the sand, she pulled out her phone and captured the image of dozens of gulls who sat on top of The Table, the boulder where Jenna had discovered Lynn Martinelli's body. She recoiled at the memory and pushed it out of her mind, replacing it with a lovely daydream. One day soon, she would bring Lucy to play on this beautiful beach where Merrill had brought Lucy's mother, aunt, and uncle when they were children. She imagined the two of them collecting shells and sea glass, stones and feathers, just as she had done with Dina, Mickey, and Jason. They would picnic on the natural benches made of driftwood and Merrill and Lucy would wade a few yards into the lake and then swim out to The Table. Reality intruded and Merrill put that part of the plan on hold. First, she would have to take swimming lessons herself before she could allow her granddaughter to venture into water that came over her knees.

She looked down at Frank, the picture of contentment as he trotted along beside her. Something about this perfect moment in time, incongruous as it seemed, made her think about the tragic death of Lynn Martinelli. Such a waste. And Alexandra Sheldon. An abandoned, abused child who had turned into a jealous, violent woman.

Suddenly, Merrill felt an unseen force stop her forward motion. What she was experiencing in this moment was not unfamiliar. She recognized that it was her psychic antenna connecting with something. At this point in her life, she had learned to trust her instinct or intuition, whatever this gift was that she possessed. She had actually tried to explain what it felt like to her friends one Thursday night at Larry's. "There are physical aspects to it that I can't ignore when it happens. It starts as a sudden heaviness in the pit of my stomach, immediately followed by light-headedness. In that dizzying moment, I feel a kind of joy, the kind I feel when I'm researching something and I know I'm seconds away from a key discovery."

She turned and looked out again at the unusual cloud bank hanging over the lake. Her thoughts returned to one day being with Lucy here at the beach. They would talk about the "pictures in the clouds," describing for each other the "drawings" they saw in the sky. She squinted as she had as a child herself, trying to decide what picture Mother Nature had painted in the heavens this evening. What she saw at that moment took her breath away. She looked up and down the shore at the many people walking the beach this evening. No one else appeared to notice this astonishing picture surrounding the sun. It seemed meant for Merrill's eyes only.

When she turned back and stared out at the story in the clouds, she saw a little girl wearing a crown. She was seated on her sky throne, point-ing straight ahead at Merrill. This had to be the same royal child who had come to her through Victoria Erikson! Another realization sent a shiver up her spine. That Spirit child had not been a child at all! Merrill turned away from the vision and broke into a run. Because she had been open and trusted her gut, as Richard had told her to, she knew where to find this "princess."

Frank kept up with her as she jogged toward Shore Acres. The sun was a giant orange globe on the horizon, and the once mystical cloud formation a shapeless blob by the time the two reached the seawall that protected Lynn Martinelli's beach front from wild Lake Erie storms. Merrill lifted her short-legged friend over the barrier and set him down on the grass "Come, Frank," she said, as she ran toward the miniature Queen Anne storage shed. It was padlocked, as she knew it would be, but she recalled Mike Farrell's trick and she grabbed two rocks that edged the pond.

"A Princess named Anne bearing gifts," she said out loud, as she ran back to the structure.

The sunlight had all but disappeared as she used the rock technique to unlock the padlock. Making her way through lawn equipment and expensive water toys, she moved quickly through the building to the narrow stairway that led to the turret. She didn't want to risk carrying Frank up to the second floor, and his short legs would make the climb dangerous for him. "Stay, boy," she said. He uttered one little whine of protest, but he obeyed and sat down at the bottom of the stairs.

When she stood on the top stair, she was surprised at how dark the room was in the early evening. Then she saw the reason for the lack of light. The turret's six signature windows were covered by room-darkening shades extended downward to their limit. Merrill pulled out her phone and turned on the flashlight app. With it, she traced the circular expanse of the space. This was a room she could live in. The massive window moldings were incredible. The white wood paneling that went halfway to the top of the turret was stunning. Had there ever been a storage building with such attention paid to the historical detail of the period and the main house it was emulating?

Merrill turned her attention to the contents of the room. There were some odds and ends of furniture and an empty steamer trunk. Another kayak and a long board leaned up against a far wall. She knew that Farrell and his assistants had removed some old computers from the room, but the team had found nothing else worthwhile, at least nothing that would corroborate that Alex Sheldon had murdered Lynn. The cops had left the rest of the stuff, mostly in storage bins, for Lynn Martinelli's children to sort through.

Flashlight pointed along the walls, Merrill walked the circumference of the room. Suddenly, she tripped over what she guessed was a long-board paddle. "Damn it!" she yelled as she thrust out her arms to break the fall. From below, Frank began to bark in earnest. "I'm okay, boy. Calm down," she shouted toward the stairs.

In the fall, she had dropped her phone, and the flashlight had turned off. She was shocked at the sudden pitch darkness of the space. Cursing her clumsiness, she began feeling for her phone as she got on her hands and knees and crawled. Pressing against the wooden paneling as she crept, a sudden give in the wall stopped her. She pushed against it and the panel opened. Merrill couldn't see them, but as she explored with her hands in the blackness, she could feel them. Packages. Most of them felt like they were no more than twelve inches square, wrapped in what felt like paper, the kind grocery bags were made from.

In that moment, Merrill remembered her Fitbit with its illuminated dial. It cast just enough light for her to crawl back to the center of the room and her phone. She turned on the device's flashlight again and stood for a moment, directing the light to the opening in the wall.

She kneeled down and counted the packages. Ten. As much as she wanted to start tearing the paper wrapping to discover what was inside, she knew she couldn't risk contaminating the evidence that could possibly convict a murderer. If the police could find among those packages the journal where Alex Sheldon had written her sentiments regarding Lynn Martinelli, be they love or hate or both, this discovery might very well be the nail in the murderer's coffin.

Merrill's pulse raced. She needed to get these packages to the Deputy Sheriff. More than likely Johnny was still on the road. She would call Mike Farrell and tell him to get here with an evidence kit, ASAP. From the main room below, Frank began barking loudly.

"It's okay, Frank, I'll be there in a minute," she shouted. The sound of the shed door opening made her wish she had kept silent. Could it be a neighbor who had seen the light in the turret, checking on Lynn Martinelli's property? She turned off the flashlight and stood in the dark, listening.

"Go on, doggie," a familiar woman's voice said.

Merrill felt sick to her stomach as she heard the storage shed door close, but Frank continued to bark from outside the little Queen Anne. Hurrying back toward the secret panel, Merrill pushed on it and it closed. She reached into her bag and pulled out the stun gun.

As Lynn Martinelli's killer reached the last step and stood before her in the turret space, Merrill knew that her pink device would be no match for the revolver that was pointing at her. "Hello, Mrs. Connor. I've come to retrieve some things that are mine," the woman said.

Merrill struggled to keep her voice steady. "Things that would incrimi-nate you, you mean. It may be too late for that, Alex."

"Where are they?" the woman screamed.

In that moment, Merrill could hear the same desperation she had heard at the top of the stairs in the Sidey's Building. The librarian was not used to acting without thinking, but that's what she did. Her quick movement to-ward the murderer startled the woman and she froze for just enough time for Merrill to act. Their height difference left her no choice but to push the device into Alex's ribs, even though Johnny had said it wasn't the most vul-nerable spot. Miraculously, the woman dropped the gun. It clattered onto the floor and Merrill fled down the staircase. Three steps behind her, the revived killer followed. She could hear Frank as he continued to disturb the calmness of the summer night with his alarmed barking.

Merrill reached for the door handle. And that's when the barking stopped and the lights went out.

## CHAPTER FORTY-FIVE

# STUNNED

"ARE YOU KIDDING?" Merrill tried to sit up, but an instant wave of vertigo forced her head back to the pillow. "She hit me with a paddle?" she asked Johnny for the third time.

"She did. A longboard paddle."

Merrill couldn't help it, she had to say it. "Well, I guess she's had practice with that method of taking someone out."

"And if you hadn't had that stun gun…"

She raised her hand and felt her bandaged head. "I feel terrible."

"You have a pretty serious concussion," Johnny said, "but the x-rays showed that there are no fractures."

"Oh, my God, please don't tell my kids," she begged.

"They're on their way," he said. "and I know they'll blame me for this, and they're right to do that. Your talents are observation and research. And the podcast. That's why I hired you in the first place. From now on, I need to keep you out of harm's way." Johnny Lovallo was not good at hiding his emotions, Merrill knew. But this one she had never seen him display before. It was fear. The guy looked like he had seen a ghost.

"Where is Alex Sheldon?" she asked him.

"Mayville. At the jail, being interviewed by the FBI. Farrell and I questioned her for a couple of hours," Johnny said.

"What did she tell you?" Merrill asked.

The color was returning to his face, and Johnny took a deep breath. "She confessed to the murder of Lynn Martinelli. She said she had planned it for weeks, even though she says she regrets it. She misses her, she says." Johnny stopped. "Are you sure you're okay with this? You should get some rest," he said, as he got up out of the chair.

"Don't you dare leave! I need to hear everything she said to you!"

The Deputy Sheriff sat back down. "Okay, okay! Just don't get upset, please!"

Merrill nodded and took a deep breath as Johnny continued. "She admitted that she and the doctor had never been lovers. Apparently, for a very brief time, Lynn Martinelli had a profile up on a dating website. That's where Sheldon found her. She never revealed that to the therapist, though. And she did admit that the therapy actually helped her for a while. She was sure that Dr. Martinelli had the same attraction for her that she had for the therapist. But on the day that she had decided she would tell her about her feelings for her, before she could, Lynn suggested that she see another professional. And that's when everything started to go to hell. She described herself as having a 'burning fury' from the time Dr. Martinelli 'fired' her from her practice. She says she fought the compulsion to physically harm her, but she couldn't accept that the doctor was abandoning her, just as everyone in her life had done. You sure you're okay, Merrill?" he asked, pouring each of them a glass of water from the pitcher on her bedside table.

"Yes, thanks. Keep going, please," she said.

"Between Alex's ability with computers and her familiarity with some of the doctor's routines, she had an advantage and thought she could get away with murder. Late in the afternoon of June 10th, she parked two blocks away from the house and hid in the woods across the street until around 6:30, when she headed toward the beach, doing her best to look like Dr. Martinell's ex-husband. She snuck behind the seawall down to the beachfront just as Lynn Martinelli was putting her life vest on. The poor woman didn't see it coming. Alex came up on her from behind and bashed her at least twenty times with the paddle. She thought she was dead when she picked her up and put her in the kayak. But in the last instant of her life, just before her murderer pushed the Oru out into windy Lake Erie, Lynn Martinelli reached up and tore the necklace from Alex's neck. She must have dropped it into the water, which is several feet deep at that spot. Sheldon tried to find it, but the sun was setting and she lost sight of it."

"And then she took the murder weapon and the clothing and put them in Peter Martinelli's storage shed," Merrill said.

Johnny nodded. "She had read that he had an open house that day, and so she knew he wouldn't be home." The two remained silent for several seconds.

"Her plan was to leave town, maybe the country, but when the Oru registration came back on her, she had to fabricate the whole ex-lover story."

"Why in the world did she come back to the scene of the crime the night that she clobbered me?" Merrill asked. She didn't want to admit to Johnny that she wasn't exactly sure what day or night this current one was, either.

"One of those "gifts" you discovered in the wall was Alex's journal. In her own words, it described the love/hate relationship with her therapist, including detailed options for murdering her; one was the plan for killing her and setting her afloat in the kayak. She knew it would seal her fate if the police found the journal, so she came back to Shore Acres to make sure that wouldn't happen."

"Instead, she found Yours Truly there and gave her a good whack on the head. I guess she could have done a lot more to shorten my life span," Merrill said.

"Oh, she intended to. When we got there, she was pouring gasoline used for the lawn equipment around the perimeter of the little Victorian shed. That decision should get her another ten years in prison," Johnny said.

Shock mixed with vertigo washed over Merrill and she fell back on the pillow. Just then the curtain around her bed was pushed open and Jenna walked in with Frank on a leash. "The nurse said she didn't care if he was a service dog. He has to be leashed," Jenna complained.

Merrill sat up and said, "Hi, Frank! I guess I'll never get to dog sit for you again. But we had a good time until we almost got murdered, right?"

Frank did what Frank did best, which was to wag his tail at warp speed and look soulfully into the eyes of any human who needed reassurance. "In a way, Frank saved you," Johnny said. "I stopped at your house when I got back into town that night and the place was dark, even though your car was in the driveway. I rang the bell and pounded on the door. No answer, so I texted you, but there was no response. So I looked at the app on my phone and Frank's collar tracker located him. It seemed very weird that you would have gone to Shore Acres for any good reason, so Farrell and I jumped into the patrol car and raced to Dunkirk."

After her three visitors left, Merrill closed her eyes with the intention to sleep, but the harrowing thoughts and visions she tried to push away kept coming. She couldn't believe how close to death she had come. Maybe it was time to rethink this whole CI thing. When her three adult children entered her hospital room an hour later, the horrified looks on their faces told Merrill where they stood on the issue.

## CHAPTER FORTY-SIX

# LUCKY

THE LABOR DAY weekend brought thousands of visitors to the beaches of Lake Erie, but by Monday, the permanent residents could expect a much less crowded experience. Merrill had counted on this when she made the plans for the holiday celebration finale.

Her kids and their families had come on Friday and would spend until Tuesday morning between her house and Jason and Craig's condo. This meant that Lucy would be visiting her grandmother in Westfield for the first time. Merrill had borrowed a Pack 'n Play from Doris Breonski at the library, and Lucy's parents had brought the vast array of other equipment the three-month-old required.

Shortly after Lucy and her family arrived, Merrill carried the baby from room to room in the house, pointing out anything she believed would hold the infant's attention. When she got to the Shed, she hugged the baby closely and told her all about her grandfather as she held her in front of each of his paintings, sculptures, and photos. "Lucy, you would have loved him, and he would definitely be head over heels for you," she said. The baby's wide blue eyes glanced back and forth from her grandmother's face to each of Richard's creations.

By Monday, Merrill's kids agreed that they couldn't eat another morsel or drink another sip of anything, but by dinner time, no one could resist the grilled lobster, salt potatoes, or corn on the cob. After they cleaned up, Merrill made an announcement. "We're going to end this beautiful weekend at the beach. Grab your sweatshirts, bug spray, wine, and S'mores makings. I've got some friends starting a bonfire at Boulder Point. And at 10 p.m. the town is putting on the last fireworks display of the summer at the pier."

Sherry, Kate, and Johnny were true to their word and were already at Boulder Point with Frank at their heels as they gathered wood for the fire. Kate shouted to Merrill's group as they got out of their cars. "Pick up some small pieces of driftwood on your way here, please. We need to keep this going!"

When they reached the fire, there were hugs all around, except for the handshakes for and by Johnny. Merrill's friends had lined up flat pieces of driftwood and some sizeable rocks in a ring around the fledgling bonfire, and her kids had brought camp chairs, too. The baby was content in the sling that hung from her father's shoulders. Next year, Merrill thought with a smile, they would be chasing after her all over this beach.

The sun was setting much more quickly than it had a month ago and an orange moon was rising over the lake. "Sit down, Mom," Jason said, pointing to the chair next to him.

"I will. I'm just waiting for Jenna. There she is!" she said, as she watched the *Mermaids' Tears* van pull into a parking space. She hurried to meet her and when the two women entered the circle, each was carrying a large bag with the mermaid logo from Jenna's shop.

Johnny was adding wood to the fire. He looked up and said, "What's in the bags?"

Merrill regarded all of their faces, highlighted by the glow of the bonfire. A ring of people whom she loved. "Well, this is a party. For each of us. We have so much to celebrate!"

"Such as...?" Mickey said.

"A long weekend," Craig said.

"Yes," Merrill said. "That too. And so much more! We are so very fortunate. I wanted to focus on that tonight."

Jason spoke. "We're fortunate you're still on the planet, for instance," he said looking from his mother to Johnny.

"I'll second that," Johnny said.

"Take a seat, please, Sheriff," Merrill said. "You too, Frank. Jason, you can open that wine and start pouring, if you would." As her son did her bidding, she began the speech she had been planning since that July day when she woke up in the hospital.

"I want to tell you all about a beachcombing experience I had with Jenna this summer," she began." We found some beautiful glass that day. Go ahead, please, Jenna," she said, pointing to the bags at her feet. As Jenna passed out *Mermaids' Tears* boxes to each of them, Merrill continued. "But we also found these little white stones that day, too, and Jenna had collected dozens more over the years. You can go ahead and open your presents now," she said to the group. "The fact that the stones were such a uniform size and shape surprised me, and I asked Jenna what they were."

Jenna came and stood by Merrill's side as she explained. "These really are not stones," she said. "OOHs" and "AHHS" traveled around the circle as each of them opened their packages. "They are part of an organ of the Sheepshead fish, of which we have plenty in Lake Erie. When the fish die, this bonelike structure can be found for miles up and down the beaches. People call them Lucky Stones."

"Look closely at your gift. You'll see that the stones have what looks like an "L" etched into them. That's why they're called Lucky Stones," Merrill told them.

Around the circle, Merrill heard her friends' and family's exclamations of "Cool!" "Pretty!" "Beautiful!" She waited until it was quiet again. "For my children and their partners, we thought pinkie rings with an inset Lucky Stone would be a good choice."

There was an outpouring of agreement as Merrill continued. "Like I said a minute ago, we are all so fortunate. First of all to have one another," she continued. Sherry and Kate held up the earrings Merrill had sketched and Jenna had made. Pieces of lake glass, aquamarine for Kate and cobalt for Sherry, dangled from a Lucky Stone.

"There have been some milestones this summer and they should be celebrated, too. Lucy's birth is one," her grandmother said.

"Look at this!" Dina held up the mobile that Jenna had created for Merrill's granddaughter. It was a cascade of multi-colored pieces of sea glass and Lucky Stones.

"Frank says, 'thank you,' ladies," Johnny said, holding up the new collar with the Lucky Stone sewn on in the center.

"Well, becoming certified as a service animal is a big deal," Merrill said. "And some of us have heroically survived a very difficult time." She turned to Jenna and clinked her wine glass with her friend's. Jenna had overcome the trauma she had encountered on Boulder Point and Merrill was proud of her. The two women had decided on a silver chain for each of them with silver beads separating three Lucky Stones. They walked around the circle, showing off the necklaces.

Merrill stopped in front of Johnny and quietly told him, "I wasn't just referring to the Lynn Martinelli case as your difficult time." She didn't have to explain that she truly admired his bravery for facing the tragedy of their daughter's death with Melissa.

"I know that. And I love them, Merrill," he said fingering the cufflinks that were two Lucky Stones set in gold bezels. "But one of these stones is upside down. It looks like a J...Oh, I get it!" J L, that's me!"

"I thought they would look nice with the tux you'll be wearing when you receive your award in Albany next month," Merrill said.

"What award??" Sherry and Kate asked together.

Before he could shrug their question off, Merrill explained that the Chautauqua County Sheriff had nominated Johnny for a prestigious award. "Johnny has been selected from all of the Deputy Sheriffs and Undersheriffs across the state to receive the Distinguished Service Badge of Honor." She reached into the pocket of her cutoffs and read from a piece of paper. "In recognition for exceptional dedication, commitment, and exemplary service."

Everyone but Frank and Lucy clapped and shouted words of congratulations to the Sheriff. The bonfire was casting light on Johnny's reddening face. "Well, thanks. But I certainly am indebted to my whole team for the service we provide, including Merrill Connor, of course."

Each of Merrill's children turned and looked at their mother. "Mom?" Jason said.

"Yes. I guess this is as good a time as any to let you all know. I'm leaving the Sheriff's office." The only sound was a large piece of dry wood exploding. It shot embers and sparks of light up toward the sky. "Rather, I'm taking a leave for a few months," Merrill said. "I'll be doing some traveling that I've delayed since Richard's passing. I'll be taking *A Deeper Dive* on the road, though. The podcast will continue with a lot of remote technical support from Jason. Sherry is going to help me find places to stay along my journey. In the meantime, Johnny and I will be working on a more refined job description for me, one that will take more advantage of my librarian skills and less …"

The first of the fireworks display interrupted her, and the group all turned toward the lighthouse pier down the beach. Except for Merrill, who continued to look at each of them. As a burst of purple glitter lit up the sky, she grasped one of the Lucky Stones on her necklace and smiled.

## ACKNOWLEDGEMENTS

Thank you to my beta readers, Kathy Holser, Susan Penn, Gary Madar, Joe Pace, Susan Breon, Marjorie Switala, and Kathryn Richmond for their astute and constructive advice. A special thank you to Kathy Holser, sea glass collector and jewelry maker, for her expert opinions, and to Joe Pace, LCSW, for his knowledge of mental health therapies and the laws of New York State as they concern patient treatment plans used in court cases.

Thanks to my husband, Gary, for his love and support throughout the months as I wrote and rewrote Boulder Point.

Thanks to my multi-talented son, Jesse Stratton, who gave me valuable story development notes. If you're looking for a terrific book coach, let me know. I'll send you his website. Susan Penn, my talented college roommate came up with an initial idea for a cover for the book, which I will use in promoting the novel. But in the end, Jesse Strattton designed and created the cover for this book. I love it! Thank you, Jesse, for your hours of work.

Lastly, to my faithful readers throughout these past ten years. Thank you for telling me, "Your book made me think." Thank you for asking me, "When is your next book coming out?" Thank you for recommending my books to your family, friends, and book clubs. Your support has inspired me to keep on doing what I love.

And for those of you who have asked, "Is there going to be a sequel?" I can finally answer, yes. Here it is!

## About the Author

Deborah Madar is a native of Western New York and lives with her husband Gary in Bemus Point. They have four children and nine grandchildren. Debbie taught high school and college English for many years before opening her laptop and her imagination to the "what if's" that she loves to explore in her books. BOULDER POINT is her fourth novel.

If you enjoyed BOULDER POINT or any of Debbie's books, please consider posting a review on Amazon, Goodreads, or on the social platform of your choice.

CONTACT DEBORAH
http://www.deborahmadar.com
On twitter - @Deborah Madar
Facebook.com/DeborahMadar
Instagram.com/debmadar
Goodreads – Deborah Madar

www.ingramcontent.com/pod-product-compliance
Lightning Source LLC
Chambersburg PA
CBHW071147260626
47162CB00003B/944